r

'Why are you doing this, Beth?'

Guy was sitting on the bed beside her, positioned so that he did not prevent the candlelight from falling on her face. She smiled, but he detected a wariness at the back of her eyes.

'Does there have to be a reason?'

He did not reply. Desire still raged through him, and he had to work hard to fight against it.

'You think that you can seduce me, so that I will not betray you?'

'No! I—'

He put a finger on her lips.

'Do not lie to me, Beth.'

She sat up, pulling up the neck of her night-gown, not realising that the flimsy covering did nothing to hide her body. It merely heightened her charms.

'I th-thought I might persuade you…'

'I am not so cheaply bought!'

AUTHOR NOTE

THE DANGEROUS LORD DARRINGTON sees the return of a favourite of mine: Guy Wylder, the older brother of Nick, my hero from WICKED CAPTAIN, WAYWARD WIFE. I always planned that both the Wylder brothers should have their own book, but Guy has had to wait a little while! He is the Earl of Darrington and, while he is the more serious of the two brothers, he has gained a reputation as a dangerous flirt. Woe betide any woman who loses her heart to him!

Fate brings Guy to Malpass Priory, where he finds Beth Forrester, a beautiful young widow. She is not impressed by his title, and is wary of his reputation, but when she is obliged to accept his help in clearing her brother's name she finds the Dangerous Lord Darrington to be a true friend.

This romantic adventure has everything—a spooky old house, French *émigrés*, greedy villains and wicked villainesses. And of course it has a hero and heroine who are clearly made for one another. But they both have secrets and must learn to trust each other before they can find happiness.

Happy reading!

THE DANGEROUS LORD DARRINGTON

Sarah Mallory

First published in Great Britain 2011
by Mills & Boon, an imprint of Harlequin (UK) Limited.
Harlequin (UK) Limited, Eton House, 18-24 Paradise Road, Richmond, Surrey TW9 1SR

© Sarah Mallory 2011

ISBN: 978 0 263 21840 4

Harlequin (UK) policy is to use papers that are natural, renewable and recyclable products and made from wood grown in sustainable forests. The logging and manufacturing process conform to the legal environmental regulations of the country of origin.

Printed and bound in Great Britain
by CPI Antony Rowe, Chippenham, Wiltshire

Sarah Mallory was born in Bristol, and now lives in an old farmhouse on the edge of the Pennines with her husband and family. She left grammar school at sixteen, to work in companies as varied as stockbrokers, marine engineers, insurance brokers, biscuit manufacturers and even a quarrying company. Her first book was published shortly after the birth of her daughter. She has published more than a dozen books under the pen-name of Melinda Hammond, winning the Reviewers' Choice Award in 2005 from Singletitles.com for *Dance for a Diamond* and the Historical Novel Society's Editors' Choice in November 2006 for *Gentlemen in Question*.

Previous novels by the same author:

THE WICKED BARON
MORE THAN A GOVERNESS
  (part of *On Mothering Sunday*)
WICKED CAPTAIN, WAYWARD WIFE
THE EARL'S RUNAWAY BRIDE
DISGRACE AND DESIRE
TO CATCH A HUSBAND…
SNOWBOUND WITH THE NOTORIOUS RAKE
  (part of *An Improper Regency Christmas*)

THE DANGEROUS LORD DARRINGTON
features characters you will have met in
WICKED CAPTAIN, WAYWARD WIFE

**Did you know that some of these novels
are also available as eBooks?
Visit www.millsandboon.co.uk**

For TGH

Chapter One

The news that Dangerous Lord Darrington was staying with Edwin Davies at his Yorkshire hunting lodge had spread, but it posed something of a dilemma for those fond mamas with unmarried daughters. Guy Wylder, the Earl of Darrington, was a bachelor and it was generally agreed that it was time he settled down and produced an heir. There had been a serious scandal in his younger days, but most parents were prepared to overlook that in view of his wealth and his title. However, the earl resisted all attempts to lure him into matrimony; any young lady who forced herself too openly upon his attention was likely to suffer, for the earl would embark upon a furiously intense flirtation, setting tongues wagging and leading the young lady in question to suppose that he had quite lost his heart. Then, just when she was in daily expectation of receiving an offer of marriage, the wicked earl's ardour would cool and he would have difficulty remembering her name when they next met.

Such behaviour had caused more than one young lady to go into a decline and, despite Lord Darrington's wealth and wickedly handsome appearance, all sensible parents now went out of their way to warn their daughters against encouraging the earl's attentions. Unfortunately, in Guy's opinion, there were not enough sensible parents.

On this occasion, however, precautions proved unnecessary. Mr Davies's shooting party at Highridge comprised only gentlemen;

apart from an occasional sighting at the White Hart, the sporting company kept very much to Mr Davies's extensive acres or rode over the largely uninhabited hills and moors that stretched eastwards to the coast.

'I shall be given the cut direct when I go into the town,' was Mr Davies's laughing complaint. 'To have had a peer of the realm staying with me and not paraded him at one assembly. My neighbours will be ready to pluck any number of crows with me!'

'Davey, you know I came here only because you promised me a couple of weeks' sport in the company of friends,' replied Guy.

'And that's what you have had, but I cannot see what harm there would have been in attending a dance or two in the town.'

One side of the earl's mobile mouth lifted a fraction.

'Ah, but that is sport of a different kind, Davey, and *we* would be the quarry.'

They had been roaming the hills for some time, climbing to ride along the ridge that looked over the lush green farmland to the west and the hills and moors of north Yorkshire to the east. Guy stopped for a moment, taking in the view.

'That is always a danger, of course,' remarked Davey, bringing his horse to a stand beside him, 'but surely the cautionary tales about your cavalier behaviour towards the fairer sex give the ladies pause.'

Guy shook his head.

'Some, perhaps, but not all.' He added bitterly, 'I might be a veritable Bluebeard and some parents would still be offering their daughters to me. It seems my title and my fortune outweigh every other consideration!'

'Your fortune and title certainly mean you are constantly mentioned in the society papers. Those damned scoundrels who write the *Intelligencer* are happy to print any amount of gossip about you.'

'That scandal-sheet!' Guy's lip curled. 'Ignore it, I do. What they cannot find out they make up, and as long as it is only about my amorous adventures it does not bother me at all. Besides, if the scandals are bad enough, perhaps those ambitious mamas will finally give up the chase.'

'I know the gossip doesn't bother you, but it does anger your friends. Take the latest *on dit* about the Ansell chit, for example.'

'By heaven, I dance twice with a girl and immediately I am thought to be in love!'

'Well, her mother thought so, at all events. Told everyone you had invited them to Wylderbeck.'

'They invited themselves. Ansell started telling me how his daughter was interested in architecture and that she had heard such wonderful things of Wylderbeck. I told 'em they were welcome to take a look at the old house.' Guy shot his friend a quick glance, his grey eyes glinting. 'I hope they enjoyed it. I had a letter from my steward last week saying they had come hotfoot to Yorkshire, only to be told I was not at home! My housekeeper showed 'em around the house and suggested they could put up at the Darrington Arms.'

Davey laughed, but shook his head at him.

'A devilish trick to play, Guy.'

'One becomes weary of being constantly pursued. Scandal goes some way to reduce the problem.'

'I sometimes think you are happy for people to think you betrayed your country,' muttered Davey, frowning.

'If you think that, then you are a fool,' Guy retorted. 'I regret my youthful folly more than I can say, but the damage is done. However, I prefer that the news-sheets and the *ton* should talk about my scandalous love life and leave the past alone. It may be forgotten now, but the smear is there, and always will be.'

'But it could be erased—indeed, it was never more than a salacious rumour, but your withdrawing from politics was taken by some as an admission of guilt. Come back to London,' Davey urged him. 'There are many in government who know your worth and would welcome your help, especially now, with the unrest in France.'

'Mayhap I will, but I would be happier to do that if those matchmaking dragons would leave me alone.'

'There is a simple answer to that,' remarked Davey. 'Take a wife.'

'Never!' Guy shook his head, laughing. 'Now that…' he grinned, kicking his horse into a canter '…is a step too far!'

A speedy chase along the ridge followed but when they reached the highest point Guy brought his horse to a stand and looked around him, enjoying the freedom of the wide open space. He thought he could smell the sea on the light breeze, even though they were nearly thirty miles from the coast.

'Are you sorry now that you suggested we should stay on here?' he asked as Davey came alongside him. 'Would you have preferred to go on to Osmond's house with the others?'

'Not at all! Much as I like having a large party at Highridge, I prefer this: we can do away with ceremony, rise when we wish, do what we want and talk or not, as the mood takes us.'

Guy reached across to lay a hand briefly on Davey's shoulder.

'You have been a good friend to me, I appreciate that. Always there to support me, even when the whole world thought the worst—'

'Nay, there were plenty of us who realised you were not to blame, even though you preferred not to defend yourself. Too chivalrous by half, Guy.'

'What would you have had me do?'

Davey scowled. 'Put the blame squarely where it belonged.'

Guy shook his head.

'The woman had fled the country: my protests would have looked very ungallant.'

'Gallantry be damned,' exclaimed Davey. 'You gave up a promising career for that woman and robbed the country of a most able politician! Your talents have been wasted, Darrington.'

'Not at all. I have spent my time putting my estates back into good heart. My father almost bankrupted the family, you know, with his profligate ways. And it was useful to be in the north while my scapegrace brother Nick was away—I could keep an eye upon his estates.'

'But it must be five years since he settled down. Surely you might make a push now to return to politics.'

'To be subjected to ridicule and constantly reminded of my disgrace?' Guy stared out across the hills. 'No, I thank you!' He gave himself a mental shake. 'But this is dismal stuff for such a fine September day! Let us press on. What else did you wish to show me?'

Realising confidences were at an end, Davey pointed to the northwest.

'Thought you might like to visit Mount Grace Priory. I know the family, so there will be no difficulty seeing the ruins. I know you have an interest in antiquities of that sort.' He grinned. 'Not quite in keeping with the image of the Dangerous Lord Darrington, which is why I didn't suggest it while the others were here.'

Guy laughed. 'Much I care about that! But you are right, they would not have enjoyed such a visit.' He glanced up at the sun. 'But it is midday already—is there time?'

'Of course. We can spend a couple of hours looking at the ruins, then take the lower route back to Highridge, stopping at Boltby. The inn there is famous for its dinners.'

'Very well, then, let us go to it!'

In perfect accord the two gentlemen set off at a canter, enjoying the freedom of the hills before they were obliged once more to descend to the lower ground.

The ruins of Mount Grace had occupied most of their afternoon and by the time they set off again for Highridge the sun was far to the west.

'Looks like rain is coming,' observed Guy, eyeing the heavy grey clouds building on the horizon.

'We should crack along if we are to avoid a soaking,' agreed Davey. 'Come along then; mayhap we'll forgo dinner at Boltby and cut across country. What do you say?'

'Why not? We have been jumping these walls for the past couple of weeks; my horse is accustomed to it now.'

Davey laughed.

'It will be the muddier route, but that will make the roaring fire and rum punch all the more enjoyable when we get home!'

Davey led the way through the winding lanes for another mile before turning off on to a narrow track. As they left behind them the little villages that lined the main highway the country became ever more barren and soon they were riding across a wilderness with no houses in sight. Guy glanced up at the sky. The sun had disappeared behind thick clouds the colour of lead and the air was heavy with the threat of rain.

'How much farther is it?' he asked as they slowed down to a walk, resting the horses.

'About another five miles,' replied Davey. 'I am sorry we did not think to bring our greatcoats. If this rain comes down, it will be heavy, I fear.'

Guy shrugged.

'No matter. We may yet beat it.'

'We may indeed. We can at least cover the next mile or so at speed, if we cut across the fields.' With that Davey spurred his horse and they were off again, galloping across the large, rectangular fields. Guy's powerful hunter took the dry stone walls in his stride, but he silently cursed his friend's recklessness as they scattered sheep and a herd of milch cows in their headlong flight. The daylight was reduced to a gloomy twilight and a soft rain had started to fall as they thundered towards another grey stone wall. It was not particularly high, but as they approached it Davey's bay mare stumbled. They were too close to stop and she made a valiant effort to clear the wall, but a trailing hoof caught one of the topstones, sending horse and rider tumbling to the ground.

Guy did not hesitate. He put his own horse to the jump, but reined in as soon as he could, turning back to help his friend. His heart sank when he saw the mare on the ground, legs flailing, and Davey trapped beneath her. Quickly he dismounted and dashed across to the stricken pair. The bay rolled over and clambered to her feet. She stood, trembling and snorting, but appeared otherwise unhurt as Guy dropped to his knees beside his friend.

Davey's face was ashen and one leg was twisted in an unnatural position. He opened his eyes and looked up at Guy.

'Pushing…too…hard,' he gasped.

'Don't talk and keep still,' barked Guy. 'I need to see just what damage you have done to yourself.'

'Damned fool,' muttered Davey. 'Light was going…didn't see the rabbit hole…'

There was the thud of heavy boots as two farmhands ran up.

'We saw the fall from the road, sir,' called the first, grimacing as he gazed down at the injured man. ''Owt we can do?'

'We need a doctor,' said Guy. 'And somewhere to take him out of this rain.'

'There's the barn on t'other side o' beck,' offered the second man, coming up. 'Or t'owd Priory just over there.'

Guy followed his pointing finger and noticed for the first time the outline of a steeply roofed building in the distance.

'The Priory would be best, if it is inhabited.'

'Oh, aye, Lady Arabella will be at home. She never leaves the place these days.'

Guy nodded. Quickly he gave instructions for the men to fetch help while he removed his jacket and threw it over Davey. He sat by his friend's head, leaning forwards to shelter him from the worst of the drizzling rain.

'This is a damned nuisance,' muttered Davey, wincing.

'Don't try to move. We will carry you to that house yonder and soon have you comfortable again.'

'Comfort, hah! Didn't know my legs could hurt so much.'

'You are growing soft, then,' retorted Guy, secretly relieved to know his friend could still feel pain. He was no doctor, but he suspected at least one leg was broken, but he hoped there would be no more serious damage. He took his friend's hand. 'Don't worry. Help will be here soon.'

Davey gave a slight nod and squeezed Guy's hand, then his eyes closed and his head fell to one side. Only the tiny pulse throbbing at one side of his neck told Guy his friend was still alive.

* * *

Guy had no idea how long he had sat beside Davey, the sky grow-ing ever darker and the rain falling steadily. It felt like eternity, but he guessed it was less than an hour later when he heard the wel-come sound of voices. Half-a-dozen men arrived with a donkey pulling a small cart. Guy tried to ensure that Davey was lifted as carefully as possible into the cart, but he was profoundly thank-ful that his friend was still unconscious. He winced when the cart rocked on the uneven field; by the time they reached the gravelled drive leading to the old Priory he felt as if he had been walking for miles.

The stone building towered over them, a black, looming shadow against the leaden sky, but the warm glow of lamplight shone from several of the windows and an oblong of light spilled out from the open doorway and illuminated the steep stone steps leading down to the drive. As they approached, the black outline of a woman could be seen in the doorway. She hurried down the steps and handed a blanket to one of the men.

'Here, you can use this to carry him indoors.'

Silently Guy watched as the woman issued instructions, direct-ing the men in the best way to ease the unconscious man on to the blanket and how to hold it to cause the least movement as they made their way up into the house. He stopped for a quick word with the groom who came running out to take charge of the horses, then followed behind the ragged cortege, unheeded as they made their way through the echoing hall and up a wide stone staircase to a small chamber where a maid was hurriedly building up the fire.

Guy retired to the corner, reduced to a spectator. He was ready to advise if necessary, but the young woman was supervising the men as they laid Davey on the bed and Guy did not think he could im-prove upon her instructions. He watched her as she moved around the room, the candlelight glinting on her flame-red hair. Despite his concern for his friend, Guy found himself wondering how old she was: not a girl, that was certain, for she carried herself with assurance, speaking to the men—all known to her by name—in a calm, low voice. She was dressed in a grey gown that showed her slender figure to advantage and she moved with a youthful grace and agility that was very pleasing to the eye. She was clearly used to running a household. Was she perhaps the Lady Arabella the men had mentioned? He broke off from his reflections as the sound of a hasty footstep in the corridor announced the arrival of the doctor. A large, cheerful-looking man appeared in the doorway.

'Ah, Mrs Forrester, good evening to you!'

That answered one of Guy's questions.

The doctor approached the bed, saying cheerfully, 'So this is the young man I have been summoned to attend, is it? Thrown from his horse, I understand.'

'Yes.' Guy stepped out of the shadows. 'The mare came down on top of him.'

'Hmm.' The doctor frowned down at the unconscious form now laid out upon the bed. With a sudden movement he began to take off his coat. 'Then I must get to work. The rest of you should leave me now—except for your footman, ma'am. I will need him to help me undress my patient.'

'I will help you do that,' said Guy quickly.

The doctor gave him a searching look.

'I think not, sir. You would be advised to get out of those wet clothes or I shall end up with two patients instead of one! Mrs Forrester, perhaps you will take care of that—and get the rest of these men out of here! They have served their purpose and should all go away now!'

The red-haired woman immediately moved towards the door.

'Of course. Thank you, everyone. If you would like to go down to the kitchens, Cook has prepared a bowl of punch for you all.'

'Does that include me?' asked Guy as he filed out of the room behind the others. The young woman's large, dark eyes regarded him solemnly. She gave no sign that she had noticed his attempt at humour.

'No, sir, you may wait for your friend in the great hall. I will have refreshments brought to you there.'

Guy followed her back down the stairs. He had not realised how chilled he had become until he felt the heat coming from the fire blazing in the huge fireplace. Thankfully he moved towards it.

'And just who is this man dripping water all over my floor?'

The imperious voice stopped him in his tracks. He looked round to find an old woman standing on the far side of the room. She was dressed in severe black with a black lace cap over her snow-white hair and she was leaning heavily on an ebony cane. She looked very regal and Guy glanced down at his mud-stained clothes.

'I fear I must present a very dishevelled appearance, ma'am, and I beg your pardon.' He gave her his most elegant bow. 'I am Darrington.'

'The Earl of Darrington?'

'The same, madam.'

Behind him he heard the young woman's sharp intake of breath and smiled to himself. She had clearly not thought him of such consequence!

'Well, you will catch your death of cold if you remain in those wet clothes! Beth, my dear, what are you thinking of?'

'But Tilly and Martin are—'

'If the servants are busy, then you must take the earl upstairs, girl. Immediately!'

'I assure you, ma'am,' Guy began, 'I would as lief stay here beside the fire—'

Mrs Forrester interrupted him. 'My grandmother is right, my lord, you should change,' she said. 'Pray forgive me for not thinking of it sooner. Follow me, if you please.'

She led him away, up the stairs and through the twisting, turning corridors. As he followed he tried to take in his surroundings. The entrance and great hall were obviously very old, probably part of the original priory, but there were signs that the house had been extended in Tudor times to make a comfortable residence. The whole building had an air of antiquity and demonstrated the family's pride in its heritage. Everywhere was filled with fine old furniture and paintings from previous centuries; he guessed that the coffers pushed into odd corners would be found to contain a mass of unwanted objects that the old lady could not bring herself to throw away.

The young woman opened the door to a snug bedchamber with a cheerful fire burning in the grate. She walked across the room and lifted a large white cloth from beside the washstand.

'Use this to dry yourself. And if you remove your wet clothes, I will arrange for them to be cleaned and dried.'

She avoided looking at him and, almost before she had finished speaking, she was back at the door, whisking herself out of the room before he could thank her.

Guy stripped off his wet clothes and rubbed himself down with quick, powerful movements that forced the blood around his chilled body. There was a knock at the door and he looked out. The passage was empty, but a brightly patterned bundle of cloth was lying at his feet. Shaking it out, he found it was a wrap. Unlike the fashionable silk banyan that his valet would have laid out for him on his bed at Highridge, this garment was made of fine, soft wool, warm to the touch and infinitely comforting as he shrugged himself into it and fastened the ties at the waist. It was a little short, but otherwise a good fit. He was rubbing the worst of the wet from his hair when there was another soft knock on the door. It was Beth Forrester, holding a tray in her hands. His instinct was to take it from her, but some spirit of mischief made him stand aside, so that she was obliged to enter the room and carry the tray across to a table.

'I thought you might like a little bread and wine,' she said, not looking at him. 'My grandmother has asked me to look out some clothes for you, so that you may join us for supper later.'

'Thank you. I should be honoured to do so.' As he shut the door she whirled around, startled, and for the first time looked directly at him. Her eyes were a deep, dark brown, too beautiful to hold such anxiety as he read in their liquid depths. He said soothingly, 'Please, stay a moment—Mrs Forrester, is it not? I would like to talk to you.' She eyed him warily and he smiled. 'I am naturally anxious to know how my friend goes on.'

'Doctor Compton is still with him. There is no news yet.'

'Ah, of course.' He moved towards the dressing table. 'May I use this comb?'

She nodded and stood silent as he tidied his damp hair.

'Is this your bedroom?' His question brought her eyes to his face again and with a little smile he lifted a silver-backed hairbrush from the dressing table. 'There are red hairs in it.'

She nodded again.

'It was the only bedchamber with a fire. With Tilly and Martin both occupied it seemed the most sensible thing.…' She trailed off, a delicate flush mantling her cheeks.

'It is not at all sensible to let a strange man into your bedchamber,' he murmured, guessing her thoughts. 'But I am extremely grateful. I only hope your husband will understand.'

'My husband has been dead these six years, sir.'

'I am so very sorry.' He paused. 'Is this his banyan I am wearing?'

'No, it—it is my brother's, but it was always far too big for him and he never wore it. I should go…'

'Please, do not run away!'

'I am not— I mean, I must find some clothes to fit you, if you are to join Grandmama for supper.'

She stood before him, like a deer poised for flight, but still Guy stood in her way.

'And will you be at supper, too?'

'Of course.'

'Very well, I will let you go.'

He stepped aside, but even so in the small chamber there was only just room for her to walk by him to reach the door. He forced himself to keep still as she passed within inches of him and as she went by he breathed in the unmistakable scent of lemons.

Chapter Two

Beth's composure only lasted until she reached the corridor. As soon as she was out of sight of the bedroom door she collapsed against the wall, her legs trembling so much she could barely stand. What on earth was she about, to enter the room with that man in there, naked save for a thin wrap that clung to every contour of his body? As soon as she realised he was not going to take the tray from her she should have placed it on the ground and walked away, not carried it into the room. She was well aware of Lord Darrington's reputation as a dangerous rake—as well walk into a lion's den! A laugh bubbled inside her. He was certainly built like a noble beast. That clinging wrap had left little to the imagination and, although he was so tall, his broad shoulders and slim hips were to her mind perfectly proportioned. Her mouth had grown quite dry when she had watched him pulling her own ivory comb through his hair—for one reckless moment she wished it was her fingers that had been driving through those thick, dark locks. Beth closed her eyes, shocked by her reaction to this stranger. Was this what happened to widows when they had been alone for several years? The caresses and intimate moments she had shared with her husband had never seemed very important to her, yet now she was imagining herself locked in the arms of the earl and sharing heady, passionate kisses…

Beth took another deep breath and forced herself to be calm. The tingle of excitement she had felt when he looked at her was purely nerves, brought on by the unexpected events of the evening. She had been caught unawares. Now she must pull herself together: there was much to do before she could sit down for supper.

'So, my lord, you found something to fit you!'

Lady Arabella Wakeford looked formidable in her black-and-silver gown when Lord Darrington entered the great hall some two hours later. He walked up to her chair and gave a flourishing bow.

'As you see madam. The embroidered coat is perhaps more suited to St James's than Yorkshire, but much better that I present myself to you attired in this than a dressing gown.'

Standing beside her grandmother's chair, Beth thought the earl looked magnificent in the coat, waistcoat and breeches of striped-blue velvet. The coat and waistcoat were embroidered with yellow flowers and leaves around cut-glass lozenges that twinkled in the candlelight. The clothes hung a little loosely save across his broad shoulders where the coat was stretched tight, but she agreed with him: she could not have endured to sit at supper with him dressed only in that revealing wool wrap. She lifted her eyes to his face and the wicked glint in his eye made her believe he could read her thoughts. She blushed hotly.

'Since there is no man here to introduce us and my granddaughter seems to have lost her tongue, I suppose for formality's sake I must do it myself.' Lady Arabella held out her hand to the earl. 'You have the honour of addressing Lady Arabella Wakeford, widow of the last Sir Horace Wakeford and daughter of the Marquess of Etonwood. And this,' she continued, once he had kissed her fingers, 'is my granddaughter, Mrs Elizabeth Forrester.'

He bowed. 'Mrs Forrester.'

Beth dipped a curtsy, not sure if she was most relieved or disappointed that he did not reach for her hand. However, his forbearance pleased her grandmother, who thawed a little towards her guest.

'My granddaughter is a widow. It is Mr Forrester's court dress that you are wearing,' Lady Arabella informed him.

'Indeed?' murmured the earl. 'I am honoured to step into his shoes. And very pleased, too.'

Beth's eyes narrowed. Was he trying to flirt with her? She said pointedly, 'You may find they are too big for you, my lord.'

'The clothes *are* a little large for you around the middle,' agreed Lady Arabella, catching only part of Beth's words. 'But Forrester was inclined to corpulence.'

Darrington's eyes were on fire with unholy amusement while Beth seethed inwardly. She was thankful that her grandmother did not notice and continued to address the earl.

'I saw you entering your friend's room a little earlier, my lord. How does he do now?'

'He is sleeping, ma'am. I saw Dr Compton before he left and he explained that Mr Davies has broken his right leg.'

'Yes,' Beth replied. 'And he thinks there are a couple of broken ribs. He is also a little feverish, but I had feared it would be much worse. You may have confidence in Dr Compton, my lord. He is an excellent physician.'

The earl nodded. 'He has set the leg, but I fear Davies cannot be moved for a while yet—' He broke off as a door opened.

'I am so sorry to be late, Grandmama!' said a pretty, musical voice. 'With all the excitement no one remembered to collect the eggs, so I told Cook I would do it, and then my gown got so muddy I was obliged to change it!'

Beth stepped forwards.

'Sophie—let me present you to the Earl of Darrington. My sister, my lord.'

She watched as Sophie made her curtsy to the earl and was relieved when they showed no more than polite interest in each other. In Beth's eyes Sophie was uncommonly pretty, with her dark-honey curls and pansy-brown eyes, but she was only eighteen and had not yet enjoyed a season in town. Beth was afraid that the sudden entry into her world of a handsome and attractive peer of the realm might well cause her to lose her head and her heart, a complication that Beth could well do without. She listened as Sophie enquired politely after the health of Mr Davies and commiserated with the earl upon his soaking.

'Such a pity that Beth only kept Forrester's old court suit,' she said, eyeing the elaborate coat with disfavour.

'I would have borrowed a lackey's raiment if one could have been found to fit me. The alternative was to keep to my room until my own clothes are dry.'

The smile that accompanied these words startled Beth, for it softened the earl's rather sombre features and warmed his eyes. She felt again that delicious tingle running through her.

'Ah, such elaborate garments are not seen much now outside London, more's the pity,' sighed Lady Arabella. 'But something plainer might have been more comfortable for you, my lord. Beth my dear, could you not find something of Simon's for the earl?'

'They would not fit, Grandmama.' Beth caught the earl's look of enquiry and added briefly, 'My brother, sir. It was his wrap I gave you.'

'He died eighteen months ago,' added Lady Arabella.

'My condolences, ma'am. Was he—?'

Beth turned quickly to her grandmother, interrupting him.

'Here's Kepwith to say supper is ready for us. Shall we go in?'

Lord Darrington came forwards to offer Lady Arabella his arm.

'We keep to the old ways here, my lord,' she said as he led her into the dining room. 'An early dinner and supper at ten. At my age I do not want to be eating dinner in the evening and supper at midnight, as I believe is quite the fashion now in town.'

'But that makes perfect sense if one is at a ball, Grandmama,' put in Sophie. She smiled across the table at the earl. 'Not that I have yet been to a ball—a *real* ball, that is. But I shall do so next year, when Beth takes me to London.'

The earl turned toward Beth.

'You go often to town, Mrs Forrester?'

'No, I have never been. I—'

'Beth hasn't been away from Malpass for years,' put in Sophie. 'Except to go to Ripon to stay with her friend—but next year she has promised to take me to London for the Season. Of course, she will be Mrs Radworth by then—'

'Sophie!' Beth's knife clattered to her plate. 'Pray do not chatter on so. Lord Darrington does not want to know all our business.'

'But it is no secret,' stated Lady Arabella. 'Do you know Miles Radworth, Lord Darrington?'

'No, ma'am. I have not had that pleasure.'

'He has a property in Somerset, I believe, but he is currently renting a house in Fentonby. He came to bring us news of my grandson's death.' Lady Arabella stopped, her old eyes suddenly dimmed.

'I am very sorry, ma'am.'

The earl's words hung in the uncomfortable silence, broken only by the crackle of the fire and the soft padding of the butler as he walked from chair to chair, refilling their wine glasses. Beth was about to speak when Lady Arabella rallied and began again.

'My grandson was drowned at sea, you know. In the Bay of Biscay. He had been making the grand tour. It was very good of Mr Radworth to come all this way to tell us.'

'And it was not all bad news,' added Sophie brightly. 'He took one look at Beth and fell violently in love!'

'Indeed?' The earl's grey eyes rested on Beth.

'Yes.' Sophie nodded. 'And they are to be married.'

'Then I offer you my congratulations, Mrs Forrester.'

'Thank you.' Beth uttered the words quietly, keeping her eyes lowered.

'You and your friend are quite far from home, I believe,' remarked Lady Arabella.

'Yes, Davies has a hunting lodge at Highridge. I am staying there as his guest.'

'You must consider yourself a guest here,' came the gracious reply, 'until your friend is fit enough to return to Highridge.'

'No!' Beth coloured, and added quickly. 'What I mean is, surely there can be no need for Lord Darrington to stay. We can look after Mr Davies perfectly well.'

'But I should like to remain with my friend, if Lady Arabella permits,' the earl responded.

'But it is only a few miles to Highridge, and I am sure you would be much more comfortable there.'

'Nonsense, it is more than ten miles.' replied Lady Arabella. 'Lord Darrington must stay here, if he wishes. We have room to spare.'

'But…but we do not have so many staff—certainly not as many as an earl is accustomed to.'

'Oh, this earl is not at all high in the instep, I assure you,' came the mild reply. 'And I am quite undemanding.'

Again that amused glint in his eyes. Beth found it quite infuriating.

'To have you in the house as well as an invalid will create a great deal of extra work, no matter how undemanding you may be,' she ground out.

'I shall send to Highridge for Davies's valet to join us,' replied the earl, smiling in a way that made Beth long to hit him. 'He will be able to nurse his master and look after my very minor requirements. And I am sure that some of the other staff from Highridge would come, too, if they could be of use.'

'There is not the least need for anyone to come,' retorted Lady Arabella briskly. 'Really, Elizabeth, you are behaving very oddly this evening. My lord, I assure you we have sufficient servants to deal with everything that is required. You catch us at a disadvantage today because I gave some of my people permission to go to the market, leaving only a couple of maids and one footman to attend us. I have no doubt the rest are all returned now, but by all means bring your friend's manservant—and your own, for that matter, if you wish—we will find room for them all.'

'Since you do not object, ma'am, I shall summon Peters, who is Mr Davies's valet, and Holt, my groom. I shall not require my own man to attend me, although I will ask him to pack up my clothes and send them over.'

'That will be perfectly acceptable, my lord,' Lady Arabella responded regally, her frowning gaze fixed upon Beth. 'As the daughter of a marquess,' she said pointedly, 'I think I may be expected to know how to entertain an earl.'

'Yes, Grandmama.' Beth looked down at her plate and acknowledged herself beaten. 'I beg your pardon.'

* * *

Guy said little for the remainder of the meal; when Lady Arabella announced that the ladies would retire to the drawing room and leave him to enjoy a glass of brandy alone, he bent his mind once more to Beth Forrester's outburst. She had been quite determined that he should not stay. It could only be that she was uneasy with his presence. They lived very isolated here, but perhaps she was aware of his dubious reputation. Perhaps he should not have teased her so. Certainly it had been wrong of him to keep her talking alone in the bedroom, but she was a married woman, or at least a widow, not an ingenuous schoolgirl. He sipped at his brandy. One thing was certain, he wanted to remain at Malpass Priory at least until he knew that Davey was recovering well. He would apologise to Mrs Forrester and assure her that he would in future be the model of propriety. That should ease her mind.

Having made his resolve, Guy drained his glass and made his way to the drawing room, where he was disappointed to find only Lady Arabella waiting for him, the younger ladies having retired. However, she assured him that his room had been prepared and beckoned to the hovering footman to show him the way. With an inward smile Guy bowed over the beringed hand held out to him and prepared to leave. He had been dismissed for the evening.

Chapter Three

Martin the footman showed Guy to his room, a comfortable chamber that bore all the signs of having been a gentleman's bedroom.

'Was this Mr Forrester's room?' he enquired, glancing around him.

'No, my lord, this was Mr Simon's room,' offered the footman. 'My lady wouldn't have anything changed in here after she heard he was drowned and you will find the press still full of his clothes. But Mr Simon was much smaller than your lordship, so the mistress has searched out one o' Mr Forrester's nightgowns for you. And Mrs Forrester said to tell you that your own clothes will be brought to you in the morning.'

Nodding, Guy dismissed the servant. He removed his coat and draped it over the back of a chair, glad to be free of the restriction about his shoulders. He glanced at the clock on the mantelpiece. It was not yet midnight and, despite the excitement of the day, he did not feel sleepy. He prowled around the room, inspecting the sporting prints upon the walls and idly flicking through the few books that were stacked carelessly on the mantelshelf. The room had a cluttered, lived-in look, as if its master was expected to return at any time. The only exception to this was the dressing table, which was bare of the brushes and combs that one would expect to find in a gentleman's room. He supposed that Simon Wakeford had taken these items with him when he went travelling and they would have been lost at sea. He felt a sudden sympathy for Beth Forrester. His own brother, Nick, was a sailor and Guy could well imagine the pain of losing him. How much worse must it be for a widow, left to shoulder the burdens of running this old house and at the same time looking after her grandmother and her younger sister?

'Not that it is any of your business,' he told himself, coming back to the fire and throwing himself down into the chair. 'She has made it very plain that you are here on sufferance, so do not waste your sympathy where it is not wanted.'

He began to unbutton his waistcoat, but stopped when he heard a faint cry break the silence. Before he undressed he should look in on Davey and make sure he was comfortable. Picking up his bedroom candle, he let himself quietly out of the room. The borrowed shoes he had worn at supper were too loose to walk without tapping noisily on the polished boards of the corridor and he left them behind, padding silently through the darkened house until he came to the door at the top of the stairs.

There was a faint line of light beneath the door and as he entered the room he saw that a single lamp glowed on a side table, illuminating the curtained bed, but leaving the corners of the room in deep shadow. A movement beside the fire brought him to a stand.

'Mrs Forrester!' She rose as he whispered her name, the dim light muting her fiery hair to a deep auburn. He continued, 'I heard someone cry out and thought perhaps he might be...'

Guy waved towards the figure in the bed. She looked discomposed and took a step as if she would leave the room, then thought better of it.

'Mr Davies has not moved,' she said quietly. 'It must have been a peacock, or some night creature that you heard, my lord. The night time is full of noises.'

He nodded. 'Of course. But why are you here, ma'am?'

'Doctor Compton suggested someone should sit with your friend tonight,' she said softly.

'But he did not mean you, ma'am.'

She spread her hands. 'I wanted to be sure he was comfortable. Besides, the servants need to be fresh for their duties in the morning.'

'And you do not?' He placed his candle on the mantelshelf before turning his attention to the figure in the bed. 'How is he?'

'Still sleeping. He grows a little restless now and again, but nothing serious.' She added with a thread of humour in her voice, 'It is very tedious keeping watch over a sleeping man.'

'Then may I sit with you for a while?'

'Oh, no—that is, I did not mean to imply...' Beth trailed off, disturbed lest he should think she had been hinting for him to stay.

'Of course not, but surely a little company would be welcome to while away the long night hours.'

Beth could not deny it. With a little nod she resumed her seat beside the fire and motioned him to a chair opposite, her eyes dwelling for a while on his stockinged feet.

'Ah. I did not wish to wake the household by clumping along in those court shoes.'

'I did not hear you approach; that is unusual for this house—the building is very old, you see. It is full of rattling doors and creaking boards.'

'I was aware of that as I came along the landing earlier this evening. A person with a more fevered imagination might well have thought there were spirits abroad.'

'The wind does howl through the corridors and rattle the locks.' She was glad of the opportunity to explain away any noises he might hear in the night. 'Some guests think they hear voices, others declare the Priory to be haunted. All nonsense, of course. I hope you will ignore any strange sounds, my lord, and remain comfortably in your bed.'

'You may be sure I shall, madam.'

They lapsed into silence. After a few moments the earl said slowly, 'I am glad of this opportunity to speak to you, Mrs Forrester. We have given you a great deal of extra work, I fear.'

'Think nothing of it, my lord.'

'But you were very much against my remaining here overnight.'

'Oh, no! It was... I mean—if I was ungracious, my lord, I beg your pardon.'

'There is no need. I quite understand, given the circumstances.'

Startled, Beth looked up. What did he know, what had he guessed? 'My lord?'

'To have me walk in, wearing your late husband's clothes. I should have realised how distressing my appearance must be to you.'

'Oh.' She breathed again, relieved. 'I have been a widow for nigh on six years, sir. I barely remember that suit of clothes. Besides, you are nothing like my husband.' Beth wished she had not spoken. Would he think she was trying to flirt with him? She added hastily, 'I mean, sir, that Mr Forrester was a very *good* man.'

'As I am not?'

'I have no idea!' she retorted, flustered.

He laughed at her. 'I beg your pardon, madam. I could not resist the opportunity to tease you.'

Beth pressed her lips together, determined not to respond, but she could feel the heat in her cheeks and was aware that in other circumstances she would quite enjoy his teasing.

She was thankful when a groan from the bed claimed their attention. Mr Davies was stirring. He was muttering incoherently and Beth picked up a cloth and dipped it into the small bowl on the bedside table.

'Lavender water,' she explained as she gently wiped the patient's brow. 'It is very soothing.'

However, on this occasion it did not calm Mr Davies, who continued to mutter and began to move restlessly in the bed.

'Perhaps you should leave him to me?' suggested Lord Darrington as the injured man cried out and began to curse when the movement tore at his cracked ribs.

'My dear sir, I am no schoolroom miss! I have heard much worse from my husband and my brother, I assure you. We must give him some laudanum,' she decided. 'Can you support his shoulders, my lord?'

The earl proved himself surprisingly useful in a sickroom, using his strength to gently raise his friend while Beth administered the drug. He continued to hold him up while Beth turned the pillows and straightened the covers. Soon Mr Davies was growing calmer again as the laudanum began to take effect and Beth could return to her seat. She wondered if the earl might retire now, but instead he sat down again. Neither of them spoke, yet the silence was not uncomfortable. It was surprisingly companionable sitting together, listening to the steady, rhythmic breathing of the man in the bed and Beth did not wish to break the spell. Her eyelids drooped and she dozed.

It was some time later that Beth woke and noticed that the earl's bedside candle had burned itself out and the fire was reduced to glowing ash. She reached for the poker, but the earl forestalled her.

'Allow me.'

She sat back in her chair and watched him as he knelt before the fire, stirring up the embers before building it up with small logs from the basket. He was still wearing the embroidered waistcoat she had found for him. The strings had been pulled tight across the back to make it fit and the white sleeves of his shirt billowed out, accentuating the wide shoulders that she knew lay beneath the soft linen. His movements were quick and assured and he soon coaxed the fire into a blaze. Beth gazed at his face as he sat back on his heels and regarded his handiwork. He had a handsome profile, she decided. The straight nose and sculpted lips would not have looked amiss on a Greek statue, although the heavy black brows and the line of his jaw were a little too strong to be called classical.

He turned his head at that moment and she found herself unable to look away, her gaze locked with his rather hard grey eyes. A presentiment of danger swept over her. She had become far too complacent; it was the middle of the night and they were the only beings awake in this twilight world. Her throat dried. There was a distant cock crow somewhere outside the window.

'The servants will be stirring soon.' Her voice sounded strained. 'Perhaps you should retire, my lord.' His brows rose and she went on, 'I know one should not listen to gossip, but I am well aware of your reputation, my lord. We subscribe to the London *Intelligencer*...'

'Ah. That explains a great deal.'

She heard the dry note in his voice and added quickly, 'I am aware that much of what they write is untrue. No one knows better than I—however, it is not wise to be alone.'

'But we are not—we have Davies here as our chaperon, after all.'

A twinkle of amusement banished the harsh look in his eyes and she found herself responding with a smile.

'So we have, my lord. But there are some hours yet until breakfast and you should get some rest. You need not be anxious for me,' she added quickly. 'My maid is coming to relieve me shortly.'

'Then if there is nothing else I can do for you, I shall return to my room.' He stood up.

Intimidated by him towering over her, Beth rose, but even when she drew herself up her eyes were only level with his mouth. She was momentarily distracted by the curve of his lips and the tiny lines on each side of his mouth, indicative of laughter. An entertaining companion. The thought occurred to Beth and was instantly dismissed. She had no time for such luxuries.

'Thank you, my lord, for your assistance.'

'It was my pleasure, ma'am.'

With a slight bow he left the room. As soon as the door closed Beth was aware of a chill of loneliness wrapping itself around her.

Chapter Four

Lady Arabella did not believe in the modern notion of nuncheon and it was usually close to noon before she left her apartments to break her fast. By that time Beth had normally been up for hours and busy with her household duties, but after a night keeping watch in the sickroom she had slept the early morning away and was roused by her maid coming to tell her that Dr Compton had arrived to see his patient.

The hour was therefore quite advanced by the time Beth made her way to the breakfast table. Lord Darrington was already there and appeared to be upon the very best of terms with his hostess. They were bandying names unfamiliar to Beth as she came in and she heard her grandmother sigh.

'Of course I never go to town now and most of my old friends have passed on, so I am no longer in touch with the world.'

'Nonsense, Grandmama,' said Beth bracingly. 'Sophia and I read the London papers to you every day!'

'Including the *Intelligencer*?' murmured Guy.

Beth avoided his laughing eyes.

'But that is hardly the same,' stated Lady Arabella. 'I was telling Darrington he should go to town more.'

'London holds no charms for me,' said the earl apologetically. He was dressed once more in his fine wool riding jacket and tightly fitting buckskins, but all traces of mud and dirt had been removed.

'I am pleased Mrs Robinson managed to clean your clothes for you,' said Beth as he rose and held out a chair for her.

'Yes. They were delivered up to me earlier this morning. Please thank your housekeeper for me. However, I shall be happier once Holt has arrived with my baggage. I would prefer to wear something a little more formal—and my own!—before I sit down to dinner again.'

Beth refused to respond to his charming smile.

'There is not the least need for you to put yourself to the inconvenience of staying another night—'

'That is enough, Elizabeth.' Lady Arabella's voice cut across the table. 'I have invited Lord Darrington to stay with us for as long as he wishes.'

'But our household cannot be what the earl is accustomed to,' objected Beth.

Lady Arabella silenced her with the wave of her hand and turned again to the earl.

'My granddaughter appears to think we are not good enough for you, Darrington. I do not know why. The Wakefords can trace their line back before the Conqueror and my own family rose to prominence in the time of good King Hal. Your own title, I believe, was not created until the time of Charles the Second.'

The earl nodded. 'That is correct, ma'am. I am a veritable upstart.'

'That is not what I meant at all,' protested Beth, flustered. 'I was...concerned for your comfort, sir.'

His sceptical look brought the colour flooding to her cheeks and she was pleased when Sophie arrived to create a diversion. Her young sister was prettily polite to their guest and enquired solicitously after his friend's health.

'I have not yet seen him this morning, Miss Wakeford, but I believe he is comfortable.' The earl looked an enquiry at Beth, who nodded. He continued, 'I am much in Mrs Forrester's debt. She attended Mr Davies throughout the night.'

'Ah, then that accounts for her crotchets this morning,' remarked Lady Arabella with no little satisfaction.

Normally Beth would have laughed off such a comment, but the fact that the earl was present to hear it made her feel out of reason cross. She turned to her sister.

'Sophie my love, will you have time to help me today? We need to gather more comfrey leaves.'

'More?' said Lady Arabella. 'But you went out collecting comfrey only last week. Surely you have enough?'

'Rudge tells me the old mare requires another poultice, ma'am,' Beth explained patiently.

'Then let him go and gather the leaves,' retorted her grandmother. 'He is, after all, the groom—or he could send the stable boy.'

'Really I do not mind going,' said Sophie quickly. 'I know exactly where to find the best comfrey plants and shall collect a whole basketful. Then we shall have leaves to dry as well as fresh ones to use now.' She smiled across the table at Lady Arabella. 'You need have no fear, Grandmama. I shall be back in time to read the papers to you while you are resting before dinner.'

'You have both forgotten our guest may need entertaining.'

The earl shook his head. 'Not at all, my lady. I am very happy to amuse myself.'

'Lord Darrington is, of course, welcome to join us on our expedition,' Beth offered politely but Guy did not miss the look of relief that crossed her features when he declined.

He said, 'I expect the carriage to arrive from Highridge at any moment and I propose to take a stroll along the drive to look out for it.'

'Then if you will excuse us, we will collect our baskets and be off. Come, Sophie.'

The two young ladies disappeared, Lady Arabella made her way to the morning room, declaring that she was going to write her letters, and Guy was left alone. After assuring himself that Davey was still asleep, he made his way to the entrance and descended the steep stone steps to the drive. It was a bright, sunny morning with just a hint of autumn in the air and it was hard to believe that only the night before he had followed the farmhands as they carried Davey's body through the rain, up these same steps and into the house. He looked around him with interest at the old building. The original refectory with its gabled roof now housed the main entrance and great hall. Beside the steps was an ancient arched doorway, leading to the undercroft. Intrigued, Guy tried the door, but it was locked. Wandering on, he soon spotted the stable block and made his way across to it. He noted with approval the tidy yard and quickly strode across the swept cobbles and through the high-arched entrance to the stables. Inside he found an iron-haired groom inspecting Davey's bay mare. The man touched his cap when he saw Guy approaching.

'Rudge, isn't it?' Guy addressed him pleasantly and nodded towards the mare. 'No injuries, I hope?'

'No, sir, she's in fine fettle. As is your hunter, my lord. We brushed 'em down, fed and watered 'em as we would our own. They was a bit shaken, but they're both as good as new, now.'

'Well, that's good news.' Guy smiled. 'I would not want to add to your work when you already have one lame horse to worry about.'

'Sir?'

'Your mistress said this morning there was an old mare needed a poultice.'

Slowly the groom shook his head. 'Not in these stables, my lord. I check them all every morning and I'd know if there was summat wrong.'

Guy frowned for a moment, then shrugged.

'No matter, mayhap I misunderstood her.' He heard the rattle of an approaching carriage. 'Ah, that should be Mr Davies's man—and my groom. I hope you will be able to accommodate Holt in your stables, Rudge? He is a useful man, and of course he will defer to you,' he added quickly, making a mental note to talk to Holt before he set him to work.

Guy made his way back to the front drive in time to see his travelling chariot sweep into view. Holt was riding on the back seat and jumped down nimbly even before the carriage had stopped. A few words sufficed to send him hurrying off to the stables and

Guy was then free to observe Peters, Mr Davies's diminutive but very efficient valet, and the various trunks and bags that he had brought to the Priory.

In a very short time Peters had made himself at home in the sickroom, unpacking the bags and even finding time to shave his master in readiness for Dr Compton's next visit. However, Guy would not allow the valet to remove Mr Davies's borrowed nightshirt until the doctor had pronounced the patient well enough to be moved. Davey himself, sleepy from laudanum and irritable from discomfort, swore roundly and wished them at the very devil, his outburst bringing a rare smile to his servant's rather austere countenance.

'It is good to see that you are recovering, sir,' he murmured as he walked out of the room with the shaving apparatus.

'Damn your eyes, why did you have to send for him?' grumbled Davey. His fair hair was ruffled and his boyish face was uncharacteristically glum.

'Because he is the best person to look after you,' returned Guy, unperturbed. He perched himself on the edge of the bed. 'But tell me truthfully, how do you feel?'

'Like the very devil! I don't think there is a part of me that doesn't hurt. Can't laugh or cough without a stabbing pain in my ribs, my wrist feels as if it's sprained and my leg—' He glanced up and Guy saw the anxiety lurking in his guileless blue eyes. 'Is it…?'

'Broken, nothing more serious. The doctor has set it and thinks it should heal perfectly, if you will be patient.'

'And where are we? I don't recognise this house, nor the servants.'

'Malpass Priory, near Fentonby. It is the home of Lady Arabella Wakeford. Do you know her?'

Davey frowned. 'No. I've heard the name, though.'

'So have I.' Guy frowned. 'Cannot quite recall where I have seen it. They are a very old family, I understand.' A smile tugged at the corners of his mouth. 'The Wakefords were ennobled long before the Wylders gained their earldom.'

'Well, their house is certainly old enough,' remarked Davey, staring at the gracefully arching window with its leaded lights. 'But thankfully they have had the wisdom to renew the mattress on this old bed! Have they put you up, too? Are you comfortable?'

'The room is comfortable enough.'

Davey did not miss the hesitation in Guy's tone and he said bluntly, 'Are we inconveniencing the family?'

'I am not sure.' Guy rubbed his chin. 'The old lady seems happy enough to have us here and they were quick enough to take you in last night, but I have the distinct impression her granddaughter doesn't want me here.' He shrugged. 'Perhaps I am unjust. It may be that she is uneasy having gentlemen in the house. The old lady lives here alone, you see, with her two granddaughters—there was a grandson, but I understand he died at sea some eighteen months ago.'

'That will be it, then,' said Davey sagely. 'The women are afraid of being ravaged by the Dangerous Lord Darrington! Don't worry— I'll soon make it known that you are house-trained and only seduce women who throw themselves at you.'

'Thank you, my friend, but I would prefer you to say no such thing.' Guy noted his friend's pallor and rose. 'All this talking has tired you. Rest now until the doctor arrives. I could send for your own doctor from Helmsley if you prefer, but Compton seems able enough.'

'No, no, I don't want anyone else fussing over me.' Davey waved his hand. 'Go away, now, and let me sleep. And tell Peters to keep out of my sight until after the sawbones has been to see me!'

Encouraged by his friend's return to spirits, Guy went out. He intended to go back to his own room and check his bag to see what changes of clothes his man had sent for him, but the sound of voices coming from the great hall drew him instead to descend the stairs.

He observed a tall, fashionably dressed gentleman standing before the fireplace. He had removed his Holland hat of brushed beaver to display a heavily powdered wig tied back into a queue with a green ribbon. He wore brown breeches and highly polished topboots, and the gloves and cane that lay on the bench beside his hat suggested he had arrived on horseback.

As Guy reached the bottom stair the man became aware of his presence and swung round towards him. He subjected Guy to a searching scrutiny before giving a little bow.

'You must be Lord Darrington,' he said pleasantly. 'Allow me to present myself. Miles Radworth, at your service.'

Ah, thought Guy. *The fiancé. That might explain the underlying reserve.*

'Kepwith has been telling me of the accident,' continued Mr Radworth. 'I trust your friend has sustained no serious injury?'

'A few cracked ribs and a broken leg, but nothing more, we hope. We are awaiting the doctor now.'

'Excellent, excellent. Let us hope he has good news for you. You will be wanting to get your friend back to his own house, I don't doubt.'

Guy met Radworth's smile with one equally bland.

'All in good time,' he responded. 'Lady Arabella has been most hospitable. We are very comfortable here.'

'Ah. I'm glad to hear it,' came the insincere reply.

A rustle of skirts made both men look towards the door.

'Miles! I did not expect you here today.'

Beth Forrester came in, pausing to remove her straw bonnet, and at that moment the sun shone in through the high window in the gable wall, bathing her in a golden glow. Guy could not but appreciate the effect: her red curls flamed about her head, accentuating the whiteness of her skin and the deep, liquid depths of her brown eyes. With the grey redingote hanging open from her shoulders and her white skirts billowing as she moved, Guy was suddenly reminded of an oil painting he had seen once, by one of the old Italian masters: an angel descending to the earth. As if to confirm his impression the glinting sun created a halo around her flaming head as she tossed aside her bonnet and held out her hands to Miles Radworth.

'I had not planned to come,' he said, lifting her fingers to his lips, 'but when word reached me that there had been an accident—'

'But not to me.' She smiled up at him, her fingers squeezing his briefly before she disengaged herself and moved away. 'You have met Lord Darrington?'

'We introduced ourselves,' murmured Guy. 'Was your search successful, ma'am? Did you find the leaves you required?'

'Yes, two full baskets! I gave them to Sophie to take to the still room rather than trail them through the house.'

'Comfrey leaves, was it not?' he asked. 'To make a compress for your lame horse?'

She shot a quick look at him.

'Why, yes, comfrey has many uses. We shall dry some, of course. The weather is turning now and the leaves are dying back, so this was our last opportunity to gather them.' She turned to Miles Radworth again. 'So you rode over to assure yourself that all was well here? That was kind.'

He bowed. 'I was hoping you might invite me to stay for dinner, even though Lady Arabella might look a little askance at my informal dress.'

Guy wondered if he imagined the heartbeat's hesitation before her reply.

'But of course, Miles, that would be delightful. You know us too well to stand on ceremony, so you will not be offended when I say that I shall be obliged to leave you to entertain yourself for a while. I am expecting Dr Compton here at any moment to attend Mr Davies.'

'I have no wish to add to your burdens,' Radworth replied quickly. 'Perhaps there is something I can do, read the newspaper to Lady Arabella, for example. You know you may trust me to do that.'

She smiled at him. 'Yes, of course I do, Miles, but Sophie has offered to read to Grandmama, so there really is nothing for you to do.'

'You insist upon treating me as a guest,' he said in a low voice. 'Come November…'

'Come November everything will be different,' she responded quietly. 'For today, however, perhaps you could show the earl the library, Miles? You are almost as familiar with the rare books and artefacts in there as I am.'

'Thank you, but I had planned to accompany Mrs Forrester and Dr Compton to the sickroom,' put in Guy, mildly irritated by the thought that others should organise his time.

'Is that quite necessary?'

Radworth's question was posed lightly, but Guy found his hackles rising.

'Perhaps not, but perfectly understandable,' Beth interposed smoothly. 'I have no doubt Lord Darrington is anxious for his friend. In fact, we will go upstairs now, my lord, if you wish, and make sure all is in readiness. Doctor Compton is no stranger here and will make his own way up when he arrives. So, Miles, I pray you will make yourself comfortable in the library and I will join you again as soon as I can.'

Thus dismissed, Radworth nodded and walked away. Neither Guy nor Beth moved until the library door had closed behind him.

'As a matter of fact, I have just come down from Davies's room,' said Guy. 'He was looking tired so I promised he would not be disturbed again until the doctor's arrival.'

She raised her brows at him. 'But you did not think to say so before I sent Miles away?'

'I did not think Radworth desired more of my company.'

'He is anxious that you should not impose upon me.'

'You are very quick to defend him.'

Her chin went up a little. 'Of course. We are betrothed. Besides, he has been very kind to us. A true friend.'

Guy met her eyes, trying to interpret her look, half-defensive, half-defiant.

'And you will marry him in November.'

'Yes.'

Even to Beth's own ears the word sounded stark and cold. It should not be, for she was very happy about her forthcoming marriage, was she not? It was merely that she could not look forward to that happy day until she had resolved the problem that weighed upon her spirits.

'Then Davies and I must be very much in your way,' said the earl.

She wanted to disclaim, but honesty tied her tongue and it was with relief that she heard the doctor's hearty voice at the entrance. Moments later Dr Compton was striding across the hall.

'Good day to 'ee, Mrs Forrester, and to you, my lord. Glad to see *you* haven't been laid up after your soaking yesterday! And how is my patient, awake by now, I hope! Passed a reasonable night, did he? Good, good. Well, then, take me to him!'

Beth soon realised that she was not needed in the sickroom. Mr Davies's valet was eager to attend his master, so she left him taking instruction from the doctor, with the earl standing by, ready to lend a hand if necessary. Doctor Compton cheerfully dismissed Beth, promising to find her and give her his report before he left.

She went downstairs, but after staring at the library door for a few moments she decided against joining Miles and instead made her way down to the lower floor.

Beth emerged a short time later, shaking the dust from her skirts before hurrying back to the great hall where she spotted the butler coming out of the library.

'Kepwith, is Dr Compton still upstairs?'

'Yes, madam.' He gave a little cough. 'I am to fetch refreshments for Mr Radworth, madam. He informs me he is staying to dinner.'

'That is correct. Perhaps you would see to it that another cover is laid, if you please.'

The butler bowed, hesitated, then said anxiously, 'Is that wise, ma'am? In the circumstances…' His meaning was not lost upon Beth.

'Perhaps not,' she said quietly, 'but it cannot be helped.'

'But if he should become restless, madam, and cry out again—'

She put up her hand to stop him. 'Tilly will make sure that does not happen again. There is no reason our guests should find anything amiss, Kepwith, as long as we keep our heads.' She looked up to see the doctor and Lord Darrington coming down the stairs. 'Very good, Kepwith, that will be all. Well, Doctor, how is Mr Davies?'

'Progressing, Mrs Forrester, progressing, but I would as lief he was kept very still today. Lord Darrington suggested carrying him in his own travelling chariot, loaded with cushions, but even so I would not wish to move him yet. We shall see how he goes on after another night or so. I shall return again tomorrow, madam. Until then Davies's man is on hand now and he seems a competent fellow. He will look after his master.'

He began to move towards the door.

'But what should I give him for fever?'

Doctor Compton stopped. 'Put your mind at rest, madam, the fever has passed now.'

'Of course, but if he should wake up…'

'A few sips of water, perhaps, or have some lemonade on hand, if you wish.'

'Nothing stronger?' Beth persisted. 'He may be in pain and I have used up the laudanum you left us. I'm afraid I spilled some of it on the floor this morning.'

The doctor smiled at her. 'Why this sudden anxiety, Mrs Forrester? This is most unlike you.'

She spread her hands. 'I am concerned that Mr Davies should be comfortable.'

'Well, make him up a saline draught, if you wish, it will do no harm. And if he is in pain—which I do not at all anticipate as long as he is kept quiet—I have more laudanum in my saddlebag, I'll give it to your butler. Now, I must get on. Come along then, Kepwith, if you please! I have two more patients to call upon today.'

Beth watched the butler escort him to the door, then turned to find the earl waiting for her in the great hall.

'You may be easy, Mrs Forrester. Peters is a good man and will know how to look after his master, I am sure.'

'Yes, of course. I m-merely wanted to ensure Mr Davies does not have a disturbed night.' She added lightly, 'Poor Mr Radworth will think I have forgotten him! Shall we go into the library, my lord?'

He declined gracefully. 'I wish to check all is well with my groom.'

'As you wish, my lord. You may recall we dine early at Malpass. Shall I send a man to help you dress in, say, an hour?'

He shook his head. 'Peters can do all I require—you look incredulous, Mrs Forrester. I told you I am not at all high in the instep.'

She was disarmed by his smile and as she gazed into his cool grey eyes she found herself thinking that it was no wonder he broke so many hearts. The click of heels on the marble floor recalled her; a footman was making his way to the library, a tray bearing a decanter and glasses balanced on one hand.

'Oh, heavens. Miles!' Her hands flew to her mouth and with a quick glance of apology towards the earl she hurried off.

Chapter Five

When Beth went upstairs to change for dinner she decided not to wear the grey silk laid out in readiness, but asked her maid to fetch her new lavender silk gown with the white muslin petticoat.

'Ah, dressing up for Lord Darrington, are we?' giggled Tilly.

Beth frowned at her. 'Not at all. Mr Radworth is staying for dinner.'

'So you won't be wanting to hide your charms beneath a white fichu?'

'That is enough of your insolence!' Beth grabbed the fine muslin scarf and arranged it becomingly to fill the low neckline of her gown. She said, trying to sound severe, 'I do not know why I put up with you, Tilly.'

Her maid merely laughed at her. 'Because you know I love you and Sophie and Lady Arabella very dearly. And because no one else can dress your hair quite so well. So do sit down now, Miss Beth, and let me brush your curls for you.'

Beth had submitted to her maid's ministrations and was rewarded by the look of approbation that she received from Miles Radworth as she entered the drawing room. She was disappointed to receive no such acknowledgement from Lord Darrington, who was conversing with Sophie and Lady Arabella on the far side of the room. He glanced across when she came in, but made no attempt to approach. As Miles took her hand and murmured any number of flowery compliments, Beth watched the earl from the corner of her eye, noting that he gave all his attention to her grandmother. She was piqued; she did not need Miles to tell her that the lavender silk set off her copper-coloured curls. One glance in the mirror had informed her that she presented a very striking figure, and while she would have been offended if the earl had been so impolite as to ogle her, she would have liked to see some sign of appreciation from him.

'…what do you say to that, my love?'

She dragged her attention back to Miles, who was obviously wanting an answer to his question. She summoned up her most charming smile. 'I beg your pardon, Miles, I do not understand you?'

'I was merely suggesting, in my roundabout way, that since you have done nothing yet about your bride clothes, I should take you to York. I am sure Lady Arabella can manage perfectly well without you for a few days.'

'Ah, Miles, how thoughtful, but there really is no need. I intend to go and stay with my good friend Maria Crowther in Ripon and I will be able to buy everything I need there.'

She excused herself and moved towards Lady Arabella. The earl rose as she approached.

'Mrs Forrester.' He bowed and held the chair for her. 'Perhaps you would like to sit next to Lady Arabella?'

Beth inclined her head and sat down, but she could not relax while the earl remained standing behind her. It took great strength of will not to turn her head to see if his hands were still resting on the back of her chair. She forced herself to say something.

'Grandmama, I hope Sophie has taken care of you this afternoon?'

'Of course, as she always does,' replied Lady Arabella. 'Such a good girl, and she reads so beautifully, not a hint of impatience when I am sure she would rather be elsewhere.'

'Not at all, Grandmama!' Sophie cried out at this and the old lady chuckled and patted her cheek.

'Perhaps, my lady, you might allow me to read the newspaper

to you tomorrow,' offered the earl, moving around to stand beside Miles Radworth. 'It would be a little something I can do to repay your hospitality.'

'Aye, and I have no doubt you would do it admirably with that deep, smooth voice of yours,' agreed the lady.

'Oh, but I am very happy to read to you, Grandmama,' said Sophie quickly.

'So, too, am I,' declared Beth. 'We do not need to trouble the earl with such a task.'

'What, would you deny me the company of such a handsome gentleman?' Lady Arabella's eyes twinkled with mischief. 'I do believe they want to keep you for themselves, Darrington.'

The earl gave a little bow. 'I am flattered, my lady.'

The inconsequential thought entered Beth's mind that his dark hair, cut short to collar length and with its tawny highlights glowing in the candlelight, was much more attractive than Miles's curled and dully powdered wig. She scolded herself silently. She had invited Miles to take dinner with them, so it was unjust to make any comparison when he had not been able to change for dinner. She must not contrast his velvet jacket with the earl's dark coat that seemed moulded to his form, nor should she compare topboots and riding breeches with satin knee-breeches and stockings that showed Lord Darrington's athletic limbs to great advantage. When it came to ornaments, she thought the honours equal, for apart from a large signet ring and the diamond that flashed discreetly from the folds of his snowy cravat, Lord Darrington had only his quizzing glass, hanging about his neck on a black ribbon. Miles, however, wore an emerald pin in his neckcloth and was sporting a few fobs and seals at his waistband, as well as his ornate watch. No, she would not compare them, nor would she dwell on the fact that with his splendid physique, the earl looked very like the heroes that had once filled her dreams. Her marriage to Joseph Forrester had taught her to put aside such romantic notions. It had been a struggle to curb her impetuous nature, but Joseph had soon taught her that a husband did not want a wife constantly hanging on his arm or displaying affection. She did not think her life with Miles would be any different, for her feelings for him were well-regulated, unlike the disturbing turmoil Lord Darrington roused in her.

Looking up, she met his amused glance and her face flamed. She hoped he could not read her thoughts!

A glance at Miles showed that he was not too happy with the conversation and she said quickly, 'Grandmama, you are very wicked to tease us so. We must not forget that when Dr Compton calls tomorrow he may declare Mr Davies well enough to return to Highridge and we will be obliged to say goodbye to our guests.'

'And very sorry I shall be to see them go,' declared Lady Arabella. 'The Priory has been far too quiet since Simon died. We have become positively reclusive.'

'You know I would willingly move in, my lady,' offered Miles, 'if it would comfort you to have a man in residence.'

Lady Arabella stared at him for a long moment, her face quite impassive. She said at last, 'Thank you, Mr Radworth, but no one can replace my grandson.'

The silence hung uneasily about the room. Beth rose in a whisper of silk.

'Shall we go in to dinner?'

Beth did not enjoy her meal. Lady Arabella presided over the table with her usual grace, but although the two gentlemen were perfectly polite to each other, Beth was uncomfortably aware of a tension in the air. Even Sophie cast uneasy glances at them. When she considered the matter dispassionately she did not think that any blame could attach to Lord Darrington, who was seated next to Lady Arabella and responded to her questions and remarks with perfect ease and good humour. Miles, however, was above being pleased. He found fault with every dish and, although Lady Arabella did not appear to notice his ill humour, his barbed remarks made even Sophie lapse into uncharacteristic silence. He was also drinking heavily, calling for his glass to be refilled with such regularity that Kepwith was obliged to fetch up another bottle.

The covers had been removed and the dishes of sweetmeats placed upon the table when matters came to a head. Miles was reaching for a dish of sugared almonds when his cuff caught the edge of his wineglass and sent the contents spilling across the table. The earl quickly threw his napkin on the pool of wine as Miles jumped up, cursing under his breath.

'No harm done,' said Beth, placing her cloth over the earl's. 'We have contained it. Sophie, if you give me your napkin, too, I think that will do the trick.'

'I beg your pardon, that was dashed clumsy of me,' muttered Miles, standing back and watching proceedings. 'That last bottle was bad.'

'Very possibly,' said Beth in a tight voice.

A footman brought in more cloths to finish wiping the table.

'There, all is well again,' remarked Lady Arabella. 'Pray sit down again, Mr Radworth.'

'Aye, I will, but first I am going down to the cellars to find a decent bottle!' He grabbed the butler's arm. 'Give me the key.'

'Sir!' The butler's exclamation was a mixture of outrage and alarm.

Sophie gasped. Beth put a hand on her shoulder, aware that the earl was watching them.

'There is no need for that, Miles.' She kept her voice calm. 'Kepwith shall bring another bottle if you wish for one.'

'Aye, I do wish it, but I'll have none of his choosing. It's my belief he is fobbing you off with poor stuff and keeping the best for himself.'

'Nonsense,' said Beth sharply. 'I do not keep disloyal staff. Neither do I allow my guests to venture into the servants' domain.'

Her hauteur had its effect. Miles glared at her, but she held his gaze steadily and at last he resumed his seat, saying with a little laugh, 'You are quite right, m'dear. Plenty of time to discuss how the household is run once we are married, eh? Very well, Kepwith, you may go and find another bottle of claret, and be quick about it!'

Lady Arabella led the ladies away to the drawing room soon after, and Beth was not surprised that the gentlemen did not tarry over their port. Miles seemed to realise that he had gone too far and tried to approach Beth and apologise, but she would have none of it, turning a shoulder to him, only relenting when he announced he was leaving shortly after they had drunk tea together and humbly begged her to accompany him to the door.

'My dear, I can only apologise for my outburst,' he said, unclipping his watch and putting it safely in his waistcoat pocket.

She shrugged. 'The effects of inferior wine, I collect.'

'Not only that, Elizabeth. I fear I was jealous of seeing Darrington so at ease here.'

She blinked. 'You are jealous of the earl? You have no need, I assure you. I have no interest in him at all!'

'Ah, but what if he is interested in *you*?' said Miles. 'I observed how often he watched you this evening.'

'No, I am sure you are mistaken,' she cried, her colour heightened.

'I think not. I fear he may wish to fix his interest with you.'

She raised her brows. 'How can he, when I am already betrothed to you?'

'Betrothed, yes, but how I wish we were wed!' He pulled Beth into his arms. 'I would have married you the moment you came out of mourning—'

'I know, but we must give Grandmama time to grow accustomed. You have been very forbearing,' she said softly. 'Pray, Miles, be patient for a little longer.'

'Why must we wait?' His arms tightened. 'You are no innocent schoolgirl, Beth—can you not tell how much I long for you? You need have no worry that I am making you false promises to get you into my bed. The contract is signed, 'tis only the priest's blessing we are lacking—'

'Good heavens, Miles, would you have the shades of this old place rise up against us?' she asked him jokingly. She placed her hands against his chest and held him off when he would have kissed her. 'But, to be serious, Miles, the church vows are very important to me. I would have nothing spoil our wedding.'

She gazed at him steadily and was relieved when the hot, ardent look died from his eyes and he smiled at her.

'Very well, my love, you know I can deny you nothing.'

He pressed a last kiss upon her fingers and took his leave. Thoughtfully Beth made her way back to the drawing room.

'Has Mr Radworth gone now? I cannot say I am sorry,' declared Lady Arabella. 'How oddly he behaved tonight. I do hope he is not sickening.'

'I am sure he is not, Grandmama. I think it is as he says, a poor wine.'

'More like the quantity,' put in Sophie bluntly. '*You* did not feel any ill effects, did you, my lord?'

Beth frowned at her sister. She could not be happy about the way Grandmama and Sophie had taken to Lord Darrington. It would be better for everyone's peace of mind when he and his friend had gone.

Guy noticed the change as soon as Radworth had left the Priory. Lady Arabella's outward demeanour did not alter, but he sensed she was a little more at ease. Sophie, too, became more talkative. Only Beth remained aloof, but Guy suspected that might be because she was embarrassed at her fiancé's behaviour.

He was still pondering on the events of the evening when he made his way up to Davey's room after supper.

He found his friend propped up in bed and thumbing idly through one of the newspapers that littered the bed. He tossed it aside as Guy came in and greeted him with a cry of relief.

'Darrington, thank heaven you are come! I thought I should expire with boredom!'

Guy grinned at him. 'You are looking much better, old friend, and sound much more like your old self. How are you?'

'Everything still hurts like the very devil, but only if I move.' Davey beckoned him forwards. 'Come and sit down here and tell me all that is going on downstairs. Have you kissed any of the ladies yet?'

Guy laughed. 'Only your broken ribs prevent me from punching you for that, Davey! Of course I haven't! Lady Arabella is a matriarch, born to command, and her two granddaughters are both completely ineligible, one being a schoolgirl, the other a widow.'

'A very beautiful widow, if Peters is to be believed.'

'True, but she is also about to be married.'

'And her future husband dined with you tonight?'

'Why on earth should you want me to tell you anything?' demanded Guy irritably. 'You know it all already.'

'Devil a bit! Peters has passed on the little he has gleaned. Most of it was nonsense about the ghosts that walk during the night. Peters tells me some of the servants even swear they have heard wailing and crying in the gardens after dark! Tales set about by the housekeeper, I suspect, to keep them in their own beds at night! I'm hoping you can give me all the details about the family.' Davey put his head on one side and narrowed his eyes. 'And by your frown I'd say something is puzzling you.'

'Aye,' said Guy slowly. 'It is.'

He related the details of his evening and at the end of it Davey merely nodded.

'Seems simple enough to me. The widow is marrying a fool. Nothing unusual in that.'

'Not such a fool that he hasn't tied up the business all right and tight,' retorted Guy. 'Over the port he made a point of telling me that the contracts were all signed, and even if Mrs Forrester should cry off now all the property would pass to him.'

'Does she want to cry off?'

'No—that is—I cannot say. I do not believe she is in love with him. The story goes that Radworth brought news of the brother's death to the family, fell in love with the widow and had been courting her ever since. I don't think the old lady is too enamoured of him, though.' A smiled tugged at his mouth. 'It should prove a stormy marriage—I saw the way she ripped up at Radworth when he threatened to go down to the cellars himself! I had the impression she might actually call upon the servants to restrain him, if he had persisted.'

'It's the red hair,' muttered Davey. 'It might look glorious, but she'll make the very devil of a wife.'

They fell silent and Guy realised that Davey was looking rather pale. He stood up.

'Thankfully, the problems of the Priory are nothing to do with us and I for one cannot wait to leave them behind! With good fortune, by this time tomorrow we shall be back at Highridge. Now sleep well, my friend. I shall call on you again in the morning.'

Guy made his way to his room where he was pleased to see the fire had been built up and a small basket of logs placed on the hearth beside it. Peters had unpacked his nightgown and it was draped across the bed, a pale, ghostly spectre in the shadows. A gusty wind was blowing, stirring the curtains that covered the ill-fitting leaded window and causing the occasional puff of smoke to blow into the room. Guy regarded the old stone hearth with disfavour and thought longingly of his own house, refashioned in the past ten years to provide such modern conveniences as small, iron fireplaces that threw out more heat and kept the smoke going up the chimney. Even Davey's hunting lodge seemed luxurious in comparison to the Priory!

Guy was not used to keeping such early hours and as he put his coat over the back of a chair and kicked off his shoes he knew that sleep would elude him for some time yet. He picked a book at random from the mantelpiece and threw himself into the chair beside the fire, adjusting the candles to give him as much light as possible on the page. It was one of the volumes of *Tristram Shandy* and Guy was happy to amuse himself for an hour. He heard the board creak outside his room as someone padded along the passage. It was not the brisk step of a servant going about his business, but rather a slow, creeping tread. If they were trying not to disturb him, then their efforts were wasted, he thought sourly as another cloud of smoke belched from the chimney. He gave a wry smile. Perhaps Mrs Forrester was correct; he was grown too puffed up in his own conceit. He had stayed in much more uncomfortable houses in the past and never thought to complain. He stirred up the fire and threw a couple of small logs on to the flames, making up his mind that he would read until these had burned down, then go to bed.

The wind died down and the house grew quiet. The silence of the room settled around Guy and the slow tick, tick of the clock lulled him until he began to doze over his open book. He jerked himself awake. This would not do, he thought, stretching. He should go to bed.

At that moment he heard a cry. It was like a shout in the distance. It was not loud, and he thought that if he had been asleep it would not have roused him, but now he froze, his ears straining to catch the least noise. He heard the soft thud of a door closing, a murmur—it could have been the wind, or low voices, he could not be sure—then the definite sound of feet hurrying past.

Guy hesitated. Perhaps Lady Arabella had been taken ill, or one of the servants. It was none of his business, after all, and they would not thank him for his interference. But perhaps it was Davey—he hoped Peters would wake him if that was the case, but Guy could not be sure. Snatching up his bedroom candle, he opened the door and stepped out.

The passage was empty and silent. Moonlight filtered in through the mullioned windows at each end of the corridor, creating grey patterns on the floor. To his left the passage led to Davey's room and the stairs down to the great hall, to his right it continued the length of the old building, then turned and provided access to the rest of the house. Guy walked towards Davey's room. There was no bead of light from beneath the door, no sound save the sighing of the wind outside. As Guy stood, indecisive, a sudden cold draught hit his back. He might have put it down to imagination if his candle had not blown out. He turned. The cold had passed, as if a door somewhere in the house had been opened briefly.

Guy put down the candlestick. There was sufficient moonlight pouring in through the windows to light his way. He padded along the corridor in his stockinged feet, the only noise he made came from a creaking board. When he reached the end wall he hesitated. Mrs Forrester had led him this way to her own room, so he knew the passage led away into the Tudor wing of the house with the family's apartments. He had no business here, but he was curious to know who might be about in the house in the middle of the night. Treading carefully, he made his way through moonlit passageways, past a series of doors in the polished-oak panelling until he rounded a corner and saw the dark rails of a narrow staircase before him. That would lead up to the servants' quarters and down to the kitchens. His ears caught the soft sound of a footstep and at the same time a faint glow appeared in the stairwell as someone began to ascend from the basement. Quickly Guy drew back out of sight. It was most likely a servant, who could continue up the staircase to the bedchambers above. He strained to listen, heard the lightest footfall, the slight creak of a board, barely had time to note the approaching glow before a figure came around the corner and stopped with a small shriek of terror to find him blocking the way. Guy had the advantage of knowing someone was approaching, but he was surprised to find himself gazing into the terrified face of Beth Forrester.

'Do not be afraid.' Guy reached out and took the lamp from her shaking hand, holding it up so that she might recognise him. 'I heard noises and thought I might be of assistance.'

She was shaking so much that he put out his free hand and caught her arm, feeling her trembling beneath the thin sleeve. She had changed her silk evening gown for a more serviceable closed robe in some dark colour. Her hair, free of lace and feathers, hung in a thick braid over one shoulder, gleaming in the lamplight like a trail of fire.

'I suppose I am allowed to wander where I will in my own house!' she retorted in a fierce whisper, pulling her arm free.

'Could you not ring for a servant?'

She was regaining control. Guy noted that her large, dark eyes were no longer dilated with terror, although her look was still guarded.

'It is not my habit to rouse my maid from her bed when I am perfectly capable of finding my way to the kitchen.'

She's hiding something, thought Guy. Was there a man, perhaps? An assignation with someone other than her fiancé? He thought not. He hoped not. She had roused his admiration with the calm way she had dealt with Davey's injury and, despite her coolness towards himself, Guy had thought her honest and honourable.

But he had been wrong about a woman before and it had cost him dear. He allowed his eyes to travel over her again. Would a woman go to meet her lover wearing such a homely gown? True, the soft wool clung to her figure, accentuating her tiny waist and the soft swell of her breasts, but its long sleeves and high neck looked almost Quakerish. What he had first thought was a pattern around her skirts at a second glance was seen to be dust. He frowned.

'Where *have* you been, Mrs Forrester?'

'That,' she said haughtily, 'is none of your business. Now, if you will please give me the lamp, I will show you back to your room.'

'Surely I should be escorting *you*.'

Her eyes flashed scornfully, but she said sweetly, 'But I wish to assure myself that you find your way safely back to your room, my lord.'

'Are you afraid I might discover your horrid secret?'

Her eyes flew to his face and he was startled to see the stark terror in their depths again. He stepped closer.

'My dear Mrs Forrester, pray do not look so alarmed. I was jesting.'

He noted the pale cheeks, the way the tip of her tongue ran nervously across her full bottom lip. Only a few inches separated them. He had to steel himself not to reach out and pull her to him. Her eyes were locked on his. They were cocooned in the lamplight and for a long moment neither spoke. Guy did not even breathe.

Oh, heavens, what is happening to me? The thought screamed in Beth's head while her eyes remained fixed on the earl. His blue-grey eyes, hard as granite, held her transfixed. Even in his stockinged feet he towered over her, like a bird of prey hovering over its victim. Yet she was not frightened. Instead she felt an irrational desire to close the gap between them, to cling to the earl and allow him to take the cares of the world from her shoulders.

No! With enormous effort Beth tore her eyes away. The impression that they were imprisoned together in a bubble of lamplight was merely an illusion and she must break free of it. She must stay strong and keep her own council.

She swallowed, cleared her throat and said huskily, 'Thank you, but I am not alarmed.' She added in a stronger voice, 'Neither am I in the mood for funning.'

She reached for the lamp, her hand trembling as her fingers brushed the earl's. She held the lamp aloft and led the way back through the darkened house. The earl walked beside her, his long, lazy stride easily keeping up. Neither spoke until they reached Guy's bedchamber, where a faint shaft of light spilled out from the open door.

'It is never wise to leave your bedside candles burning unattended, Lord Darrington.'

'I hope I shall not have cause to do so again.'

'You had no *cause* to do so tonight.'

In the doorway he turned to face her and they stood, irresolute, as if neither of them wished to bring the moment to an end. But Beth knew that was mere foolishness. Lord Darrington had received only the barest civility from her while he had been at the Priory and must be longing to return to more hospitable surroundings. For her part, the sooner the earl took himself and his friend back to Highridge the better.

Beth put up her chin and, bidding the earl a chilly good-night, she turned and hurried back to her own room.

Chapter Six

'Elizabeth, my love, you are looking haggard this morning. Far too pale.'

Lady Arabella's greeting as Beth took her place at the breakfast table was direct and to the point. Beth ignored the earl sitting opposite her. It really was of no consequence to her that he was looking as if he had spent an undisturbed night with an army of servants to shave and dress him.

'I did not sleep well, Grandmama.'

'I think I know the reason for that.'

Lord Darrington's remark brought Beth's eyes to his face, her heart plummeting, then soaring to her throat, almost choking her as she waited fearfully for him to continue. He held her eyes for a long moment.

'It was the wind,' he said blandly. 'It was rattling the window for most of the night.'

The suffocating fear was replaced by anger. He was teasing her! He met her furious glare with a look of pure innocence.

'Would that be it, Mrs Forrester?'

Relieved laughter trembled in her throat at his impudence. 'Yes, my lord,' she said unsteadily. 'I think you must be right.'

'If the blustery wind kept you awake, I am sorry for it, my lord,' declared Lady Arabella. 'I cannot think it would affect Beth, however. She has lived here long enough to grow accustomed to it.'

'Thankfully it does not appear to have disturbed everyone,' said

Beth quickly. 'I saw Peters on my way downstairs and he told me Mr Davies passed a very peaceful night.' She threw a quick look towards the earl. 'I am hopeful Dr Compton will declare him fit to travel today.'

Sophie came in at that moment, hurrying towards the table, words of apology tumbling from her lips.

'Grandmama, I beg your pardon for being late, I have been helping Mr Davies with his breakfast—'

Beth almost spilled her coffee at this artless speech. 'Sophie! There was no need for that, especially now that Peters is here.'

'I know, Beth, but I heard the most dreadful clatter as I passed his room and the door was open so I peeped in, just to ask how Mr Davies went on, and I could see that his valet was having difficulty because his master had thrown his spoon across the room.' She twinkled. 'I fear poor Mr Davies is quite uncomfortable, you see. He told me his wrist hurt far too much for him to feed himself.'

'Couldn't hurt that much if he could hurl his spoon at his valet,' remarked the earl.

'I fear the pain from his injuries had made him short-tempered,' said Sophie innocently. 'So I offered to help him with his porridge. He was very grateful, I assure you.'

'I am sure he was,' murmured Beth. She suspected that few gentlemen would object to being attended by a pretty young lady and she had to admit that Sophie was looking particularly fetching this morning in her yellow muslin gown and with her soft brown hair curling around an open, smiling face.

'I have no objection to Sophie visiting the sickroom,' pronounced Lady Arabella. 'It is not as though Mr Davies is infectious and I am sure the sight of her will raise his spirits. But I must insist that she does not do so unaccompanied.'

'No, indeed, Grandmama,' Sophie assured her earnestly. 'Peters was in attendance all the time. And I should like to help—perhaps I may read to Mr Davies later...'

'Let us wait to see what Dr Compton says when he calls this afternoon,' put in Beth quickly.

'Well, I do not see that he will object,' returned Sophie. 'And since Grandmama approves, I shall go back to sit with Mr Davies when I have broken my fast. Peters is going to let me know when he has made his master presentable, for Mr Davies insists upon being shaved before I visit him again.'

Sophie applied herself to her breakfast, unaware of the effect of her words upon her sister.

'It does appear that Davies is vastly improved this morning,' murmured the earl as he helped himself to another slice of cold beef.

Beth did not reply. She hoped he was improved enough to leave the Priory. She had cares enough without adding a blossoming love affair between her sister and the invalid.

She was just emerging from the wine cellar when Kepwith announced that Dr Compton had arrived.

'The earl was waiting for him on the drive, madam,' the butler informed her. 'He has taken him up to the sickroom.'

'Has he indeed?' declared Beth, angrily shaking the dust from her skirts. 'And who gave him the right to do that?'

Kepwith bent a fatherly eye upon her. 'Now, Miss Elizabeth, you know the doctor never stands upon ceremony in this house and would have gone up anyway.'

'That is not the point,' she declared, stripping off her apron and hurrying to the stairs.

She entered the sickroom just as the doctor was pulling the bed-clothes back up over the patient.

'Well, now, things are mending very nicely indeed,' he declared. 'Your ribs will be sore for a few weeks, I dare say but I think if you are careful there is no reason why you shouldn't sit out of bed…'

'Does that mean Mr Davies could manage a carriage ride?' asked Beth hopefully.

'To take him home, you mean?' replied the doctor. 'Well, I don't see any reason why…' his jovial gaze went past Beth and after an infinitesimal pause he continued '…why he shouldn't be fit enough to travel in a—um—a week or so.'

Beth swung round. The earl was standing behind her, his countenance impassive.

'I thought, Doctor, that you said Mr Davies was much improved,' she said suspiciously.

'He is, my dear Mrs Forrester, but one cannot be too careful with a fracture such as this.'

'It is still as sore as the very devil,' added the patient, giving Beth a soulful look.

'But I am informed the earl's travelling carriage is very comfortable,' Beth persisted. 'And I am sure we can find mountains of cushions to protect Mr Davies's leg.'

'Out of the question,' returned the earl. 'I could not go against the doctor's advice.'

'No, it would not be wise.' Doctor Compton shook his head. 'Let us give it another week and I will call again.'

'A week!' cried Beth, dismayed.

'Well, there is little point in my calling before that. Time is the great healer, madam!' He picked up his bag. 'You may send for me if there is any change, but if not I shall call again in a se'ennight.'

With a cheerful word of farewell the doctor went out and Beth followed him, closing the door upon the two gentlemen.

'If I were a more sensitive soul,' remarked Davey in thoughtful tones, 'I should think our hostess was wishing me at Jericho.'

Guy grinned at him. 'Not *you*, Davey, it is I she wishes to see gone from the Priory.'

'And I thought you shared the sentiment. Why, man, only yesterday you were saying how much you wanted to leave.'

'That was yesterday.'

'Well, I must say it suits me very well to stay, especially if Miss Sophie is here to entertain me.' He looked up at Guy, an added glow in his blue eyes. 'Is she not an angel?'

'She must be if she could persuade you to eat porridge!'

'Yes, well, it isn't so very bad, you know, especially when served up by Miss Sophie.'

'She will provide you with a very pleasant diversion,' laughed Guy.

'But that does not explain your change of heart,' Davey persisted.

'I made sure the old sawbones was going to say I was ready to go home, then he caught your eye and changed his mind.'

'There is some mystery here, Davey, and I am intrigued.' Briefly he told Davey about meeting Beth in the corridor.

'So she has a lover,' said Davey, shrugging. 'That is not so unusual.'

'No, I don't think that is it,' said Guy slowly. 'When I discovered her last night she looked truly terrified. And little things do not add up, such as telling me she is making poultices for a lame mare when the groom knows nothing about it, and strange noises in the middle of the night.'

'Perhaps she keeps her husband locked up in the dungeons,' declared Davey, his lips twitching. 'I fear you have been reading too many Gothic novels, my friend. Perhaps you should accept the fact that Mrs Forrester is not enamoured of the great Lord Darrington.'

'I am not such a coxcomb,' protested Guy. 'No, there is some mystery here and I want to get to the bottom of it.'

Beth soon realised that she was the only member of the household who was unhappy at the doctor's verdict. Lady Arabella declared herself delighted to have company at the Priory, especially since the earl was content to while away an hour or two each evening playing backgammon with her. Beth was disappointed that Sophie did not share her anxieties. Although she did not neglect any of her duties, Sophie spent all her spare time with Mr Davies, entertaining him with card games and word puzzles or reading to him. After two days of this behaviour Beth tried to remonstrate with her, pointing out that all the time she spent with Mr Davies left the earl with nothing to do but to wander about the Priory.

'I have hinted to him that he might as well go home and leave Mr Davies to us, but he will not.' She twisted her hands together. 'I fear he suspects something.'

'Oh, nonsense, you are in a panic over nothing,' replied Sophie. They were alone in the library and she was running her fingers along the spines of the books, searching for a title.

'He is forever asking questions.'

'He is merely taking an interest, as any guest would. Besides, he will not trouble us today. He has gone out riding and is not expected to return until dinnertime.' Sophie pulled out a book. '*Vathek*—I wonder if Mr Davies would like Mr Beckford's novel?'

Beth regarded her with a mixture of amusement and exasperation. 'I do not think it matters, as long as you are the one reading it.'

'No, I am sure that is not true,' said Sophie, blushing a little. 'He…he is a very pleasant gentleman, do you not think so?'

'Excessively,' declared Beth. 'But he must do without you for a little while, because I am expecting Miles to call this afternoon and I will not be able to read to Grandmama, so I will be obliged if you will do so. And I need you to make up another poultice.'

Sophie's expression immediately became anxious. 'Could we not take Dr Compton into our confidence?'

'No, I dare not do that. We must keep our secret as long as we can. Besides, I do not think he is so bad as he was and I hope, with careful nursing, we will bring him through.'

Sophie gripped her hands. 'You know I am only too happy to help where I can. I will go down for an hour before I read to Grandmama. But you will not object if I read a little to Mr Davies after that?'

Having given her assurances, Beth watched her sister dance out of the room. To be sure, the idea of a burgeoning romance between Sophie and Mr Davies was a little worrying, but it was good to see Sophie smiling again, despite all the anxiety that hung over them.

Perversely, when Miles Radworth called and showed every inclination to sympathise with her for having Mr Davies and the earl with her for at least another week, Beth found herself making light of the matter.

'Ah, it is your sweet nature that makes you so compliant,' said Miles, raising her hand to his lips. 'I do not like the idea of you being here on your own.'

'But I am not on my own,' she protested. 'And there is no denying that the earl is very good with Grandmama. He takes her for a gentle airing in the grounds on sunny days and entertains her royally each evening. And even Sophie is proving useful, reading to Mr Davies and keeping him amused.'

'I wish you would let me stay, at least while the earl is in the house.'

'No, Miles, especially *not* while Lord Darrington is here!'

'You are thinking of my behaviour the other day,' he said ruefully. 'Will you not accept my apology for that?'

'I have already done so, but since you declare it was jealousy that made you lose your head, I think it best if you spend as little time as possible here at the moment.' She smiled at him. 'Now, my dear, if you want to please me, take me for a stroll about the gardens, for I have been cooped up in the house all day!'

They spent a pleasant hour walking through the grounds of the Priory and Miles exerted himself so much to please that Beth found her anxieties about her forthcoming marriage fading. They were making their way back to the house when they encountered Lord Darrington coming from the stables.

'Ah.' Miles cast a rueful glance at Beth.

She squeezed his arm. 'I have told you there is no need to be jealous of the earl, Miles. Pray be polite to him, for my sake.'

'I shall be more than polite,' murmured Miles. 'You will see that I can be the perfect gentleman! Good day to you, my lord. You have been riding, I see. Have you been far?'

The earl stopped and waited for them to come up to him.

'Around the park, then as far as Fentonby. I wanted to gallop the fidgets from my horse—he has been eating his head off in the stables and it was time I made him work. You have a fine estate here, Mrs Forrester. The land is in good heart.'

'Thank you,' she replied, pleased with this tribute. 'I work closely with my tenants to maintain it. My father impressed upon me the value of a well-run manor.'

'Ah, but the true value of Malpass is the Priory,' remarked Miles. 'True, the building is but a small part of its glorious past, but it is filled with the most exquisite antiquities. A perfect gem. Priceless.'

Beth laughed.

'Is that how you see it? Much as I love it, I confess sometimes in winter I long for a modern building with well-fitting windows and snug, draught-free rooms! What is your preference, Lord Darrington?'

'Wylderbeck, my own house, was rebuilt by my grandfather less than fifty years ago and has even been improved since then.' He added apologetically, 'No evidence of antiquity there, I'm afraid.'

Beth dropped back a little, allowing the gentlemen to converse uninterrupted. A little knot of anxiety was twisting itself inside her. She had told Miles he had no need to be jealous of the earl, but now she realised that was not quite true. When Beth had been a girl she had dreamed of meeting someone like Darrington, a tall, handsome lord who would sweep her off her feet, but it had never happened. Instead she had married Joseph Forrester, a good, stolid man some years her senior.

It had not been an unhappy marriage, but Beth could not pretend that she had ever felt a soaring, blazing passion that made her want to give up the world for love—in fact, she was inclined to believe it did not exist beyond the covers of the novels in the lending library. With a sigh she tore her eyes away from the two men in front of her. She was engaged to Miles Radworth: he was kind, loyal—witness his patience in courting her for over a year!—and would prevent the loneliness she was very much afraid would be her lot once her grandmother was gone and Sophie had married, which she surely would. It had been her free choice to accept Miles Radworth's offer of marriage and she would not complain.

To reward Miles for his generous behaviour towards the earl, Beth invited him to stay for dinner, but he refused.

'I have an early start tomorrow. I am off to Staffordshire, to Granby Hall, for the sale.'

'Is that Prudham's place?' asked the earl. 'I heard he was done up.'

'Aye. He is having to sell everything to pay his debts. Thought I would take a look. I believe he has a fine collection of ceramics.'

'Miles collects rare and beautiful objects,' explained Beth, smiling.

'Which is why I am marrying *you*, my love.' He kissed her fingers.

Beth flushed and pulled her hand free. For some reason she felt uncomfortable at his display of affection in front of the earl. Then, afraid Miles might be offended, she stepped closer and slipped her hand through his arm.

'Let me take you both in to Lady Arabella. Sophie is reading to her in the morning room and I am sure she would like to drink a glass of canary with you...'

Beth had seen a juggler once at the May fair and the image of the man came to her mind several times over the next few days, remembering his intent gaze as he concentrated upon keeping several clubs flying, never letting them drop or collide. She felt very much as if she was juggling the pieces of her life, looking after Grandmama, discouraging Sophie from spending all her time in the sickroom with Mr Davies, entertaining the earl while making sure Miles so did not feel too neglected. On top of all this were her nocturnal visits to the cellars from where she would emerge shortly before dawn and fall into bed to sleep for a few hours before the whole round would start again.

Such was her exhaustion that she fell asleep over her book when she was reading to Lady Arabella.

'My dear child, what is the matter with you?' demanded her grandmother, banging her stick upon the floor. 'I have a good mind to summon Dr Compton to take a look at you.'

'I am perfectly well, Grandmama,' Beth assured her. 'I am just a little tired, that is all.'

'Tired!' cried Lady Arabella. 'You are looking positively hagged, girl! Of course your pale skin makes the dark circles look worse than they are, but even so—! Ring the bell, Beth, and I will tell Kepwith to send for the doctor.'

'No, no there is no need for that, Grandmama. He will be calling the day after tomorrow to see Mr Davies, so I will have a word with him then, if you wish. I am sure Mr Davies is well enough to return to his own home now, and that of course will mean a lot less work for me. I am sure I shall be able to rest more once the gentlemen are gone from the Priory.'

'I do not see how Mr Davies and Lord Darrington have made so much work for you,' reasoned her grandmother, frowning. 'Davies has his own man to look after him and the earl is perfectly amiable.'

'He may be amiable, ma'am, but he is none the less a guest, and I would be failing in my duty if I did not look after him.'

Her grandmother stared at her through narrowed eyes.

'Has he tried to make love to you? No need to colour up so, child, since you and Sophie read to me from the *Intelligencer*, you know the earl's reputation as well as I.'

'And we have always agreed that most of it is salacious gossip and should be ignored,' retorted Beth, aware that her cheeks were glowing. 'And if he did try to flirt with me I am quite capable of giving him a set-down.'

'Hmmph.' Lady Arabella snorted. 'In my day entertaining a charming gentleman would not have been considered such an onerous task!'

Beth held her peace. She would have found it easier to entertain the earl if he had not been quite so charming. He tried hard to put her at her ease, but all the time she was guarding her tongue against any unwary utterance.

Beth had hoped after dinner that evening she might slip away to her room for an hour, leaving Sophie and her grandmother to entertain the earl until supper, but her plans were foiled when Lord Darrington expressed a wish to see the ruins of the Priory.

'Davey and I had been visiting Mount Grace on the day of the accident,' he explained. 'I believe the remains of Malpass Priory extend beyond the walled garden.'

'You will find traces of the old abbey walls throughout the grounds, if you know where to look,' said Lady Arabella.

'We used to play amongst them when we were younger,' added Sophie. 'We made up the most outrageous stories of knights and dragons.'

The earl glanced out of the window. 'It is a very fine evening. Perhaps Mrs Forrester would be my guide.' He smiled. 'I will undertake to protect her from lurking dragons.'

Despite the tug of attraction she felt at his smile Beth was about to decline, but a moment's reflection convinced her that if she did not accompany the earl he would go exploring on his own, and heaven knew what he might find.

'Very well, my lord, if Grandmama will spare me.'

'Aye, take her away,' declared Lady Arabella, waving her hand at them. 'Mayhap the evening air will put a little colour in her cheeks!'

Thus on a mild September evening Beth found herself wandering through the Priory grounds with Lord Darrington. She had buttoned her pelisse against the cool breeze, but had decided against bringing her parasol for there was little strength in the setting sun.

'The walled garden is in what we believe to have been the cloister,' she told him as they made their way between the flowerbeds. 'The remains of the abbey itself are in the wilderness beyond the yew hedge.'

'In those woods?' The Earl pointed to a small iron gate set into the old cloister wall. 'I had looked through there, but the gate is locked.'

Beth reached into her pocket. 'And I have the key!' She pulled out a large iron key and fitted it into the lock. It turned, giving a satisfying clunk and with a little push the gate swung open on its well-oiled hinges.

'Is it necessary to keep it locked?' asked the earl, following her through the gateway.

'Perhaps not now—when we were very young Grandmama insisted upon it, because the wilderness is bounded on one side by the river and it is very overgrown, with hidden shafts leading down to underground chambers. Our mother died when we were very young, you see, and Grandmama was responsible for us.'

'Yet your sister said you played here.'

She chuckled. 'Once we found out where the key was kept we would come here whenever we could.' As they emerged from the belt of trees she spread her hands to take in the view. 'What child would not think this a fairytale playground?'

Ahead of them lay the ruined walls of the old abbey. The outline of the nave could clearly be seen and the west wall with its arched window still stretched towards the sky.

'Most of the stone was taken to build the extension to the present house. What was not required was left very much as you see it now. Shall we go in?'

She moved towards what was left of the south transept, picking her way across the jumble of stones. She took him around the ruins, pointing out the area of the choir and the presbytery, and a beautifully formed little doorway that would once have led to the side chapel, but now looked on to nothing more than a grassy square.

'When we were children this would be our castle,' she told him, her head full of fond memories. 'Or the deck of a great galleon, or even a cave in the depths of an enchanted forest.We had such adventures here!' She sighed. 'What a pity it is that we have to grow up.'

'Do you still hanker, then, for adventure?'

She tilted her head on one side, considering the matter. 'Everything was so easy then—there were happy endings for us all.'

'And now?'

She knew the earl was standing very close behind her. She could feel his presence. Her heart began to thud almost painfully against her ribs. Slowly she turned. He was so close she had to raise her head to look at his face. She tried to speak lightly, as much to herself as to the earl.

'Now it is time to put away such childish thoughts and do one's duty.'

He reached out and took hold of the single red ringlet hanging down to her shoulder. 'Doing one's duty sounds very dull work,' he murmured, winding the curl about his finger.

Beth was finding it difficult to breathe. He was so close she could see the fine stitching on his coat, smell the tang of cologne that hung about him and, although she kept her eyes on his face, she was all the time aware of his fingers playing with her hair.

'I—um—have grown too old for adventures.'

He smiled suddenly and she was taken aback by the force of his charm. He said softly, 'My brother Nick would not agree.'

'Then your brother is a dangerous man.' She kept her eyes locked on his face, willing herself to keep still, willing him not to look away. The wrong word, the wrong move and this brittle, beautiful moment would shatter. Her whole body was tingling. Just standing still, looking up at this man, she felt more alive than she had ever done before. She wanted it to go on for ever.

In that same instant she knew she must end it now. She knew his reputation with women and she was determined he would not seduce her. It would endanger not only her own happiness, but everything she held dear. Looking away from him was like tearing her flesh.

'We should go back.' Her throat was dry, the words a mere croak. Regret, keen as a knife, sliced through her as his hand dropped and the contact was broken.

'Is there no more to see? Can one reach any of the underground chambers?'

Beth forced herself to concentrate on what he was saying. 'Good heavens, no,' she said. 'They have all collapsed.'

'Not the ones under the house, surely?'

'Oh, no, but they are used only for storage now. There is nothing of interest there.' She shivered. 'It is growing cold. Let us return to the house.'

'Very well.'

In silence they walked away from the ruins and back through the trees, where a slight breeze set the leaves sighing overhead and one or two fell slowly to the ground, reminding Beth that summer was over.

By the time they reached the cloister garden again a cold chill had settled over her heart. Something had changed. *She* had changed. Lord Darrington held out his arm and Beth took it, her fingers resting lightly on his sleeve, wondering how it was possible to feel so very different in such a short space of time.

No words had been exchanged, the earl had not kissed her—

they had not even touched, yet Beth knew that in that brief, sunlit moment she had been unfaithful to Miles Radworth.

Guy noticed that Beth said very little at supper. He frowned. When had he started to think of her as Beth and not Mrs Forrester?

Guy hoped he had not given himself away when they were looking at the ruins of the church. He had watched, entranced, as she flew around the old building, drawing his attention to the exquisite carving on an old pillar top, pointing out a gargoyle still clinging to the west wall. She had been like a sprite, a will o' the wisp, darting here, there and everywhere, so that when at last she stood still he caught her red-gold ringlet to keep her there. She had grown very quiet then. Did she know how much he wanted to kiss her? More than that. He wanted to ravish her, to possess her completely. But it would not do: she had shown no signs of wanting to flirt with him. She might succumb to him in the magic of the moment, but afterwards, the tears, the recriminations—she was betrothed to Radworth, as good as married. True, Guy's name had been linked with married women, but they had always pursued *him*. It was not his habit to come between a man and his wife.

For the first time he was glad of the early hours kept at the Priory, and after looking in on Davey he retired to his chamber and threw himself down upon his bed, his hands clasped behind his head. Damnation, she had got under his skin! How long had it been since any woman had done that—nine years, ten? And it had to be one as unobtainable as that first, disastrous love affair. The guttering of his bedside candle told him it was getting late and he began to undress. His ears caught the sounds of stealthy movement outside his room. He was no nearer to solving the mystery at the Priory, but suddenly he didn't care. All he wanted to do was get away. Davey was recovering well now. When the doctor called the day after tomorrow he would make damned sure he was declared fit enough to travel and they would leave Malpass Priory and its mysteries behind them.

Chapter Seven

Beth did not know whether to be most relieved or sorry when she saw Lord Darrington riding out early the next morning. Kepwith told her that the earl had breakfasted alone at a most unseasonal hour and had left instructions that they were not to wait dinner for him.

She busied herself with household duties and surprised her sister by raising no objection when Sophie suggested that Mr Davies could be carried downstairs to the drawing room so that he could listen to her play on the pianoforte. Lady Arabella offered to act as chaperon and Beth was free to throw herself into a frenzy of cleaning, but no matter how busy she was she could not keep her mind from wandering back to the golden evening in the ruins of the Priory church. When Miles Radworth called to see her late in the afternoon she made a great effort to greet him affectionately.

'How was your trip to Staffordshire?'

'I bought a few pieces of Meissen, but nothing very much.' He raised his head. 'Do I hear music?'

'Yes. Sophie is entertaining Mr Davies in the drawing room. Would you like to join them?'

'No, I would much rather have you to myself. I want to talk to you about your guest.'

'Mr Davies?'

'No, the earl.'

'Oh?' Beth raised her brows.

Miles took her arm and led her towards the library. 'You know I have never been happy about you having him stay when there is no man here to protect you.'

'I am well aware of the earl's reputation, Miles, and I am quite capable of repulsing his advances. Not that he has made any, which is a sad reflection upon my charms—or lack of them!—do you not think?'

He frowned as he shut the library door upon them. 'This is no time for levity, Elizabeth. If Darrington has made no move upon you, it is because he knows he would have me to answer to. I would have you under no illusion about your guest.'

Beth walked over to the sofa and sank down, wanting to tell Miles to keep his counsel. 'Is this necessary?' she asked, keeping her voice light. 'I have every hope that he will be gone in a few days.'

'That is good news,' replied Miles heavily. 'It offends me that a man of such unsavoury reputation should be staying at the Priory.'

'He is certainly capable of making himself agreeable. He is on the best of terms with both Sophie and Grandmama, but since he shows no inclination to flirt with any of us—'

'It is not just that.' Miles took a turn about the room, like a man struggling with some unpleasant subject. He said at last, 'The man is no better than a traitor.' Beth stared at him and he continued, 'It is an old story and thus you may be forgiven for not knowing of it. When I went to Granby I met an acquaintance who spends a great deal of time in town and remembers the scandal. Darrington passed Government secrets to the French.'

'I do not believe it!'

Beth's response was instinctive. It was much easier to believe the earl a libertine than a traitor. After all, she had experienced his charm, and although she had little experience she thought she could understand a man being carried away by lust.

'It was hushed up, of course,' Miles continued. 'Nothing was ever proved and Darrington is related to some of the foremost families in the land. He was making a name for himself in the government, too, but was forced to give it all up once his reputation was tarnished. Any man who would betray his own country is a scoundrel, Beth! You would do well to distance yourself from him, especially when we are trying so hard to avoid a scandal in your own family—'

'Yes,' she said quickly. 'We agreed we would not discuss that.'

'Once we are married, my dear, never one word of recrimination or reproach shall pass my lips.' Beth stared at him. She did not like the insinuation. As if reading her thoughts he said quickly, 'I have offended you. Believe me, Elizabeth, I wanted to do no more than put you on your guard.' He gave a little laugh. 'Lord Darrington has a fearsome reputation with the fairer sex and I fear I am a little jealous of him.'

'And I have told you there is no reason to be anxious for me,' she said, keeping a rein on her temper. She rose, wanting to bring the *tête-à-tête* to an end. 'I do not believe you need be concerned about the earl. His friend is recovering well and I have every hope that Dr Compton will declare him fit to travel tomorrow. After that we need have no further dealings with the earl. Shall we join the others now?'

Beth put all thought of their discussion to the back of her mind as she took Miles into the drawing room. Greetings were exchanged, Mr Davies's health was briefly discussed, but when the party settled down and Sophie continued her recital, Beth found herself going over in her mind everything Miles had told her about the earl. She did not want to believe it, but Darrington himself had admitted he rarely went to London these days. Her experience of men was limited, so perhaps her judgement was at fault. He might well be a cunning and unscrupulous deceiver.

It does not matter, she told herself firmly. *It means nothing to me. In a few days he will be gone, and everything will be as it was.*

Beth rose early the following morning; by the time she joined Lady Arabella and Sophie for a late breakfast she was able to inform them that Dr Compton had already visited his patient.

'He has said Mr Davies is well enough to travel back to Highridge tomorrow morning.' She added mischievously, 'It seems Mr Davies suffered no ill effects from your piano playing yesterday, Sophie.'

'But surely he would be better not to undertake such a journey for a few more days.' Sophie cast a beseeching glance at her grandmother. 'Being carefully carried downstairs bears no comparison to being driven ten miles in a jolting carriage!'

'Are you casting doubts upon the comfort of my travelling chariot, Miss Sophie?' Beth looked up quickly to see the earl standing in the doorway. He had been out riding and brought with him an aura of health and vigour as he strode into the breakfast room. Beth felt again a *frisson* of excitement, of attraction, at the sight of him and fought it down, telling herself it had nothing to do with the earl, it was merely her own weakness. He was not even looking at her, but was smiling at Sophie and there was laughter in his voice as he addressed her. 'I vow I am mortified.'

Sophie had very quickly come to regard the earl as a friend, thought Beth ruefully, and now she merely waved away his joking comment.

'I am sure his lordship's carriage will be very comfortable,' declared Lady Arabella.

'Yes, but—'

'We cannot trespass upon your hospitality any longer, Miss Sophie,' the earl interrupted her gently. 'You have all been most kind, but Mr Davies and I must return to Highridge tomorrow. There are any number of matters that have been left unattended since this accident.'

'Yes, of course.' Sophie nodded.

'We will find cushions and blankets to support Mr Davies's leg,' offered Beth, noting Sophie's anxious face.

'Thank you.' She tried to ignore his smile, forcing herself to believe it was insincere. He continued, 'Perhaps Miss Sophie would oversee the arrangements for the patient's comfort.'

This suggestion met with immediate approval and when it was decided that Mr Davies should be carried down to the drawing room again, Beth realised that she could expect no help from her sister for the remainder of the day. This did not worry her overmuch; knowing that Sophie and the earl would spend their time entertaining Mr Davies and Lady Arabella, Beth knew she would be able to attend to her own business without fear of interruption.

Guy should have been pleased—he had done his best to avoid Beth Forrester and so far he had succeeded admirably. A full day's riding yesterday had meant he had not seen the bewitching red-head at all and so far today he had shared only a few words with her over breakfast. He had spoken with Dr Compton when he had arrived to see Davey and made it very clear that he was now anxious to get his friend home with all speed. The good man had not failed him and all was now arranged for them to leave in the morning.

He was enjoying a lively game of Halfpenny Loo with Davey and Sophie in the drawing room; Lady Arabella was dozing in her chair and Beth had excused herself, saying she had work to attend to. With luck, thought Guy, he would only have to endure one more dinner and supper in her company before leaving the Priory for good.

Guy caught himself up. Endure? He was being unfair; that was not the way to describe what he felt in her company. No, her company was not a penance. It was the loss of it that would be difficult.

Having seen Davey taken carefully back to his room and delivered into the hands of his valet, Guy changed into his dark coat and satin knee breeches in readiness for dinner, but he did not hurry downstairs. Beth had shown little desire for his company since their walk together in the ruins of the old church and, much as he wanted to see her, he decided it would be better for them both to spend as little time together as possible. He therefore remained in his room until he judged it almost time for dinner to be announced. His soft-soled shoes made little noise on the boards and his descent into the great hall was not noticed by the two people deep in conversation there. Beth and her butler were standing to one side of the staircase, talking earnestly. Their voices were hushed, but the bare stone floor and walls of the chamber meant their voices floated up the stairs to meet him.

'He's very restless, ma'am,' Kepwith was saying, an anxious note in his usually expressionless voice. 'I don't think he should be alone. Perhaps Miss Sophie...'

'No.' Beth's reply was emphatic. 'We will not worry Sophie with this. I will go down to him as soon as we have finished dinner.'

'I wish you would let me send for Dr Compton, madam.'

'And so I shall, if the situation warrants it, but I do not think it is so very bad. You will let me have the keys after dinner and I shall attend—' She broke off when she became aware of someone on the stairs and glanced up at him.

Good God, what have I done to deserve such a look?

It was gone so quickly that Guy could almost believe he had imagined the horror in her eyes. Not for the world would he be so uncivil as to mention it. He said, 'I beg your pardon. I could not help overhearing—has Mr Davies suffered a relapse? He was well enough when he was taken back up to his room...'

'No, no, I was merely reassuring Kepwith that Mr Davies is going on very well.' She turned back to the butler: 'You may go now. And announce dinner as soon as possible, if you please.'

With a bow the old retainer walked away and she watched him in silence for a moment until the chiming of the clock recalled her attention. She said, 'I feared I should be the last to come down to dinner.'

He knew her society smile was designed to keep him at a distance and he responded in kind, holding out his arm to her. 'Shall we go in together then, ma'am, and brave Lady Arabella's wrath?'

Guy watched Beth during dinner. She looked serene enough, but he noticed that she merely toyed with her food and seemed distracted, almost impatient for the meal to be over. It did not surprise him, therefore, when he returned to the drawing room after spending the minimum amount of time enjoying his brandy in solitary state, that only Sophie and her grandmother were waiting for him. They were playing backgammon and Guy declined their invitation for him to take a turn and very soon he excused himself, saying there were letters he wanted to write.

He made his way directly to Davey's room, where he found his friend sleepy after enjoying a good meal and a bottle of wine.

'Has Mrs Forrester been here?' asked Guy without preamble.

'Not since this morning, when Compton called,' returned Davey, yawning.

'Are you sure you are telling me the truth?'

'Of course I am! Why should I lie to you?'

Guy frowned. 'Your leg is not paining you? Or mayhap your ribs hurt, after being carted downstairs today?'

'Nothing out of the way,' replied Davey. 'In fact, I would have been happy to be *carted downstairs*, as you phrase it, to join you all for dinner, only Compton would not hear of it. He said I could only be brought down to the drawing room in the afternoon as long as I promised to rest after that, ready for our journey tomorrow.' He sighed, wincing as the breath pulled at his ribs. 'You know Guy, glad as I shall be to get back to Highridge, I shall miss the company here.'

'One young lady's company in particular, no doubt.'

Davey grinned, his boyish face flushing.

'Miss Sophie is an angel, is she not? So accomplished, witty, delightfully unspoiled—'

'Have a care, Davey,' cried Guy, startled. 'She is also very young.'

'Eighteen.' Davey nodded. 'I shall have to go slowly, but I am in earnest, Guy. And I think she likes me, too. I wonder if my sister would come and look after me? There could be no objection then to Sophie visiting…'

Guy laughed and clapped him on one shoulder. 'You must write and ask her, once you are safely back at Highridge! But for now you must rest, my friend. We have a long journey tomorrow.'

Reassured on one point, Guy left, but other questions nagged at him as he made his way back to his room. If Kepwith was not referring to Davey, then who was he concerned for? A servant, possibly, but if that was the case why should Beth want him to believe they were talking about Davey? He rubbed his chin. She had distinctly said she would go down to him and had asked Kepwith for his keys.

He stopped. A sudden memory came to him of the night Miles Radworth had demanded more wine. Beth had been at great pains to ensure that he did not fetch it himself.

Guy began to walk again, past the door to his allotted room and through the winding passages that led to the back stairs where he had surprised Beth a few nights ago. There was no one in sight, but the clatter of dishes and voices echoing from below told him that the servants were busy. He hesitated for only a moment before setting off down the stairs. However unusual it might look, he was determined to get to the bottom of this.

He descended into darkness, for the warren of service rooms that ran beneath the main house was underground with only a few windows high in the walls of the kitchen and servants' hall, and no natural light at all in the central passageway. A single lamp glowed on the wall and it took a few moments for his eyes to grow accustomed to the gloom. The passage stretched away before him with several blocks of light spilling out on to the floor from the open doorways. There was no one in sight, but shadows occasionally fell across the doorways and the noise and chatter he could hear suggested it was the kitchens. An open door opposite the stairs showed him the lamp room and he quickly helped himself to one of the bedroom candles that were arranged neatly on a narrow shelf.

Lighting his candle from the lamp, he headed away from the kitchens to a door beneath the stairs, leading back under the older part of the house. He reasoned that the stone undercroft of the old building would make an ideal wine cellar. The same reasoning told him that if the door did indeed lead to the wine store then it would be locked and Kepwith or Beth would have the key. Nevertheless, after coming this far it was only natural that he should try the door.

It opened easily.

Guy slipped inside and closed the door behind him. A quick glance showed that his guess had been correct. He was in a large stone vault, the walls of which were lined from floor to ceiling with bottles of wine. The lower racks were grey with dust. He remembered Beth brushing the dirt from her skirts and nodded to himself. There was a chaotic pattern on the dusty floor indicating that the butler had made innumerable trips to the cellars to collect wine for the table. As Guy moved away from the door he could see more distinct footprints on the floor. The wine racks ended and he found himself walking between neatly piled trunks and boxes and the occasional piece of heavy wooden furniture, no longer required by the family upstairs. As he held his candle aloft the soft glow showed him a heavy wooden door in the stone wall ahead of him. Cautiously he tried the handle. It turned easily, silently, as if it had been recently oiled. He opened the door an inch and paused, listening intently. From the far side of the door he could hear the murmur of voices then, louder, a distinct groan. Gently he pushed the door and it swung open with a whisper to reveal another gloomy vault. This one looked as if it had at some stage been used as a stable, for there were high wooden partitions projecting halfway across the floor. A soft glow of lamplight could be seen between two of the partitions. Guy extinguished his candle, closed the door behind him and moved forwards silently, stopping for a moment as he heard Beth's voice.

'Hush, my love. Here, drink this. It will help you.'

Guy moved forwards again until he could see the little tableau illuminated by a storm lamp hanging from a hook on the wall. Beth was sitting on the edge of a low wood bed in which lay a gaunt, bearded figure, propped up against white pillows. Guy was standing outside the circle of light and they did not notice him at first. He watched as Beth held a cup to the man's lips, then she wiped his mouth with tender care. As she did so the man looked up and saw Guy standing in the shadows. His start alerted Beth and with a little cry she jumped to her feet.

'What are you doing here?' she hissed at him, planting herself between Guy and the man in the bed.

'So this explains your night-time wanderings,' he murmured, ignoring her question.

The man behind her shifted nervously. 'Who is it, Beth? Do you know this man?'

Guy raised his brows. 'Well, are you not going to introduce us?'

'Please.' Even in the dim light he could read the urgent appeal in her eyes. 'Please, go away and forget what you have seen here.'

'Beth, who is this?' The man in the bed spoke again and Guy moved to one side so that he could see him.

'I am the Earl of Darrington,' he said conversationally. 'And who are you?'

The man propped himself up on one elbow. 'Simon Wakeford. Beth's brother.'

Guy's brows went up. 'I thought you were dead.'

'So shall I be, if I am discovered.'

Chapter Eight

Beth clasped her hands together until the knuckles gleamed white. She would have given anything to prevent this meeting. Why had she not locked the cellar door behind her?

'Ah.' Simon collapsed back on his pillows. 'So you are one of our guests. It is your friend who has the broken leg, I take it?'

'That is correct.' The corners of the earl's mouth curved upwards. 'I understand now why Mrs Forrester was reluctant to let me stay.'

His eyes were upon her, but whether they held mockery or sympathy she did not know because she would not meet his look. Beth felt quite sick with anxiety. She was unsure how to deal with the situation. She heard Simon voice the question that was uppermost in her mind.

'What are you going to do now?'

'I do not know, since I have no idea yet just what I have stumbled upon.'

With a calm assurance that infuriated Beth, he dragged a three-legged stool to the end of the bed and sat down. 'Perhaps one of you would like to explain everything to me?'

'How do we know we can trust you?' Beth challenged him.

'You don't, but I am not going away now until I know the whole story—unless you intend to enforce my silence by murdering me.'

Beth threw up her hand. 'Do not joke of such things!'

A heavy silence fell over them.

'We have no choice, Beth.'

She turned to look at her brother, her heart aching at the sight of his gaunt, tortured features. Reluctantly, she nodded and turned to face the earl.

'Simon is accused of a murder he did not commit.' She gazed defiantly at the earl, but he remained silent, a look of polite enquiry on his face. She continued, 'He was in Portsmouth, on his way back from the Continent, and went to the aid of a Frenchman and his wife who were being robbed, but one of the thieves was wounded and planted a necklace in Simon's bag before he died. By then the victims had sailed for France, so he had no one to speak for him.'

'And you had no way of finding them again?' asked the earl.

'No.' Simon shook his head. 'I knew their name, but precious little else. After I escaped I tried to find them in France, but—'

Lord Darrington put up his hand. 'You went to France? I thought you had just come from there.'

'I had, but once I was accused of murder it seemed safer to get out of England.' Simon's thin hand plucked at the bedcover. 'The mob rioted in Portsmouth and broke open the gaol. I escaped with some others and took a ship to France, but it foundered.'

'Simon was injured swimming to the French shore,' put in Beth. 'He has had no proper nursing—'

'Until now.'

Beth took his hand and squeezed it. 'I am hopeful that the worst wounds are now healed.' She shot a look at the earl, 'He still has a swollen ankle and a recurrent fever.'

'Ah. That explains the comfrey leaves.' He met her eyes, but there was no reading their expression. 'So what efforts have you made to find the French couple, what do you know of them?'

'Only their name,' said Simon. 'I remember the man was considerably older than his wife.' He added inconsequentially, 'She was young and very pretty.'

Once again the earl fixed his eyes upon Beth.

'And what part did Miles Radworth play in this?'

'He was on the packet that brought Simon back to Portsmouth from his tour of the Continent. They struck up an acquaintance, and then, when Simon was accused, Miles came north to tell us what had happened. Since we believed Simon dead I thought no purpose could be served by making it known to all the family. Father was so ill and I was too busy nursing him to worry about what could not be changed.'

'Do you mean Lady Arabella still knows nothing?' interjected Lord Darrington.

'She thinks Simon was drowned returning to England,' said Beth. 'We have been at pains to keep the truth from her. It would break her heart.'

'Hence you or your sister read the newspapers to her?'

'Yes. Grandmama's sight is failing so there is little possibility of her reading anything about Simon for herself. There has been nothing in the newspapers since those early reports, but we will not take the chance of her finding out.'

The earl nodded and turned back to Simon. 'By running away you have as good as admitted you are guilty.'

Simon shrugged. 'What else could I do? If it had been only the dead man, I could have pleaded manslaughter, since there had clearly been a brawl. The jewels were a different matter.' He gave a savage laugh. 'The courts do not look favourably upon thieves. I did try to find the de Beaunes when I was in France, but I had no money and dare not use my real name, so I decided to come back to England. I managed to get a ship back to Plymouth and then began the long journey north to Malpass. I found a little work to pay my way, then the fever returned and I was laid low for weeks. But at last I made it here and Beth has kept me hidden in the undercroft ever since.'

'When did you get back?'

'Three weeks ago,' Beth answered, seeing the blank look on her brother's face. The poor boy lived in constant darkness and had little idea of the passing time.

'I take it this explains the servants' tales of ghostly noises,' remarked the earl. 'And those cries I have heard at night.'

Beth nodded. 'Yes. At the far end of this vault is the door that opens on to the drive—the one beneath the steps to the main entrance. We keep it locked, of course, but occasionally when Simon is in the grip of the fever he cries out. And Tilly has a habit of leaving the inner doors open behind her. On such occasions Simon's cries can be heard inside the house. We have been happy to foster the idea of noisy ghosts. Besides myself, only Kepwith, Sophie and my maid know that Simon is here.' She added, 'I have written to Mr Spalding, our family lawyer in London, and he is making enquiries in France, trying to find this Monsieur de Beaune and his wife. When we do, we shall be able to prove Simon's innocence.'

'And in the meantime you expect to keep his presence here a secret.'

Beth clasped her hands together. 'Yes.'

'You are aware there are severe penalties for harbouring a felon?'

'But he is not guilty!' she cried.

Simon reached out and clutched her skirts.

'The earl is correct, Beth. I should go away.'

'No. Not yet. You are not yet well enough.'

She fixed her eyes upon the earl. 'Well, my lord, will you keep our secret?' When he did not answer she rushed on. 'I have some guineas saved—'

'Money will not buy my silence!'

His harsh interruption frightened her. Had she offended him, or was he contemplating some other way she could reward him for his co-operation? A chill ran through her. She could trust her servants, whom she had known all her life, but this man was almost a stranger…

'What…what do you mean to do?' she asked him nervously.

'Nothing, until I have considered all you have told me.'

'It is the truth,' muttered Simon. 'I swear it!'

Those hard eyes rested thoughtfully upon them again, then he took out his watch. 'It is nearly time for supper. Should we not be going upstairs, Mrs Forrester?'

Reluctantly she nodded. It took a few moments to make Simon comfortable, then she led the way back through the vaults, the earl following a few paces behind her.

Beth was confident they would meet no one on the back stairs; all the staff would be busy preparing supper or taking their ease in the servants' hall. They proceeded silently back to the main part of the house. Lamps had been lit now in the corridors, showing up the dusty marks on the earl's black coat.

'I cannot go down to supper like this,' he remarked. 'And if I ask Peters to deal with it he may become suspicious.'

'I have a clothes brush in my room,' said Beth.

They had reached the door of her bedchamber and she stopped, waiting for him to take off his coat. He merely looked at her, his brows raised.

'Do you expect me to stand about here in my shirtsleeves? Will that not be equally suspicious, if I am seen?'

He was right, she knew it.

'Very well, you must come in!'

She stepped back to allow him entry, quickly closing the door behind them. There was no sign of Tilly, but the room was prepared in readiness for her mistress, with a cheerful fire blazing in the hearth. Beth went around lighting all the candles and trying not to think how the earl filled the small space. She had to squeeze past him to get the clothes brush, careful to avoid the slightest contact.

'Tell me about Miles Radworth,' he said over his shoulder as she stood behind him, brushing his back and shoulders with brisk, firm strokes. 'He brought you the news that your brother was dead?'

'Yes. He stayed in Portsmouth after the escape, and when the first reports came in of the shipwreck he waited until his own enquiries satisfied him that all hope was lost.'

'And he told you also that Simon was accused of murder?'

Her hand shook a little. 'Yes.' She resumed her brushing. 'He brought with him the newspapers carrying reports of the murder and of Simon's escape. We had heard nothing until then—it is not to be wondered at that a small note in a southern newspaper should be missed by our acquaintances here. Miles was very kind and full of regret that he had not been able to help Simon—'

'But does he believe your brother is guilty?' Beth stopped brushing. 'Well?'

'I…I fear he does.'

The earl turned to look at her, his grey eyes searching her face.

'Radworth was practically a witness to this whole affair. How can you expect me to believe your brother's innocence when he does not?'

Beth sank her teeth into her lip. It *was* a lot to ask of a man she had known for such a short time. He took the brush from her hand.

'My coat is done, I think. Allow me to return the favour.'

He dropped to his knees and began to work on the hem of her gown; Beth stared down at his dark head. His movements were confident and assured, the shoulders beneath the fine tailoring of his jacket broad and strong, capable of taking the troubles of the world, she thought. If only he would believe her.

'There.' He stood up and she quickly schooled her face into a mask of indifference. 'I think I have removed all signs that you have been in the undercroft.'

He handed her the brush again, smiling slightly. The candle-light played on his face, enhancing the smooth planes of his cheeks and accentuating his strong jaw. His black brows shadowed his eyes, making them look grey and hard as granite. Merciless. With a sudden rush of nerves she realised her situation, alone in her bedchamber with a man she had known for just over a week. She swallowed and said a little croakily, 'We must go down to supper. I—um—I will check the passage is clear for us to go out.' Moving away from him was difficult, as if she had to break an imaginary thread between them, but she forced herself to go to the door. Moments later they were in the corridor.

'I believe Radworth moved up here soon after he first came to see you.' The earl fell into step beside Beth.

'Yes. He has been very attentive.'

'Your sister puts it more romantically. She says it was love at first sight.'

She shot him a suspicious look. 'Do you find that so incredible?'

'Not at all. You are a very beautiful woman.'

Her cheeks flamed. 'I beg your pardon, I was not looking for... for a compliment, my lord!'

'I am merely answering you honestly. There must have been a

powerful inducement to make a man leave his estates and settle in the north.'

Still reeling from being called beautiful, Beth was not offended by his remark.

'You are not to think that I was so flattered by his attentions that I have not considered that,' she replied frankly. 'I have made en-quiries—he is no fortune hunter. His estate in Somerset is at least equal to Malpass. And he did not press me to a betrothal while we were still grieving for Simon.'

'And why are you marrying him? Do you love him?'

His question caught her off guard and she replied without think-ing, 'No, but—' Her step faltered. She added, trying to speak lightly, 'I must make a life of my own at some time. Grandmama will not live for ever and Sophie will undoubtedly marry.'

They were approaching the dining room and through the open door Beth could see that her sister and grandmother were already seated at the table. She stopped.

'My lord, you will say nothing to my grandmother of—of what you have seen…?'

'You have my word on that, Mrs Forrester.'

'And tomorrow?'

He shook his head slightly, the tantalising smile glinting in his eyes. 'I will make you no promises of what I may do tomorrow, madam.'

Beth closed her lips. Might he consider it his duty to turn Simon over to the authorities for trial? She was sure Miles would do so; in her mind she could almost hear him telling her that the law must be upheld, that if Simon was innocent then the courts would prove it. But Darrington was not Miles. She would not expect him to help her, but she might be able to persuade him to keep their secret. After all, rumour said he was a womaniser and now Miles had unearthed some secret from his past that cast doubt upon his integrity. The problem gnawed at her throughout supper. She said very little during the meal, allowing Sophie to chatter away while she watched the earl, trying to read his thoughts.

Miles had said his reputation was tarnished. He was a traitor and a libertine. A small voice inside told her it could not be true, but another, more insistent voice whispered that such a man could be bribed. He had said he did not want her money, but there were other forms of persuasion.

As she toyed with her food a plan began to form in her head. Across the table the earl was relaxed, smiling at something Sophie had said. He glanced across at her, still smiling, but she pretended not to notice. Beth pushed her plate away. Her appetite had quite gone, but she had made up her mind on a course of action. It should not be difficult. Dangerous, possibly; certainly abhorrent, but if it would protect Simon, then she would do it.

Chapter Nine

While Guy conversed with Sophie and Lady Arabella during supper his mind was going over all he had heard and seen in the undercroft. Beth was taking an appalling risk sheltering a fugitive, but it was her brother and Guy had a brother of his own. Nick was married now, but in his younger days he had had his share of dangerous escapades. There was no question that Guy would do the same as Beth, if Nick asked it of him.

Was Wakeford guilty? He doubted it, but he could see how events had conspired to make the boy seem so. And he *was* only a boy. Twenty-two, twenty-three…he was certainly younger than his sister. The thought of Beth made him glance across the table at her. She was pushing the food about her plate, but eating very little. And no wonder. He hoped she would understand from his smile that he meant her no harm. She would not meet his eye, so he determined that before he rode away in the morning he would make it clear that her secrets were safe. Lady Arabella was addressing him and he dragged his eyes away and his mind back to what his hostess was saying.

The family retired soon after supper was ended and Guy made his way back to his room where he found Peters laying out his nightclothes.

'I take it your master is asleep,' Guy remarked, shrugging himself out of his coat.

'Yes, my lord. Sleeping like a baby, if I may say so. And a good thing, too. We have a long journey tomorrow.'

'Ten miles,' Guy agreed. 'But we will make him as comfortable as possible. Here.' He held his jacket out to the valet. 'Take that away and make sure it is cleaned for the morning, will you? Thank you, Peters. That will be all. I will see myself to bed.'

Once Peters had gone, Guy began to pack his trunk in readiness for the morning. He thought of his own valet, kicking his heels at Highridge, and hoped he was enjoying his holiday. He would certainly have plenty to do when Guy arrived back tomorrow with a trunkful of clothes needing his attention. In his mind Guy could even now hear his faithful servant bewailing the state of his shirts, washed by some provincial laundress, and he would undoubtedly say that his master's topboots were scratched beyond repair from careless polishing by the Priory's servants.

Guy was so used to the house and its sounds by now that he barely noticed it settling down for the night; the thud as the servants shuttered the windows and the distant banging of a door, until everything was silent save for the occasional creak of the ancient timbers. He was surprised therefore to hear a faint scratching at his door. He was making his way to the door when it opened and Beth Forrester slipped into the room.

Beth closed the door softly behind her and stood with her back pressed against it, wondering if she could really carry out her plan. The earl was watching her.

She had unpinned her hair and brushed it until it shone like a coppery curtain around her shoulders, the rich colour accentuated by the pale ivory of her silk wrap.

'Mrs Forrester!'

She forced her lips to curve upwards. She must look warm, seductive. *Smile, Beth,* she silently encouraged herself. *You are no shrinking virgin; you know how it feels to be in a man's arms.*

'I have come to talk to you, my lord.' Good, her voice was a little breathless. She did not miss the flicker of interest in his hard eyes.

'Is it not a little late, madam?' he asked her, his brows raised. 'Would it not be better to talk in the morning?'

'I think not.' She took a step towards him. 'I wanted…to be alone with you.'

He reached for her hand and she knew a moment of terror. Quickly she lowered her lashes, veiling her thoughts from him. He led her to the chair beside the fire.

'Will you not sit down? You look a little pale. Peters has left me some brandy, or I could send for wine…'

'Brandy would be very welcome, thank you.' The ghost of a genuine smile pulled at the corner of her mouth. 'It would not do for anyone to know I am here.'

'Of course not.'

There was only one glass beside the decanter. The earl filled it and handed it to Beth. She took it with both hands, praying he had not seen the way her fingers trembled. His lips twitched.

'I'd wager you are not familiar with that drink, madam.'

She did not answer him. The pungent liquid was burning her throat, though she would die before she admitted as much. He leant back against the bed, his arms folded in front of him.

'What is it you wish to discuss, Mrs Forrester?'

She moistened her dry lips with the tip of her tongue. 'I—um—I hope you have enjoyed your stay at the Priory, my lord. I…I have not been as…welcoming as I ought.'

He inclined his head, saying politely, 'You have been all kindness, ma'am.'

'You are too generous.' She took another sip of brandy. Really, it was not so bad and at least it stopped her shivering. She said, 'I have been a little…cold towards you, I fear, but you know the reason for that now.'

'You were concerned for your brother.'

'Yes.' She rose. 'I thought perhaps I could…I might…make amends.'

She forced herself to stand still, hands at her sides and her eyes fixed upon his face. They were only inches apart. She saw his eyes darken and glow with something she did not understand, but suspected was desire. As if someone had opened a pot-pourri jar she was suddenly aware of his scent, a mixture of sandalwood and spices. Slowly he reached out one hand and caught the belt of her wrap, pulling her towards him. Her heart jumped and began to hammer a swift tattoo against her ribs.

You wanted to know how his arms would feel, she reminded herself as she stepped closer, eyes lowered, breast rising and falling quickly as he untied her belt and pushed the wrap from her shoulders, revealing her thin nightgown. It had formed part of her original trousseau, but had never been worn. Light as gossamer, it hid none of her charms. The strings at the neck were loose and the gown had already slipped from one shoulder. He reached up and ran his fingers lightly over the curve of her neck between shoulder and jaw. She could see the pulse jumping at his throat. He wanted her. The thought excited and frightened her. He slid his thumb under her chin and tilted her face up. She kept her eyes modestly lowered, the dark lashes sweeping her pale cheeks. She forced herself to stand passively while he cupped her face with his hands and began to cover her face with light gentle kisses. When he slid his mouth over her lips they parted invitingly and she was immediately aware of a change. The earl's mouth instantly became more insistent; he wrapped his arms around her, sliding his hands over her buttocks and pressing her against him. There was only a fine layer of muslin between her flesh and his roving fingers. Her muscles tightened, she was pressed against his groin and there was no mistaking his arousal. Instantly her body responded, hips tilting, breasts almost painfully taut. He explored her mouth with his tongue and she gave up trying to resist and kissed him back until she was quite heady with desire.

She almost groaned when he broke away and scooped her up to lay her on the bed. She reached for him, eager for him to take her, but he evaded her hands and stood looking down at her. The bedhangings were tied back and she lay in the golden glow of candlelight, her hair spread over the coverlet and her body tantalisingly visible through the fine muslin of her nightgown. She watched as his gaze ran over her. No man had ever studied her thus before.

Her husband had insisted their couplings took place in the dark, hinting that only a wanton would display herself to a man. Now, as Darrington turned away to toss his waistcoat over the chair she was shaken by doubt.

What are you doing, surely you do not think you can seduce a man as experienced as Lord Darrington?

He turned back to her at that moment and she dragged up a smile, but not quick enough. He had seen the uncertainty in her eyes and stood looking down at her.

'Why are you doing this, Beth?'

'Does there have to be a reason?'

He had positioned himself so that he did not prevent the candlelight from falling on her face, but his own countenance was in shadow. She knew he was watching her and she suddenly felt very vulnerable. At last he spoke.

'You think that you can seduce me, so that I will not betray your brother.'

'No! I—'

He put a finger on her lips. 'Do not lie to me, Beth.'

She sat up, pulling up the neck of her nightgown. 'I th-thought I might persuade you...'

She heard the anger in his voice as he ground out, 'I am not so cheaply bought!'

The words cut her like a whip and she flinched. She wrapped her arms over her breasts as shame and embarrassment burned her up.

'Here.' He picked up her wrap. 'Put that on.'

She almost snatched it from his hand, struggling into it while he stepped across to the fire and threw on more logs. His movements were quick and angry. Taking advantage of his distraction, Beth eased herself off the covers and fled.

Guy heard the soft click as the door closed and swung round. She had gone. With a muttered oath he threw himself into one of the chairs, trying to make sense of the welter of emotions that were raging through him. Anger and disappointment made a bitter mixture! What in hell's name did she think she was playing at? She was as good as married to Radworth. Guy did not think her the sort to enter into such an agreement lightly, but it might be a business arrangement, a marriage of convenience. He could not deny he was attracted to the lady and if she had come to satisfy a mutual lust he could have accepted that, but to offer herself to him, like some sort of sacrifice, and an unwilling one at that—did she think so little of him?

Sighing, he walked across to the washstand and plunged his face into the cold water. The chill sobered him, dousing any lingering desire and cooling his anger. She had come to him in an attempt to protect her brother, yet Guy remembered the way she had responded to his kiss—she was not indifferent to him, he would swear it!

And if he had taken her, if they had spent the night in passionate love-making, what then? Would she have walked away once she had extracted from him the promise not to betray her brother? No. Beth Forrester might be a widow, but she was an innocent. He would stake his life that she was far too honourable to sleep with one man and marry another.

'So you are well out of it,' he told himself as he climbed into bed. 'You have saved the woman—and yourself—a great deal of trouble!'

Back in her room, Beth locked the door and leaned against it, shaking. What had she done? How could she have been foolish enough to think that she could seduce a man? She had no experience, save for the quick, clumsy coupling she had shared with her husband years ago. When the earl had taken her into his arms and kissed her she had experienced a thrill of excitement, a pleasurable anticipation of what might follow.

If only he had not stopped then and questioned her. If only he had taken her in his arms and made love to her as she wanted him to do—perhaps she would not have had the courage to ask for his silence, but at least she would not have felt this wrenching, gnawing hunger for his touch. Even now her body was aroused, tingling at the very thought of him.

Without pausing to snuff out the candles burning on the mantelshelf, Beth threw herself on her bed and curled into a ball while scalding tears spilled over her cheeks. Her actions had done nothing but make the situation worse—she might even have made Darrington think Simon was guilty. After all, what woman would stoop to such tactics if she had nothing to hide?

'Oh, what have I done?' Beth groaned and buried her face in her pillow, but she could not forget the earl's look of angry contempt.

'I am not so cheaply bought!'

His words flayed her, but beneath her own misery was the fear that Simon might now be in more danger. A glance at the clock told her it wanted an hour or so until dawn. There was nothing she could do now until the morning. She would rise as soon as it was light, and if Darrington rode out himself, or sent a messenger for the magistrate, then she would move Simon. He was not quite so ill now, the fever had abated and there were many hiding places amongst the old ruins. It would not be very comfortable, but she would not allow her brother to be imprisoned.

She sat up with a start when she heard the boards creak outside her room. A small square of paper appeared under the door. She froze, hardly daring to breathe while she strained her ears to listen. There was no noise from the corridor and she imagined whoever was out there was standing very still. There was another faint creak. She could not be sure if she heard or imagined the soft pad of feet moving away.

Silently she slipped out of bed and picked up the paper. It was quite small and folded only once. With trembling fingers she opened it and turned it towards the light. There was only one line, written in a bold, sloping hand.

'Do not be afraid. Your secret is safe.'

Beth scanned the line again, just to make sure she was reading it correctly. She closed her eyes and uttered up a small prayer of thanks before kneeling before the hearth and offering the scrap of paper to the dying fire. It blackened in the glowing embers, flamed briefly and crumbled away to nothing under Beth's watchful gaze.

So Darrington would not betray them. For the first time since entering the earl's bedroom some hours earlier she felt a faint warmth within her. She did not doubt that she could trust him and the fear for Simon's safety eased. But her own misery did not lessen; if anything, it grew even more intense—she had misjudged the earl and what he thought of her now she could not bear to imagine.

Snuffing out the candles, Beth climbed back into her bed. With a heart as heavy as lead she pulled the covers over herself and settled down to wait for the dawn.

By the time the travelling chariot drove around to the front of the house to take Mr Davies and the Earl of Darrington back to Highridge, Beth's nerves were at breaking point. She did not join the others for an early breakfast and put in an appearance only when the servants were ready to carry Mr Davies out to the carriage. She joined Lady Arabella and Sophie on the drive, painfully aware of the earl standing beside the carriage. At any other time she would have been amused by Sophie's attempts to help; she fluttered about as Mr Davies was brought down the stairs and laid gently in the carriage, then she herself packed the extra cushions and pillows around his injured limb and tenderly placed a blanket over his legs.

'I have asked my sister to come to Highridge to look after me.' Davey addressed Lady Arabella, but Beth was not fooled, his words were meant for Sophie. 'I will have her write to you, to let you know how I go on. Perhaps you will all come and visit me,' he added. 'We would be glad of a little company, eh, Darrington?'

Beth did not listen to his reply. Instead she gave her attention to the earl's groom, riding up at that moment leading Mr Davies's bay mare and his master's hunter.

Not long now and he will be gone, she told herself. *A few more minutes and this will be over.*

The earl was taking his leave of Sophie and Lady Arabella. Beth swallowed and prepared herself. She could not avoid one last meeting.

'Mrs Forrester.'

He reached for her hand. Beth could not prevent her fingers

trembling as he raised her fingers to his lips. She forced herself to speak.

'Goodbye, my lord. And…and thank you.'

Her words were so quiet she thought at first he would not hear them, but he gave her fingers a slight squeeze and when he looked at her his eyes held nothing but kindness.

'Goodbye,' he murmured. 'And good luck.'

Guy rode away from Malpass Priory determined to put everything that had happened there out of his mind and for a while he succeeded. Escorting Davey back to Highridge and settling him in, placating his valet, who was inclined to take umbrage at not being summoned to join his master and arranging for Davey's married sister Julia to come and look after him took up all Guy's time for the next couple of days, but it was clear that once Julia was installed at Highridge, Davey was intent upon inviting Lady Arabella and her granddaughters to call. Guy immediately decided to bring his own visit to an end. He had no wish to see Beth Forrester again; he had given her his word that he would tell no one she was harbouring a fugitive, but it went against his better judgement. For the past ten years he had lived quietly, trying to forget the very public disgrace of his betrothal to a woman denounced as a spy. It would not do to allow himself to become embroiled in another woman's dubious plans.

'But you can't leave me now!' declared Davey, when Guy informed him of his decision.

'Why not? You have enough servants here to wait upon you, your sister will be here tomorrow, determined to cosset you to death, and I have no doubt that Miss Sophie Wakeford will call upon you at the earliest possible opportunity. What do you need with me?'

'Your company,' came the prompt reply. 'Julia's letter came express this morning and it says Bletchworth is not coming with her. You would not leave me to face her alone, would you?'

'Since you and your brother-in-law can never meet without arguing I think it is a good thing he is staying in Knaresborough,' laughed Guy. 'You will go on very well with Julia and you know it. Seriously, Davey, I have been away from Wylderbeck for far too long.'

'I suppose so,' said Davey, sighing. 'When do you propose to leave?'

'Tomorrow.'

'Will you not stay one more day? Julia writes that she is taking the mail to Thirsk and I would be obliged if you would meet her there and escort her to Highridge. Besides,' added Davey when Guy hesitated, 'it would look very odd for you to run off the very day before Julia arrives.'

Guy laughed. 'Very well, I shall collect Julia tomorrow and you will have the pleasure of my company for one more evening.'

Thus the following morning Guy drove to Thirsk in his own travelling chariot to await Mrs Bletchworth's arrival. Davey had asked him to make a few purchases for him while he was in the town, so Guy left his coachman to keep a watch for Mrs Bletchworth while he went off to fulfil his commission.

It was as he was returning to the inn that he saw Beth Forrester. She was some way ahead of him, an elegant figure in a dark-grey walking dress with a tightly fitting pierrot jacket, the low neckline filled with a snowy kerchief. At first Guy wondered if he had conjured her up, because she was constantly in his thoughts, but there could be no mistaking the flame-red ringlets peeping out beneath her round muslin hat. She was followed by her maid, who was carrying a cloak over one arm and a large bag. They stepped into the inn and were lost from sight.

Guy's own steps slowed. There was no reason in the world why she should not be at the same inn—after all, did she not say that she would be going to stay with her friend to buy her wedding clothes? For an instant he considered walking around the road to reach the stable yard, then he changed his mind. To go out of his way to avoid the widow smacked of cowardice.

With sudden decision he stepped into the inn. As he entered the coffee room he saw Beth sitting at a small table by the window, her maid beside her. She looked up and saw him just as she was taking a sip of coffee and immediately choked, spilling some on the sleeve of her pelisse. Her reaction gave him a certain amount of satisfaction.

'I beg your pardon, Mrs Forrester, did I startle you?' asked Guy, urbanity itself. He handed her his handkerchief and she began to mop at the coffee stain on her sleeve.

'I did not expect to see you here, my lord.' Her normally level voice was strained and she was looking decidedly nervous.

'I am come to meet someone,' he replied, sitting down at her table. 'What about you?'

'I—um—I am going to Ripon.'

'Ah, yes. To buy your trousseau.'

'Yes, I am.' She had regained her composure. 'How is Mr Davies? I trust the journey was not too distressing for him?'

'He managed it very well, thank you.' Guy patted his pocket. 'He is sufficiently recovered to send me out to buy a fresh supply of snuff. How long do you stay in Ripon?'

'I am not sure…' She looked up as the landlord approached.

'The London Mail will be here any minute, ma'am.'

Guy's brows shot up. 'London?'

Beth's cheeks flamed. He could read the indecision in her face and was inordinately pleased when she decided not to lie to him. She put down her cup.

'I have had word from our lawyer,' she said in a low voice. 'He has news of the de Beaunes, the witnesses to my brother's actions in Portsmouth. They are in England.'

Guy frowned. 'You cannot go to London alone.'

'I am not alone. I have my maid with me.'

'That is not what I mean. To travel such a long way by mail— you would be safer in your own carriage.' Something in her face made him say quickly, 'Does Lady Arabella know you are travelling to London?'

She hesitated. 'I told Sophie…'

'That is not what I asked, madam.'

'No,' she said quietly. 'She thinks I have gone to Ripon, to stay with Maria.' When he did not speak she spread her hands. 'What choice do I have? Simon is not well enough to travel. I must find these people and talk to them. Their testimony will clear Simon's name.'

'Then you should take Radworth into your confidence. He is, after all, your future husband.'

Her lips were pressed tightly together and there was a closed look on her face that gave him his answer. Guy gave an exasperated sigh.

'By heaven, madam, you cannot do this!'

She raised her chin. 'But I can, my lord, and I will. I have my ticket, and I shall go. This is not your concern. There is nothing you can do or say to stop me.'

Guy bit back a sharp retort. A movement in the yard caught his eye and he looked up to see a mud-splashed mailcoach sweeping past the window. Abruptly he rose.

'You are right. It is none of my concern,' he said curtly. 'I wish you good fortune, madam.'

Guy strode out into the yard and ran across to the mail. Moments later he was helping Mrs Bletchworth to alight.

'Darrington!' Julia Bletchworth squealed with delight as she descended from the carriage, trailing shawls, reticules and a very large swansdown muff in her wake for her maid to pick up. She threw her arms around him, oblivious of the stares and grins she received from the other travellers.

'Julia.' Guy returned her embrace, laughing. 'You haven't changed a bit, I see. Still a hoyden!'

'No, no, I am very respectable now, I assure you, only seeing you again takes me back to my girlhood, when you and Davey were grubby schoolboys and used to delight in tormenting an older sister! How are you, Guy—not married yet?'

'No, Julia, and not like to be. My carriage awaits us over there.'

He walked her across to the travelling chariot, side-stepping to avoid the ostlers who were hurrying to change the horses on the brightly coloured mailcoach. She patted his arm.

'One day, my dear, you will meet someone who will help you forget that horrid Bellington woman, I know it.'

'She is forgotten already,' he said lightly.

'Now you are cross with me and are wishing you had not come to meet me,' she said, laughing up at him. 'Very well, we will not talk of it. Tell me instead how my dear brother goes on.'

'His leg is mending well, but you will have the devil's own job to stop him getting up too soon.' He handed her into the carriage, then stepped back to oversee the loading of her two heavy trunks.

'Well, between us we shall manage him, I am sure,' she said when he returned to the carriage door.

'Ah, but you see I am leaving in the morning. I—' He broke off as the landlord put up a shout for the London Mail. Guy looked around and spotted a familiar figure coming out of the inn. 'Excuse me a moment, Julia.'

He strode towards the mailcoach where passengers were lined up to embark.

'Mrs Forrester, can I not persuade you postpone your trip until you have an escort?'

One of the guards came forwards for her bag and she handed it over. She bit her lip, her huge dark eyes fixed on his face.

'Come on, missus, we ain't got all day!'

The rough voice of one of the passengers standing behind her startled Beth. She gave her head a little shake.

'No, I cannot delay. Excuse me.' Hurriedly she followed her maid into the coach.

Guy turned on his heel and walked back to his own chariot, shaking his head over the impossibility of reasoning with headstrong women. It was not his concern, he reminded himself. And many women made the journey to London without coming to any harm. Still, the feeling of unease would not leave him.

'Well, now, can we be away from here?' demanded Julia as he came up. 'I vow I am impatient to reach Highridge.'

Guy put his hand on the open door.

'I am not coming with you, Julia.' Ignoring her astonished look and outraged demands for an explanation he issued a few, brief instructions before hurrying off to find the bookkeeper.

Chapter Ten

Beth made herself comfortable in one corner of the coach, her maid sitting nervously beside her. There was only one other inside passenger, a stout, haughty-looking gentleman who cast a disapproving look at Tilly, which made the poor girl ask Beth in an urgent whisper if she should go and sit up top.

'Upon no account,' returned Beth, directing a defiant look at her fellow passenger. 'I have paid for your ticket and want you beside me.'

The man sniffed and pulled out his watch. 'Two minutes late!' He leaned out of the window. 'Coachman—what is the delay?'

'No delay, sir,' replied the driver jovially. 'We leave when the church clock chimes the hour and not a minute before!'

Even as he spoke Beth heard the bell begin to toll. A shout went up, the coach lurched and swayed as the driver climbed up on to the box and Beth nervously smoothed her skirts, eager to be on her way. There was a sudden commotion, raised voices in the yard and the door beside her was wrenched open. A great-coated figure jumped in and the carriage pulled away even before the door was closed.

'What are you doing here?' Beth demanded as the Earl of Darrington made himself comfortable opposite her.

'I am going to London.'

His bland smile caused anger to replace her astonishment. 'Impossible!'

'Not at all,' he replied. 'I have purchased a ticket.'

'This is most irregular!' protested the haughty man. 'Your name will not be on the waybill!'

Lord Darrington raised his quizzing glass and regarded the protester. 'On the contrary,' he said coldly. 'I purchased my ticket from the bookkeeper and saw the guard write my name on the waybill before we set off. Not, my good man, that it is any business of yours.'

Beth might appreciate this masterly set down, but she was not going to own up to it. She glared at the earl. 'I have no wish for your company, sir!'

'You cannot prevent me from riding in this coach, madam.'

She bit her lip. With the haughty man regarding them with undisguised curiosity she was unwilling to embark upon a prolonged argument. She hunched her shoulder and turned to stare out of the window. The streets of Thirsk were soon replaced by open fields, but it could not be said that Beth enjoyed the view afforded her as they bowled along. She was anxious to get to London. She would not allow herself to hope for too much, but if she could find Monsieur de Beaune, if he would speak for Simon, his name might yet be cleared. She glanced across at the earl. He was sitting back in the corner, eyes closed, but she did not believe he was sleeping. Why was he here? She had seen his own carriage in the yard and had watched as he escorted the very dashing matron to it. Why then, should he suddenly buy a ticket for a London mail? Did he wish to torment her? She could not believe he would want to help her, not after the way she had thrown herself at him and been rejected. And yet…

No! Defiantly Beth closed her mind to it. To accept help from the earl would be further humiliation and she would resist that with all her might. She shifted in her seat and the earl's eyes opened. Beth was very aware that Tilly was asleep beside her and there was a gentle snore from the haughty man in the far corner. Beth knew a moment's panic—she might as well be alone with the earl.

She turned her head to stare out of the window again. Darrington sighed.

'It is going to be a very tedious journey if you mean to ignore me, madam.'

'Then I suggest you alight at the next stage, sir!'

'No, no, I am determined to help you.'

'And *I* am determined you shall not!'

He fixed his grey eyes upon her. 'What, not even for your brother's sake?'

She glared at him. 'I do not *need* your help, Lord Darrington. I am perfectly capable of doing this myself.'

He crossed his arms and said with maddening calm, 'I doubt it.'

He was trying to make her lose her temper, but Beth was not about to let that happen. She said icily, 'Then follow me if you wish, sir, and I will show you!'

They proceeded to the next stage in a stony silence. Beth thought miserably that she had never spent such an uncomfortable journey. Tilly was slumped against her in a deep slumber, squashing Beth into her seat. The earl lounged in his corner; if he was discomposed by the jolting of the carriage or the haughty man's sonorous snoring, he showed no sign of it.

The carriage jolted over a particularly uneven section of the highway and rocked precariously. Beth grabbed Tilly and pushed her back into her seat, but the haughty man was thrown heavily against the earl. The man grunted, muttered something that might have been an apology and flung himself back into his own corner.

A shadow of irritation flickered over Lord Darrington's face. It was gone in an instant, but Beth observed it.

'Such treatment as this is surely not what you are used to,' she said sweetly. 'You will be heartily sick of it by the time we reach London.'

'But I see no need for us to travel all the way to London with the mail. I have left instructions for my man to pack up a bag for me and to follow on with my own carriage. He should catch up with us by the end of the day.'

'I hope by then you will have thought better of this idiotic notion to follow me.'

'Not at all. I hope to persuade you to travel with me in comfort.'

'I am perfectly happy here, thank you.' Another violent jolt at that moment sent Beth scrabbling for the strap to prevent herself from crashing against her maid and it gave the lie to her words.

The earl's mocking smile roused Beth's fury. Biting her lip, she angrily straightened her skirts and scowled at the passing landscape.

The hours dragged by. The pressure to keep moving meant that the stops to change horses were as short as possible and even though the landlords of the various inns offered the passengers refreshments they barely had time to swallow a cup of coffee before the guard was urging them back into the coach for the next section. It did no good for the haughty man to declare that he had paid for his luncheon and would take it with him; the waiter came chasing after him and wrested away the half a fowl he had wrapped in his handkerchief before he could carry it off. Even the earl's elevated status counted for very little; the landlord might be persuaded to serve his meal a little quicker, but even he could do nothing once the coachman's shout of 'All's ready' went up and they were obliged to hurry back to the coach or risk being left behind.

Beth's surreptitious glances at the earl showed that he, too, was finding the journey irksome and each time they stopped to change horses she half-expected him to jump out and declare he had had enough and would wait for his coach to come by and take him up, but each time they pulled away he was sitting opposite her. And deep within Beth, barely acknowledged, was a sense of relief. She did not want him there, certainly she did not need him, yet all the same she was aware that she did not feel quite so alone.

It was early evening and the low sun was casting long shadows when Beth was roused from her meditations by the blast of a horn. Her first thought was that it was the guard, blowing up for an approaching turnpike, then she noticed that the earl was sitting up, his attention fixed on the window. Beth heard the sounds of a second carriage and looked out to see a team of horses moving past the mailcoach. She watched, enthralled, and heard the earl give a satisfied murmur as his travelling chariot went past, temporarily blocking the light.

'Now, Mrs Forrester, we shall be able to continue our journey in comfort.'

Beth shook her head at him.

'Now, my lord, *you* will be able to go home!'

The sun had set by the time they reached Newark and the blaze of light spilling out of the inn's many windows was a welcome sight. Beth uttered up a prayer of thanks when the guard announced that they would be stopping there overnight. Lord Darrington jumped out and she allowed him to hand her down. His grip on her hand was firm and reassuring. It would be so easy to allow him to escort her to London. Only the memory of how she had thrown herself at him and how he had refused her gave her the strength to pull her hand away.

'Madam—'

'*No!* I will not listen to you. Please, leave me alone now.' With a twitch of her skirts and a brief word to Tilly to bring her bag, Beth swept off into the posting inn, her head held high.

Guy watched her go, his eyes narrowed, until a shout claimed his attention.

'My lord!' His valet, Charles Fitton, was hurrying towards him. 'We had you in our sights for the past ten miles or so and I told Thomas to spring 'em to get past, but we couldn't do anything until we'd passed the turning for South Muskham—did you see us?'

'Yes, I did, and wondered what the devil you thought you were doing,' retorted the earl. 'I told you to follow us, not risk my coach and my cattle in a race!'

Unabashed, Fitton merely grinned. 'We did follow you, until the road was wide enough for us to get past safely. And it was never a race, those poor nags pullin' the mail being no contest for our team, m'lord. Mind you, I had to grease a few palms to have the pick of the stables at the last posting stage, I can tell you.'

'I hope you haven't spent all my money, Fitton.'

'Devil a bit, m'lord,' replied the valet, reaching into his pocket and handing over a roll of banknotes to his master.

'Thank you. Now, perhaps you will go and bespeak rooms for us—and order another room for a lady and her maid,' he added.

The inn was very busy and it took several minutes for the mail's passengers to be shown to their rooms. Beth was so tired she was tempted to lie down immediately and sleep, but she knew it would be foolish not to eat something, so she shrugged off her jacket and removed her bonnet, tidied her hair and splashed her face with water. She pulled a fresh kerchief from her portmanteau and arranged it carefully around her neck. Thus refreshed, she made her way downstairs to join the other passengers in the coffee room to await dinner. There was no sign of the earl and she knew a moment's regret. She had not wanted his company, but she was forced to admit that his presence had provided her with a certain amount of protection. Now, walking into the crowded coffee room, she was uneasily aware of the men's eyes upon her as she made her way to the table reserved for the mail's passengers. With a sinking heart she realised that most of the seats had been taken and she and Tilly were obliged to sit at opposite ends of the table. One of the outside passengers jumped up to hold her seat for her, but his gentlemanly act was accompanied by such a leering smile that Beth wished there had been a space beside the haughty man: she would infinitely prefer to be ignored than subjected to the zealous attentions of the lanky fellow who smelled of spirits and tobacco and who constantly refreshed himself from a small hipflask.

During the meal Beth fixed her attention on her dinner and tried to concentrate upon what she would do when she reached London. She would need somewhere to stay, but she hoped that if she made her way directly to Mr Spalding's office in Cheapside he would be able to recommend a hotel for her. The man with the hipflask was addressing her again, but she pretended she had not heard him and when she suddenly felt his leg pressing against hers under the table she jumped up and excused herself.

Her appetite was quite destroyed. She had never felt so vulnerable before, but then, she had never travelled alone on a mailcoach before. For a moment she wished that Lord Darrington had not left, but she quickly stifled the thought. She had said she did not need his protection and she would prove it. She just wished she did not feel quite so uncomfortable.

Beth asked a passing serving maid for directions to the privy. When she returned she would collect Tilly and they would retire to their room for the remainder of the evening. She did not think that would prove a hardship, for after such a gruelling day she thought she would be asleep almost as soon as she laid her head on the pillow.

She was returning across the yard when she heard a rough voice behind her.

'Ah. So there you are!'

The words were slurred and there was little light in that part of the yard, but she recognised the lanky form of the outside passenger. She thought that he must by now have consumed the entire contents of his hipflask. Without a word she made to pass him, but his hand shot out and grabbed her arm.

'Not so fast, my pretty. I've had my eye on you.'

'You make that sound like a compliment, sir,' retorted Beth, her lip curling. 'I assure you it is not!'

His braying laugh ended with a hiccup. 'Ah, I like a bit o' spirit in my woman.'

She tried to shake her arm free. 'I am not your woman! Now pray, let me go. I wish to go indoors.'

'And so we shall, my dear, in due course. I saw you give that swell cove the shove and thought you might be needin' a bit o' company.'

'No, thank you. Please let go of my arm.'

'Now don't be unfriendly, lass.' He pulled her closer. 'I thought we might have a drink together. Now, what do you say?'

She averted her face, grimacing at the stench of brandy and onions on his breath. The yard was empty and there was so much noise coming from the inn that she doubted if anyone would hear her if she cried out. She began to be seriously alarmed. She heard a footstep on the cobbles and turned quickly, opening her mouth to shout for help, but the words died when she saw Darrington standing there.

'I think the lady has had enough of your company.'

He spoke quite pleasantly, but Beth heard the underlying steel in his voice. However, her companion merely grunted.

'So it's you come back, is it? Well, you had yer chance, now it's my turn.'

'I think not.' Something in the earl's voice filtered through to the man's drink-sodden brain.

'Oho, so you fancy a turn up, do you?'

Beth felt his grip slacken and she quickly pulled herself free. The man advanced upon the earl, fists raised. Beth did not see what happened; in the space of a moment she was aware of a flurry of movement in the darkness, a few grunts and thuds, then the lanky man was on the floor, nursing his jaw.

'Are you hurt, Mrs Forrester?' Darrington turned his attention to Beth, but she did not answer immediately. She watched her assailant clamber unsteadily to his feet and stagger back to the inn. 'Madam?'

She looked at him, momentarily dazed by events.

'No, I am not hurt.' Indignation welled within her. 'Oh, what a horrid man. How dare he accost me in that manner!'

'He is not entirely to blame,' murmured the earl, coming over to stand beside her.

She turned on him, saying angrily, 'How can you say that?'

Despite the deep shadows she could see the gleam in his eyes as he looked down at her. She swallowed nervously, her anger replaced by another, more unsettling sensation. She stood, unable to move as his hand came up and caught one of her curls.

'You go abroad with that glorious hair uncovered—how can any man resist you?'

His voice, deep and warm now, turned her insides to water and a delicious ripple of desire swirled in her belly. His body was blocking what little light there was coming from the windows of the inn.

She had the unnerving sensation that she was about to be swallowed up in the darkness with him as he moved closer. She turned her face up towards him, unconsciously inviting him to kiss her.

'I—I did not intend…'

Her words were drowned by a burst of raucous laughter. A group of stable hands crashed into the yard, breaking the spell. The earl's head snapped up.

'No,' he muttered, taking her arm in a none-too-gentle grasp, 'you have no idea how beguiling you are, do you?'

He led her indoors, but did not stop at the coffee room door.

'Where are you taking me?'

'I bespoke private rooms for us—'

With a little huff of frustration Beth shook off his arm. 'How many times do I have to tell you that I am not going to accept your help?' she demanded, glaring up at him.

'And how safe will you feel, sleeping in your room tonight? I have seen off one fellow, but what of all the others? I saw them while you were at dinner. Not one man could keep his eyes off you.'

'You…were…watching me?' Beth did not know whether to be gratified or outraged.

'I wanted to make sure you would come to no harm.' He glanced up at the yellowed ceiling and exhaled slowly. At length he fixed his eyes upon her. 'Mrs Forrester, when you took Davies into the Priory and cared for him you earned my gratitude. I would like to repay that debt. Nothing else. I have no…designs upon your virtue.'

Her face flamed and she lowered her eyes so that he would not see her humiliation, or her pain.

'That at least I can believe!' she said bitterly.

A fresh burst of noisy laughter and cheering echoed from the coffee room.

'Do you really want to go back in there?' said Darrington quietly.

Honesty compelled Beth to shake her head.

'I have a suite of rooms above stairs, including a private sitting room and a chamber for yourself and your maid,' he said. 'I would be honoured if you would allow me to escort you to town, madam—I give you my word that you will be treated with nothing but respect while you are in my care.'

Beth clasped her hands together. The thought of spending the night in the little room allocated to her was quite daunting. She would have Tilly with her, but there was no lock on the door; after her recent experiences she did not think she would sleep at all. She glanced at her companion—she might not be able to sleep, knowing the earl was in the next bedchamber, but at least that would not be as a result of fear.

'Very well,' she said slowly. 'I will accept your escort, my lord, for myself and my maid. But I must have your assurance that you will not try to f-flirt with me.' Her cheeks reddened, but the earl merely bowed.

'I shall treat you as I should treat my sister,' he said gravely. 'Allow me to escort you upstairs, madam. I shall send Fitton to fetch your maid and bring your luggage to your new room.'

He escorted her up the narrow stairs and through a labyrinth of passages to a suite of rooms. She was a little nervous as she entered and found the earl's valet waiting for them in the cosy dining parlour, but his manner was very civil and he went off immediately in search of Tilly, leaving her alone once more with the earl. She moved towards the fire to warm her hands.

'This is much more comfortable than the public dining room,' she said to break the silence. 'Will we be able to reach London tomorrow, do you think?'

'Of course, but it will be a long day.'

'I am not afraid of that.' She turned to find him regarding her, a faint smile curving his lips.

'No, I thought as much.'

The light-headed, breathless feeling swept over her again. Her knees seemed to have turned to jelly and she sank down on a chair, folding her hands in her lap.

'I would like to make one thing clear, my lord. I will accept your escort to town, and thank you for it, but once there I will take my leave. I do not intend to impose upon you further.'

'It is no imposition—'

'Once we reach Cheapside—'

'Cheapside!'

She raised her brows. 'Yes,' she said coldly. 'My lawyer has offices there. I shall place myself in his hands to find accommodation.'

'You would be better to let me help you.'

He had walked across the room and was towering over her, menacing her peace of mind. She rose and walked across to the window.

'I may be forced to accept your hospitality for the journey, sir, but you know I do not want your help in this matter.'

'That is not the impression I had,' he flashed back at her. 'That night at the Priory you were only too keen to buy my silence.'

She swung round to find he had followed her across the room. His eyes were blazing with a dangerous mixture of heat and desire.

'That was to protect Simon,' she said unsteadily. 'No other consideration would have made me approach you!'

'I am well aware of that. And yet…' He reached out and ran his fingers down her arm. His touch burned through her sleeve. 'I had the distinct impression you were enjoying it.'

'No!' She put her hands to her cheeks.

The earl stepped closer. 'Then one of us is mistaken,' he said softly. 'Perhaps we should try that kiss again, to find out which of us is right.'

He reached for her, but her body was already moving towards him of its own accord, drawn by myriad invisible silken threads. She put out her hands and held him off, but her fingers merely slid up his jacket, moving from his chest to his shoulder. His face was just inches away, her own lifted invitingly, lips parted, every nerve end screaming for contact with him. Her heightened senses breathed in the very essence of him, the hint of spices on his skin, the scented starch in his snowy-white linen neckcloth. The curling flame of desire moved lower. Her thighs ached, her knees grew weak and she clutched at his jacket. His mouth hovered over hers; they were sharing a breath, anticipating the explosion that would occur when their lips met. Beth's head went back, her eyelids were fluttering to close when she heard the thud of heavy footsteps in the passage, recalling her to her situation. She opened her eyes and pushed her hands against his chest.

'Oh, pray, my lord, let me go! My maid...'

'Damnation! Beth, I—'

With a shake of her head she pushed him away as Fitton struggled in with Beth's portmanteau in one hand and her jacket and cloak draped over his other arm, her bonnet dangling by its strings from his fingers. Tilly followed close behind with her own small bag. She bobbed a curtsy as she followed the valet across the room.

'I'm sorry we took so long, ma'am, my lord—I had unpacked the bag and had to collect everything up again.'

Beth could only nod wordlessly. The earl had turned away and was staring down into the fire. For a few moments Beth was filled with an almost unbearable, aching longing for what might have been, but this was quickly replaced by a feeling of relief. Her hands, a moment ago clutching at his fine wool jacket, now slid over her stomach. Dizzy and confused, she muttered her excuses and followed Tilly to her bedchamber, determined not to come out again until the morning.

Chapter Eleven

Guy leaned his arm along the mantelshelf and rested his head against it, his lips moving with a silent flow of curses. By heaven, what was it about the woman that beguiled him so? Was it the flame-red hair that attracted him like some hapless moth? She undermined his control, but he would swear it was unwittingly done and he was ashamed of his reactions. He was no better than the oaf he had seen off earlier that evening. It was pure lust, of course, and perfectly understandable; she was a very beautiful woman, with her glorious hair and those dark, liquid eyes that melted his soul. Desire stirred at the very thought of her standing before him. With something like a growl he lounged across to the side table and picked up the decanter. He would have a couple of glasses of brandy and go to bed, although heaven knew how he would sleep, knowing that she was lying just feet away from him in the next room.

When Beth awoke the next morning it took her a few moments to remember just where she was, but once memory returned she dressed hurriedly and made her way to the dining room, where she found the earl already breaking his fast. He stood as she came in and greeted her politely. She responded in kind and took her seat at the table.

'Fitton and your maid have gone below for their meal,' he told her, handing her a cup of coffee. 'They would not be comfortable eating with us.'

'No, of course not.' She wondered if she, too, might be more comfortable downstairs. However, the earl said nothing untoward and she began to relax.

She was finishing her small meal when shouts and calls from the roadside informed them that the mail was about to depart. Beth went over to the window to watch it pull away. She could even smile a little when she looked at the outside passengers and saw the lanky man pull out his hipflask. He had obviously found time to refill it.

'I hope you are not regretting your decision to come with me.'

She came back to the table. 'No,' she said carefully. 'As long as you remember your promise to treat me like your sister.'

He grinned at that and she quickly raised a hand to her kerchief, almost expecting to feel her heart had escaped and was caught like a fluttering bird in its folds.

'If that is the case, I must snap and growl at you and tell you that if you are not ready on time I shall leave without you.'

Beth relaxed and warmed to the amusement in his voice. 'Goodness, if that is the case I had best go and pack up immediately!'

'No, no, there is not such a rush,' he said, laughing. 'Stay and take another cup of coffee with me.'

They remained at the table in perfect harmony. Beth could not remember what they discussed, but she was aware of a faint disappointment when Fitton and Tilly returned and the earl said it was time they were leaving. She accompanied him out to the carriage and allowed him to tuck a rug around her knees.

'I am glad it is a fine day,' she said, as he climbed in beside her. 'I do not like to think of poor Tilly and your valet sitting up behind, exposed to all weathers.'

'Is that why you bought your maid a seat inside on the mail?' he asked.

'In part. I was also glad to have her beside me for company.'

'Well, now you have me. Tell me how I may entertain you, Mrs Forrester?'

She disclaimed, flustered, 'You must not think I am in constant need of amusement, my lord.'

'Of course not. Perhaps, then, you would tell me something of yourself.'

'There is not much to tell,' she said, shyly. 'I grew up at the Priory, married, was widowed and returned to Malpass.'

'Was it an arranged marriage?'

'Yes. Papa had known Mr Forrester for many years. We married when I was nineteen, but he died within the year. His heart was weak.'

'I am very sorry. And you returned to the Priory?'

'Yes. Mr Forrester's estate was entailed and passed to a distant cousin. I have a small annuity, but I was very happy to return to my old home.'

'I have never understood how you came to inherit the Priory,' he remarked, shifting his position so that he could look at her. 'Should it not have passed to your brother?'

Beth folded her hands in her lap. 'It should, of course, but Papa changed his will when he heard that Simon was lost at sea.'

'Surely that was a little premature.'

She sighed as the memories came back to her. 'I know. When Miles came to Malpass with the news that Simon had been drowned, Papa was so ill I thought he should not be told. It could only distress him. Unfortunately, Miles called while I was out one day and Papa asked to see him. Miles tells me Papa guessed something was amiss and demanded the truth. Once he knew what had occurred, Papa immediately altered his will in my favour. He was afraid that if Simon's body was never found then there might be…complications in the Priory passing to me, so he changed his will, disinheriting Simon and making everything over to me.'

'Very convenient for Radworth.'

Her head came up at that. 'Miles had no idea that Papa would do such a thing!'

'And did your father know that your brother was accused of murder?'

She shook her head. 'I made Miles promise that he would not tell him, or Grandmama. She doted on Simon and I wanted to keep her memories of him unsullied. I was determined to clear Simon's name, if I could, so I wrote to Mr Spalding, our lawyer in London, and asked him to begin enquiries to find the French couple who had been attacked. I discussed that with Miles. He thought it a good scheme.'

'I know I have asked you this before, but if Radworth knows so much about the family, why have you not told him Simon is alive?' Beth had been dreading that question. She did not have a satisfactory explanation, even for herself. When she did not answer the earl said slowly, 'It seems to me, Mrs Forrester, that you trust your fiancé even less than you trust me.'

'I have no choice but to trust you,' she retorted. 'And believe me, Lord Darrington, I like Miles Radworth a great deal more than I like *you*!'

Beth maintained an icy politeness towards her travelling companion for the remainder of the journey. He was not noticeably dashed and treated her with such courtesy that by the time they stopped at Hatfield for their dinner she was feeling quite guilty and would have been ashamed of her behaviour towards him if she had not reminded herself that she had not asked the earl to convey her to town—in fact, he had almost forced his company upon her. However, she was honest enough to admit, when they sat down to eat in the private dining room with its cheerful fire and a sumptuous array of dishes on the table, that travelling with Lord Darrington was a great deal more agreeable than on a public coach. She therefore made an effort to engage him in civil, if rather inane, conversation while they dined. At the end of the meal the earl took out his watch.

'It will be dark in an hour,' he told her. 'Perhaps you would like to put up here for the night and finish our journey tomorrow?'

Beth shook her head. 'Thank you, but I do not wish to impose upon your hospitality any longer than is necessary, my lord. If you are agreeable, I would like to press on.'

'As you wish.' His polite acquiescence pricked at her conscience and she felt compelled to try to explain.

'I want to see Mr Spalding as soon as possible. After all, I have no idea how long the de Beaunes will be in England.' She hesitated. 'I hope you do not mind pressing on to London tonight?'

She did not add that she was unwilling to spend another night in his company, but from the look he gave her she was sure he had guessed. In fact, she was uncomfortably aware that the earl was far too good at reading her thoughts.

A combination of poor horses and an overturned vegetable cart blocking the road hindered progress on the final leg of their journey and it was gone ten o'clock when they eventually pulled up outside the offices of Spalding, Spalding and Grooch in Cheapside. Unsurprisingly, the building was in darkness and Fitton's knocking brought no response at all, save for a neighbour throwing up the window and demanding who the devil was making so much noise at that time of night. A civil enquiry from the earl elicited the information that none of the partners lived on the premises and that everyone had gone home a good hour since.

'It seems we are too late,' remarked the earl, climbing back into the carriage. 'I am very sorry.'

'Even had we not been delayed on the road we might not have been in time,' Beth responded. 'I must find somewhere to put up for the night, my lord. Perhaps you would advise me.'

The earl hesitated. 'I do not think I can do that.'

Beth froze. In the gloomy interior of the carriage she could not see his face and was not at all sure that his apologetic tone was sincere.

'And just why might that be?' she enquired in arctic tones.

The earl spread his hands. 'The only hotels I can think of that would be suitable for a respectable lady travelling alone are prohibitively expensive.' He paused. 'You have not told me how much you can afford to spend, ma'am, but I would not think your purse…limitless. Neither do I think you would agree to my paying your shot.'

'You are correct on both points,' she ground out. She looked out at the darkened street. 'I do not know yet what it may cost me to prove Simon's innocence, so I am not prepared to waste money on my comfort. Very well, I must find someone to ask—perhaps the coachman might be able to recommend a suitable hostelry.'

'If I may make a suggestion…'

'Will I like it?' she asked suspiciously.

'Probably not, but I would like you to consider it. Stay with me at Darrington House.' He hurried on as she drew a breath to reply. 'Now before you turn me down flat, madam, perhaps you would lay aside that damned pride of yours and *think*. My town house is very large. You and your maid could be accommodated comfortably and in perfect safety—we need not even see each other if that is what you wish!—and you would be able to concentrate your efforts on helping your brother.'

'And what do you intend to do?'

'I would like to help you,' he said quietly. 'I may not visit town often, but I think I am probably much more familiar with London than you are. If you do indeed want to help your brother, I think you should seriously consider my offer.'

Beth bit her lip. At that moment a rowdy group of merrymakers went past, reminding her just how vulnerable she would be if she insisted on leaving the earl's protection. If she was honest, she had spent a great deal of the journey considering just how she would go on in London. She did not doubt for a moment that the earl could be very useful.

'Very well,' she said at last. 'I will accept your offer, for my brother's sake.'

'Good.'

The earl leaned out of the window to issue his orders to his driver and the carriage moved off again. Beth leaned her head against the squabs and closed her eyes. She felt tired to her very bones and not a little despondent. She very much wanted to walk away from the earl and show him that she did not require his help, but it had been abundantly clear on the journey south that he could make things so much easier for her and she owed it to Simon to accept whatever help she could to prove his innocence. She must therefore swallow her pride and allow the earl to help, however much it irked her.

'Here we are.'

She opened her eyes as the carriage drew up outside an imposing double-fronted mansion. The earl jumped out and turned to give her his hand while his valet ran up the steps and banged loudly on the door. There were no lights at any window, but after a few minutes Beth noticed a faint glow through the fanlight and the next moment the door opened.

The butler's surprise at seeing his master would have made Beth smile if she had not been so exhausted. She allowed the earl to escort her inside, leaving Tilly and Fitton to bring in their bags.

'There is nothing ready, my lord,' said the butler, leading them into the morning room and hurriedly lighting the candles. 'Mrs Burley and I have only Joseph the under-footman and a kitchen boy here at the moment. If only you had told us you were coming...'

'I did not know myself until yesterday—you may leave the fire, Burley. I will light it while you help Fitton to prepare rooms for me and for my guest. Mrs Forrester and her maid will require a suite of rooms, I think.'

'Of course, my lord. And what about food? Mrs Burley will send the boy to fetch something as soon as it is light tomorrow, but for tonight I doubt we have anything but bread and cheese...'

'Then that is what we shall have,' replied the earl. 'Have it served in here and bring a bottle of wine, too, Burley.'

He escorted Beth to a chair. 'I should keep your cloak about you for a little while, madam, until I have a good blaze going.'

Beth was very content to sit quietly while the earl knelt before the hearth, coaxing the fire into life. She watched him feeding sticks into the fragile flames, building up the heat before carefully adding the coal. It occurred to her that he was no idle gentleman and while he might well have an army of servants at his beck and call, he was quite capable of looking after himself. She thought wistfully how comfortable it would be to have such a man to look after her, then she quickly chided herself. Miles Radworth had professed himself ready to look after her—she only had to give the word. For some reason the idea made her uncomfortable and she quickly banished it. Time to think of Miles when she returned to Yorkshire. For now she would concentrate on helping Simon.

Beth could hear sounds of activity outside the door and imagined the butler bustling about, chivvying his few underlings into preparing the house for the master. But whatever the jostle and haste outside the morning room, none of it showed on the butler's impassive countenance when he came in presently with the wine. He was followed by a rosy-cheeked woman in a black-stuff gown, the white lappets of her lace cap bobbing on her shoulders as she walked in, a heavy tray covered with a snowy white cloth between her hands. Beth guessed that this was Mrs Burley and the woman's first words were very much those of an old and trusted retainer. Most likely, thought Beth with an inward smile, one who had known the earl since he was a child.

'My lord, what a pleasure it is to see you in town again, and after *such* an age! And you've cobbled up a fire in here, sir, that's good, for the nights are going off chilly now, aren't they? But what a pity you could not send a messenger before you. We would have had everything prepared! Not but what there is little to do, for I keep all the beds aired, just as you directed, and we have only to remove the holland covers from the guest suite and light a fire there to make it ready for visitors. It's what I can give you to eat that's bothering me, though, my lord. There's hardly a bite in the house save this bread and cheese.'

'That will be more than enough for me,' put in Beth quickly. 'We dined at Hatfield, so a small meal is all that I require.'

'Well, there is the bit o' broth that I was keeping for our supper—'

'We would on no account take your supper,' broke in the earl, a gleam of humour lightening his countenance. 'Mrs Forrester will be staying for a few days, so there will be time and enough for you to show her what an excellent cook you are.'

'Well, it's very kind of you to say so, my lord, and as soon as the market opens in the morning I shall sally forth and stock up, I can tell you.' She placed her tray down upon the table and turned to beam at Beth. 'Now then, I'll leave you to your supper while I go upstairs and make sure your rooms are comfortable. And if you want anything else you just ring.' She followed her impassive husband to the door and paused again. 'Your lordship went to all the trouble and expense of having that new bell system installed and it breaks my heart to see the bells hanging there, silent and unused!' She bobbed a curtsy towards Beth, adding, 'And you let me know when you want to go upstairs, ma'am, and I'll make sure the warming pan's ready for your bed.'

Calm settled over the morning room again. The earl cast a rueful glance at Beth.

'I owe you an apology, ma'am. I lured you here with promises of lordly comfort and all we have to offer is bread and cheese. Pauper's fare! Are you sure that will be enough for you? I would willingly send out—'

'No, no, we dined so well on the road that truly I want very little,' Beth responded quickly, the housekeeper's motherly address having done much to lessen her anxiety. She removed her cloak and dropped it over the back of her chair before making her way to the table and lifting the cloth from the laden tray. 'Cheese, bread and butter, pickles—a veritable feast,' she exclaimed. 'I hope we are not taking poor Mr Burley's supper.'

'Not a bit of it. Did you not hear Mrs Burley say they are having broth tonight?'

'Ah, yes, then we may eat this with a clear conscience.' She moved all the dishes from the tray to the table and sat down. 'Will you not join me, sir?'

Guy took his place at the little table and poured two glasses of wine to accompany their simple supper. Time was of no consequence, their conversation, desultory at first, became deep and wide-ranging. The fire he had built up began to burn low, unheeded, and the noises in the street died away as they considered the troubles in France and the independence of the American states before moving on to discuss their own properties.

As the candles burned down in their sockets Guy encouraged Beth to tell him more about her life at the Priory. It soon became clear that she not only looked after the day-to-day running of the house, but also managed the Home Farm. Tasks that he left to his very able steward fell to her lot, such as looking after the tenant rent books and discussing with her farmers which crops they would be growing. At one point he put up his hands and laughingly called halt when she began to question him about winter sowing.

'I vow you are much better informed than I am,' he told her. 'My steward advises me of what is to be planted each season, but I only know if his decisions are the right ones by the results.'

'I am not so very different,' she replied, smiling. 'The tenant farms are quite small, so any failure of crops will result in hardship, more so for them than for me, so it is in their interests to look after the land. We discuss repairs and improvements and they must convince me their ideas are worthwhile before I will invest.'

'A heavy responsibility,' he replied, cutting himself another piece of cheese. 'No doubt when you are married, Radworth will look after that for you—or will he bring in a steward? You said he had another property, I believe—perhaps he intends to make that your main residence?'

'No, we shall live at Malpass, at least to begin with.'

'But it will be a relief for you to have someone to share your burdens.' She did not reply immediately and he saw that she was abstracted, a crease between her brows. 'Mrs Forrester?'

She looked up, replacing the frown with a faint smile. 'Yes. That can only be an advantage.' She tilted her head, listening as the cry of the nightwatch calling the hour filtered in through the shuttered window. 'It is very late,' she said. 'I should retire.'

She made no move and in the stillness that followed Guy realised he did not want her to go.

'There is still wine in the bottle—will you not finish it with me?'

She pushed her glass towards him in silent acquiescence and a bolt of pleasure shot through him at the thought that she, too, wanted to prolong the moment. Somehow during the course of their supper they had drawn closer together, their knees almost touching under the table, their hands only inches apart on the covers. Guy carefully refilled their glasses; he had drunk only two glasses of wine, but he felt unusually alive and painfully aware of the woman sitting next to him, conscious of her every movement, every slight change of expression.

As he handed her the glass their fingers brushed. She murmured, 'I should drink this and go to my room.'

Come to mine!

Guy wondered if he had spoken aloud as her eyes flew to his face. They were large and dark as midnight pools. At some stage she had removed her kerchief from around her shoulders and several times he found his gaze wandering to the slim column of her neck, the creamy skin unadorned by any ornament. Now he saw the nervous quiver of her throat as she swallowed, observed the quick rise and fall of her breast. With an immense effort he subdued the desire growing within him, drawing on every argument he could muster to stop himself from dragging her into his arms and covering that delectable skin with hot, passionate kisses. She was another man's bride. She was under his protection. Her brother was a murderer.

This last point brought him back to their reason for being in town. Perhaps there, at least, he might be of some use to her.

He raised his glass. 'Here's to good fortune when we see your lawyer tomorrow, Mrs Forrester.'

'Thank you.'

As she looked at him over the rim of her glass her eyes were guarded. She, too, realised their perilous position. The camaraderie they had enjoyed was at an end. Guy told himself he was glad of it—she undermined his self-control far too much for his liking.

She took a few sips of her wine and put down her glass. 'If you will excuse me, I should go…'

Immediately he was on his feet and crossing the room to ring the bell. 'Mrs Burley will be here directly to show you to your room.'

In his effort to be calm his words emerged cold and indifferent. To make up for this he took a step towards her, reaching for her hand to place a formal, parting kiss on her fingers, but she hastily moved away from him, busying herself with collecting her kerchief and her cloak.

'Thank you, you have been very kind.' She did not look at him, and when the housekeeper entered she muttered a few words of farewell and hurried out.

The rooms prepared for Beth and her maid were warm and comfortable and drew rare praise from Tilly as she helped her mistress to undress. Beth hardly heard her. She tried to convince herself that her preoccupation was due to the forthcoming meeting with Mr Spalding, but when Tilly had left her and she was lying alone in the darkness, it was the earl's image that filled her mind. He was smiling at her, his eyes warm and inviting, flooding her body with an almost unbearable yearning.

With a groan she turned over, pummelling her pillow. She would not be so foolish as to believe she meant anything to the earl. A man would bed any comely woman if he was given the chance— her own husband had told her as much, when she had found him closeted with a pretty chambermaid only a few weeks into their marriage. And she had offered herself quite blatantly to the earl, had she not? He had refused her then, angry that she had tried to buy his silence, but she thought it understandable that he had reconsidered and would now be happy to enjoy her favours; perhaps he even expected her to give herself to him, in gratitude for his assistance. He had told her he would treat her as a sister, but Beth was aware of the attraction between them. She did not think it would take much to break that fragile veneer of respectability and send them crashing into a heady, passionate affair, heedless of the consequences. It had almost happened earlier that evening, when he had given her that last glass of wine. The atmosphere had been so charged with electricity she had felt the shock of it when their fingers touched. After that she had been afraid to move, to speak, lest she should betray the naked desire burning inside her.

'You are undoubtedly a fool, Beth Forrester,' she muttered into her pillow. 'You are here to clear Simon's name. Nothing must distract you from that.'

Chapter Twelve

Beth mentally applauded the housekeeper when she was shown into the breakfast room the following morning, for there was no lack of variety in the dishes on offer.

Lord Darrington was already at the table and she returned his greeting with a shy smile.

'Thank you for sending up the writing case, my lord. I did as you suggested and dashed off a note to Mr Spalding as soon as I rose. You are very good to me, my lord.'

'Think nothing of it. I am merely thinking of the inconvenience to my people if your lawyer should be unavailable this morning.'

His smiling look gave the lie to his cool words, but Beth did not respond and merely applied herself to her breakfast. She wondered if she would ever become inured to the earl's presence. Every time she saw him she was aware of a *frisson* of excitement; he only had to smile at her for the now-familiar ache to drag at her insides, but she had to acquit him of any attempt to flirt with her over the breakfast dishes—quite the opposite, for apart from their initial exchange he ignored her, giving his attention to scanning the newspaper that lay beside him on the table.

Beth was just drinking a second cup of coffee when Burley came in with a note for her.

'Oh.' She was unable to keep the disappointment from her voice as she read it. 'Mr Spalding begs that I delay my visit to him until tomorrow, when he hopes to have more news for me.' She folded the note, adding with false lightness, 'It was as well you did not order your carriage, my lord.'

'What do you intend to do now?'

She spread her hands. 'Why, nothing. I shall be obliged to kick my heels for the rest of the day. But please,' she added quickly, 'do not think I need you to entertain me. You have a well-stocked library here, I shall be perfectly happy...'

'The devil you will,' he growled, throwing down his paper. 'You will fret yourself into a lather if you are cooped up indoors all day with nothing to do.' He rose. 'You told me you have never been to town before. Go and fetch your cloak and bonnet, Mrs Forrester. I will take you for an airing!'

When Beth stepped out of Darrington House she was surprised to see the earl's curricle with Holt at the horses' heads. He touched his cap and grinned at her, correctly reading her expression.

'His lordship told me to bring his horses back from Highridge,' Holt explained. 'Reached the stables at midnight, so I was ready when 'is lordship sent word round this morning. Which was a good thing,' he added, casting a challenging look up at his master, 'for I wouldn't trust just *anyone* to drive these beauties. Prime goers, they are.'

'I hope you did not push them too hard on the journey south,' remarked the earl, pulling on his gloves.

'If I 'ad we'd've been here before you, my lord,' replied the groom, unabashed. 'Rest assured, sir, they are well rested and rarin' to go!'

It seemed to Beth that the groom had understated the matter. The horses fretted and stamped as she took her seat in the racing curricle and once the groom had jumped away from their heads they sprang forwards, so eager to be off that she glanced back to make sure Holt had managed to scramble up into the rumble seat.

'Do not be alarmed, Mrs Forrester,' remarked the earl, as she gripped tightly to the side, 'I have never yet turned over a carriage.'

'There is a first time for everything, my lord,' she replied tensely. 'Pray do not let me distract you. Look to your horses!'

He merely laughed at that and concentrated on guiding his team through the busy London thoroughfares. The sun was shining and Beth looked about her in wonder. Everywhere was crowded with carriages and pedestrians; building work seemed to be taking place on almost every street. She marvelled at the way the earl negotiated the crowded thoroughfares. First he took her to Somerset House, pointing out to her the headquarters of the learned societies, before turning on to the bustling wharf of the Adelphi so that she could enjoy the view of its impressive vaults that supported the fashionable terraces above.

'I have never seen anything like it,' she marvelled, gazing about her in awe. 'However, I do not think I should like to live quite so close to the river.'

'No. In summer it can become quite noisome.' He glanced down at her. 'Would you like to see Carlton House?'

He drove her past the Prince of Wales's palace and whisked her up St James's Street, where several gentlemen stopped to stare at them.

'Oh, dear.' Beth shifted uneasily. 'Perhaps I should not have driven out with you. Those men…'

The earl raised his whip to salute them.

'Acquaintances,' he said briefly. 'Surprised to see me in town. No need to fret over them, Mrs Forrester. There is no impropriety in your being seen with me at this time in the morning.'

'Oh, no,' she said quickly. 'And I am enjoying it so much, thank you.'

'If you have had enough of the crowds and bustle,' he said, turning on to Piccadilly, 'let us drive to Hyde Park.'

She said doubtfully, 'Is that not very fashionable?'

'The fashionable hour is five in the afternoon, ma'am. We should not meet too many people there this morning.'

He drove on, skilfully negotiating the gates and soon the noise was left behind as they drove deeper into the park.

'This is much more peaceful,' admitted Beth, relaxing. 'I had forgotten how crowded cities could be.'

'You were not planning to go into society when you came to town?'

'Not really. I thought only of finding the de Beaunes.'

'Do you have no evening gowns with you?'

'I have brought my lilac silk,' she replied, surprised by his question.

'Good. You will need it this evening when I take you to Lady Shott's soirée.'

Immediately she was on her guard. 'Really, Lord Darrington, I do not think—'

'Sir Henry Shott was the French Ambassador at one time,' he interrupted her protests. 'He still has strong connections with the country and holds a virtual open house for every *émigré* that comes to London. I am hoping we might be able to learn something there about the de Beaunes.'

'Oh. I see.'

'I hope you do.'

She bit her lip. 'I beg your pardon. I thought...'

'I know exactly what you thought. I wish you would rid yourself of the idea that I have any designs upon your virtue!'

Guy tried to convince himself that it was true, but acknowledged that she was wise not to trust him. He kept thinking of her in his room at the Priory, lying on the bed in a gossamer-thin nightgown that only enhanced her charms and with her hair spread out over the covers like a red-gold sunset. Since that night he had done his best to disguise his desire, but it was difficult, and doubly so when she joined him in the drawing room that evening, ready to go out.

He had seen her wearing the gown before, but this time she had left off the white kerchief to display the low lace-edged neckline of the bodice. Her only ornament was a single string of fine pearls and one glossy curl hung down over her shoulder, teasingly drawing attention to the soft swell of her breasts. He longed to reach out and cup them in his hands, to cover them in kisses.

Beth recognised the leap of desire in his eyes and quickly looked away, one hand nervously fluttering towards her neck. 'I am a little out of touch with fashion, my lord. I hope this is not too plain…'

He caught her hands and raised one then the other to his lips. He said softly, 'You look beautiful.'

Beth swallowed. She was hopelessly out of her depth with this man. Bit by bit he was stealing her heart. No time to worry about that, she told herself as he threw her cloak about her shoulders. He would help her to find the de Beaunes and that was all that mattered for now.

They arrived at Sir Henry Shott's narrow town house and were shown into the crowded reception rooms, where Lady Shott greeted the earl with unfeigned delight.

'Darrington, my dear sir, I had no idea you were in town!' She held out her hands to the earl and he obligingly kissed them.

'I hope you will forgive our uninvited appearance, madam.' Beth observed her hostess almost purr under the charm of his smile. The earl drew her forwards. 'Allow me to present Mrs Forrester, of Malpass Priory near Fentonby. She is newly arrived in town.'

Beth did not miss the speculative look in the lady's eyes.

'Indeed? One of the Wakeford gels, are you? I remember Lady Arabella very well—she was the terror of the ballrooms when I first came to town. Do you make a long stay, ma'am?'

'I hardly know yet, Lady Shott.'

'Mrs Forrester is in town to meet up with an old acquaintance,' said the earl easily. 'A French couple—in fact, you may know them. Name of de Beaune.'

Lady Shott's finely pencilled brows drew together.

'I do not recall the name, but that is not to say they are not here—we have any number of *émigrés* with us, as always! Henry may be able to help you further. He is over there somewhere…' She waved an airy hand in the general direction of the crowded room before dashing off to meet more new arrivals.

The earl guided Beth across the room, nodding here and there but never stopping to speak to anyone.

'We are attracting a great deal of attention,' she murmured, trying to ignore the stares of an elderly gentleman in a powdered bagwig.

'Why should you be surprised?' the earl responded. 'You are a beautiful woman.'

'I think it is more the fact that I am with you,' she retorted, pinning on a smile as the elderly gentleman approached.

The old man ignored her and fixed his angry eyes upon the earl.

'So, you're back are you, Darrington? Surprised you have the gall to show your face!'

'Indeed, Kilton? Now why should that be?'

The earl's voice was silky smooth, but Beth's hand was on his arm and she noted how his muscles tensed beneath the sleeve.

'You know very well, sir,' blustered Kilton. 'It may have been a decade ago, but—'

'Not everyone's memory is as long as yours, Kilton.'

The underlying menace in the earl's careless drawl made the old gentleman draw back, eyes snapping.

'Damn your eyes, sir,' he hissed. 'You are a disgrace to your name and your politics!'

Beth's grip on the earl's arm tightened. Was this the treason that Miles had disclosed to her?

'My lord—'

'Come, ma'am, we must not allow ourselves to be distracted.' His faint, distant smile told her he would not discuss the matter, but as they made their way across the room she was even more aware of the stares that accompanied them. Some were merely curious, others blatantly unfriendly. However, there was no mistaking the welcome they received from a rotund gentleman with bushy side-whiskers. His jolly face broke into a beaming smile as soon as he spotted the earl.

'Darrington, my boy!'

The earl introduced him to Beth as their host, Sir Henry Shott. She was encouraged by his obvious delight in seeing them and lost no time in asking him if he knew of a Monsieur de Beaune, recently arrived from France.

'Beaune…hmm. Names rings a bell with me. Yes, I remember now. There was a Madame de Beaune came to see me a few days ago. Recently arrived from France and in need of money. I helped her sell some of her jewelry.'

'And do you know where she is living?' asked Beth.

Sir Henry shook his head. 'She would not tell me, preferred to keep it a secret. Don't be too disheartened,' he added, observing her disappointment. 'Many of these *émigrés* arrive here in desperate straits and anxious for their safety. Once they realise we mean them no harm they soon settle down.'

'Perhaps some of your other guests might know of the de Beaunes' whereabouts,' suggested Guy.

'It's possible. Old Leclerc, for example.' Sir Henry nodded towards a courtly looking gentleman in an embroidered coat and heavily powdered wig. 'He's been here for years now and makes it his business to take all the new *émigrés* under his wing. Go and renew your acquaintance with him, Guy, he should remember you, although he's a bit deaf so you might want to take him to one side.' He held out his arm to Beth and said with a twinkling smile, 'You can leave Mrs Forrester safely with me!'

Sir Henry shook his head as they watched the earl walk away. 'Sad loss to the country when that young man quit the government.'

'Indeed?' said Beth. 'That was ten years ago, I think?'

'Aye, all of that.'

'Why did he resign?' She tried to keep her voice casual.

'Oh, some scandal or another,' came the airy reply.

Beth hesitated. 'We have just met someone—Kilton—who said—'

'Now you don't want to listen to old Kilton, He has been at odds with Darrington's family for generations. Don't believe all you hear about the earl, ma'am. He has his faults but he is a loyal Englishman, that I'll vouch for! Now, madam, Darrington said you hailed from Yorkshire. Do you know Ripon? I have some very happy memories of that place…'

Beth resigned herself to the fact that Sir Henry was not going to tell her anything more about the earl's past and she allowed him to rattle on as he pleased, only requiring the odd word from her to keep the conversation going. His attention was claimed by another guest and Beth quickly excused him with an assurance that she was happy to make her own way around the room. Many of the guests were newly arrived from France and she was glad that her excellent education meant she could communicate with the *émigrés* in their own language.

She was passing a little knot of ladies when she heard one say, 'So that is Darrington's latest flirt.'

'And not a maid, this time,' replied another. 'Very wise, if he wishes to avoid another episode like the Brentry scandal!'

Their unkind laughter and knowing looks brought an angry flush to Beth's cheeks. She turned away quickly, only to find her way blocked by her hostess. Lady Shott took her arm, saying quietly, 'Come away, Mrs Forrester. 'Tis a pity some people have such a penchant for salacious gossip. And it is quite untrue, of course.'

Beth could not resist saying, 'The scandal they spoke of—was it the Miss B— mentioned in the newssheets?'

Lady Shott nodded. 'Lady Brentry was throwing the poor gel at Darrington for months and all the while she was pining for another. Not, of course, that a parson's son could compare with the rich Earl of Darrington! Then her beau got her with child and married her, but not before Lady B. had tried to put it about that the child was the earl's! Not a word of truth in it, of course.'

Beth's eyes strayed across the room to where the earl was talking with a group of gentlemen. 'How can you be so sure, ma'am? After all, so many rumours…'

'Because I know Darrington,' replied Lady Shott. 'He would not take advantage of an innocent. Besides, he was at the other end of the country when the coupling must have occurred!' She gave a little huff of exasperation. 'Not that he helped matters by giving the couple a very generous sum as a wedding present! It looked for all the world as if he was paying them off! But Darrington was unrepentant and the young couple were glad enough of the money. They have gone off now to live in happy obscurity in Wales.' She glanced up and smiled as Lord Darrington came up. 'Ah there you are, my lord. Any news?'

'I'm afraid not. Leclerc has not seen the de Beaunes, although he did say he had been asked to look out for them.'

'Madame de Beaune has family in England,' said Beth slowly. 'Perhaps they have contacted him.'

'Aye, that will be it,' nodded their hostess. 'Everyone in town goes to Leclerc for information about the French.' With another genial smile she wandered away.

'Is there anyone else here we might ask?' asked Beth, looking around.

'I doubt it. I think we must wait to talk to your lawyer in the morning. Do you want to leave?'

'As soon as may be.' Beth shivered. 'Everywhere I look I find people staring. I have never been the centre of so much attention before.'

He pulled her hand on to his arm and patted it.

'One grows accustomed,' he said lightly. 'The women are wondering who you are and the men are all jealous of me.'

'Is that all it is?' She turned to him. 'What about that man… Kilton?'

He met her glance with a bland, shuttered look.

'Kilton is an old fool. Nothing for you to worry about, Mrs Forrester. Come along, let us make one full circuit of the room and then we may take our leave.'

Despite his words she could not be easy, and even as they made their way to the door she felt someone watching her. She turned quickly and caught the glimpse of silken skirts being drawn back into the shadows.

They spoke little on the journey back to Darrington House. Beth tried to make sense of all she had seen and heard at the Shotts' house—should she be more or less wary of Lord Darrington? There was no doubt that both Sir Henry and his wife thought very highly of the earl, but Kilton's venomous look and scathing words kept coming back to haunt her. She had no doubt that he was referring to the long-ago scandal that Miles had mentioned to her. She put her hands to her temples.

'Tired?'

The tenderness in the earl's voice only added to her confusion.

'A little.'

The carriage came to a halt and she allowed him to hand her down. As the carriage moved off Guy took her arm ready to lead her up the steps and into the house, where the butler was already holding the door open for them.

Beth noticed a figure hurrying towards them, swathed in a voluminous satin cloak whose folds glinted as she moved. It occurred to Beth that it was unusual to see a woman alone on the streets in this part of town. As Guy led her to the steps, the cloaked figure put herself in front of them and they were obliged to stop.

'Good evening, Darrington.'

The earl's fingers tightened painfully on Beth's arm. The woman raised her hands and gently lifted the hood back from her golden curls. Beth glanced at Guy. He was staring silently at the woman, who raised her brows, saying in a low, musical voice. 'Are you not going to present me?' She gave a little laugh and fixed her huge blue eyes upon Beth. 'I can see you are curious to know who I am, and if he will not tell you then I shall. I am Darrington's fiancée.'

And with that she crumpled silently on to the flagway.

Chapter Thirteen

'Oh, heavens!' Beth took a step towards the lifeless figure.
'Leave her.'

She stared at Guy, unable to believe his harsh tone. 'We cannot
leave her lying here in the rain! She must be taken inside.' Beth
gestured to the butler. 'Quickly, come and help your master.' With
Beth hovering about them, Guy and Burley lifted the unconscious
woman and carried her into the house. Beth ran ahead to open the
door of the morning room, which had been prepared in readiness
for their arrival. 'Put her on the sofa here, by the fire.'

'Madam. *Beth!*'

She ignored Guy's protest as she threw off her cloak and plumped
up the cushions before the woman was laid gently down. Beth knelt
beside the sofa, pulled off the woman's gloves and began to chafe
her hands. They were not as cold as she had expected and she
looked closely at the woman's face. Surely there was conscious-
ness there, despite the closed eyes—could she be pretending? Her
mind was racing with conjecture. Guy's fiancée. The words lay
heavily on her spirits, but she tried to push them aside and concentrate on helping the unfortunate creature to recover. The woman's clothes were very fine, but there was mud around the bottom
of the skirts and her satin slippers were dirty from the street. She
wore her fair hair unpowdered, but her lashes had been darkened
and there was an unnatural colour to her cheeks. Gazing into her
face, Beth thought that she must have been very beautiful once.

She was still very handsome, but in a showy way that reminded Beth of an overblown rose.

'I have a glass of water,' said Guy. 'Let me splash her face with it. That will bring her round.'

'No need,' replied Beth. 'She is stirring.'

'How convenient.'

Beth ignored his cynical comment and spoke gently to the woman as she shifted restlessly. 'Be still. You are quite safe now.'

The woman opened her eyes and stared at her for a long moment before she fixed her china-blue eyes upon the earl.

'*Am* I safe, Darrington?'

The caressing tone was not lost on Beth. She rose and stepped away from the sofa, suddenly feeling like an intruder. 'I will leave you…'

Guy caught her arm. 'No, do not go. There is nothing she has to say to me that is private. Let me present to you Miss Clarice Bellington, and let me assure you that we are *not* betrothed—that ended ten years ago!'

'And I am no longer Miss Bellington,' replied Clarice, sitting up. 'I am now Madame Cordonnier, a widow.' She put one hand to her head. 'Since you have a glass of water there, may I have some to drink?'

Guy handed her the glass and she sipped at it while her eyes were fixed on Beth.

'Is this your latest flirt? I must say, Darrington, she is not just in your usual style. In every report I have had of you, your *amours* have been fair, very much like me…'

'That is enough,' barked Guy, a muscle working in his jaw. 'Tell me what you are doing here.'

Beth retreated to a chair by the window. Guy seemed to have forgotten her existence. His attention was fixed on Clarice, who was now casting coquettish glances at him from beneath her lashes.

'I saw you at the Shotts' party and followed your carriage. I am glad it was not too far, because I had no fare for a cab and had to follow you on foot all the way.'

'I thought you were in France.'

'Out of the way, do you mean?' Her lips smiled, but Beth could discern no warmth in her expression. 'I was there until very recently. I married Cordonnier soon after I arrived in France. But he was a wastrel and gambled away all our money before blowing his brains out. That was not such a bad thing, for I had many admirers—comtes, vicomtes, marquises…but now it is not a good time to be the mistress of a nobleman. So…I came back to England.'

'To my door.'

Clarice shrugged. 'That was not my original intention, but times have changed. It seems my…friends…no longer acknowledge me.'

Guy's lip curled. 'Can you blame them?'

'Perhaps not. I need money, Darrington. I have not a penny to my name.'

'That is not my concern.'

'That is why I have been going to Sir Henry's house. I know he looks favourably upon the French and I am always sure of a meal there. But although they have not yet thrown me out of the house, it is obvious I am not welcome there.'

'Neither are you welcome here,' was the earl's frank response.

'I cannot even pay for my lodgings.'

'Do not try to play your games with me, Clarice.'

She said tartly, 'If you will not help me, I shall be obliged to offer myself to the nearest abbess!'

'Then do so.' His callous response made Beth start forwards and Guy looked up, as if suddenly aware of her presence in the room. He said bluntly, 'Do not waste your sympathy on her, madam. I assure you she is very resourceful.'

'You cannot throw her out on to the street!'

'I—will—not have her staying in my house.'

His tone was implacable, his words made all the more chilling since at that moment the squally wind hurled a clatter of raindrops against the window. Beth walked over to stand beside him. She said quietly, 'Please, my lord. It is past midnight. No woman should be obliged to walk unprotected at this hour.'

He put his hand up and cupped her cheek, his hard, angry look softening. 'Very well. I shall send for my carriage to take her back to her lodgings.'

'My, my,' murmured Clarice, watching this interchange. 'Who is this angel of mercy?'

'My name is Elizabeth Forrester,' Beth replied. 'And despite how it looks, I am *not* the earl's mistress. He—he is helping me with a…family problem.'

'You need tell her nothing!' The earl crossed to pull the bell and the alacrity with which its summons was answered suggested to Beth that Burley had been standing just outside the door. 'Send for my chariot to come back. As quickly as possible.'

'And could I have a little food while we are waiting?' asked Clarice, wilting elegantly on the sofa.

Guy nodded and the butler withdrew, to return moments later with a tray of bread and cold meats.

For Beth the evening had taken on a dreamlike quality. The events of the past few weeks had been so exhausting, so extraordinary, that she found herself wondering if any of it was real. And now, with the night-watch outside the window calling the hour, she was sitting in this elegant room, watching the woman who claimed to be the earl's fiancée picking daintily at a supper. Clarice was completely at her ease, ignoring Beth and addressing her remarks to Guy, who answered briefly or not at all. At last she pushed aside her plate and sat back with a satisfied sigh.

'Your excellent housekeeper has not lost her touch, Darrington,' she said, dabbing at her lips with the napkin. 'I remember she could always be relied upon to provide a delicious meal, no matter what time of the night we might demand it.'

Beth fixed her attention on her hands clasped tightly in her lap. There could be no mistaking the woman's look and purring tones, although she was relieved to note that Guy did not react at all. He merely said politely, 'I am glad it pleased you.' He walked to the window and opened one of the shutters an inch. 'Now if you have eaten enough, my carriage awaits you.'

Beth watched those darkened lashes flutter.

'Even if you take me back to my lodgings I have not a penny. What will become of me when my landlady demands her rent?'

'I neither know nor care.'

'My lord!'

Beth was moved to protest, distressed by his harsh tone. Clarice merely fixed him with a limpid gaze. The earl looked from one to the other, his mouth set in a thin line. At length he said, 'Very well, wait here.'

As he left the room Clarice transferred her attention to Beth.

'Well, well—you seem to have some influence with Darrington, Mrs Forrester. Has he been hiding you at Wylderbeck?'

'He has not been *hiding* me anywhere,' retorted Beth coldly. 'I have my own property in…' she hesitated '…north Yorkshire.'

'Yes, near Fentonby, I believe.' Clarice's smile mocked her. 'I asked Lady Shott about you.' She sighed. 'He has gone to open his safe, I suppose. I wonder how much he will give me?'

'I have no idea,' returned Beth shortly. 'I only pray you will use it wisely.'

She moved away, determined not to ask questions although so many were racing through her head. The engagement had been broken ten years ago—was that when the earl was accused of being a traitor? Was that the reason they had parted?

Clarice said softly, 'He was besotted with me, you know. I hear that after I left him he vowed never to trust a woman again.'

Beth turned, putting back her shoulders as she answered coldly, 'I know nothing about that.'

'But you would like to be the woman who saves him, would you not?' purred Clarice. 'Yes, I can see it in your eyes. You think you can make him love you. Well, be careful, Mrs Forrester, or he will abandon you just as he did me!'

Hasty footsteps sounded in the hall and Beth was spared an answer. Lord Darrington came in, a roll of banknotes in one hand.

'Here.' He gave them to Clarice. 'You will get no more from me, madam.'

She ran a thumb across the edge of the roll. 'It is not much, when you think what we were to each other.' When he did not reply she fluttered her eyelashes at him again. 'You will not turn me out, Darrington? I can hear the rain pouring down outside and it is so very late.'

'All the more reason to make haste, then.' He opened the door and barked an order to a waiting footman.

Clarice pouted. 'You were not wont to be so cruel.'

'I was not wont to be so wise.'

Silence fell. Beth watched Clarice, observed her foot tapping angrily beneath the grubby hem of her gown. The tapping slowed as a speculative light entered the woman's eyes.

'You owe me more than this, Darrington. I was to be your bride!'

'As a matter of fact, madam, I owe you much less. I advise you to go now, before my patience runs out.' Burley came in to announce that his lordship's carriage was at the door. Guy said, 'Well, madam?'

'Very well.' Clarice stood up, shaking out her skirts. 'I shall leave you here with your...' Her eyes roamed over Beth, whose cheeks flamed at the insinuation.

Guy stepped forwards, shielding her from that knowing gaze. 'Get out, Clarice, before I change my mind and call the constable to remove you.'

Clarice's head came up and she shot him a look of pure venom. 'You will regret this, Darrington.'

'The only thing I regret, madam, is falling into your clutches in the first place!'

Beth heard the woman's sharp intake of breath, a swish of silk and hasty steps across the floor, then the door closed and there was silence.

Beth sank down on to a chair.

'I would you had not been here,' muttered Guy, walking to the sideboard and pouring wine into two glasses.

She recalled the blatant invitation in the woman's eyes. 'Would... would you have dealt with her differently?'

'Aye. I would have left her lying in the street!'

She did not know whether she should be most shocked or relieved by his reply. When he held out the wine to her, she shook her head.

'Thank you, but no.' She watched him empty his glass in one go. 'Would you like to…to tell me about her?'

'Clarice? No. I would rather we forgot all about her.' He shook his head at her. 'Pray, do not argue with me, madam. The woman is not worth a moment's thought. Go to bed, Mrs Forrester, and save your energies for the morning!'

Beth tried to follow the earl's advice and put Clarice Cordonnier out of her mind. It was not difficult, for she had enough problems of her own to occupy her. She rose early, eager to see Mr Spalding. Knowing it might be a long day, she had a good breakfast, helping herself to slices of ham and cold beef, followed by honey and hot, spiced bread, washed down with fragrant coffee. She had almost completed her meal when Lord Darrington came in, apologising for his tardiness.

'Fitton had put out my tawny-cut velvet, but I thought a plainer coat might be more appropriate for visiting a lawyer. Less conspicuous in Cheapside.'

Glancing at the earl, Beth secretly considered he would never be inconspicuous, however plain his coat. His height and bearing commanded attention. He had chosen to wear an olive-green coat with silver buttons over a paler waistcoat and immaculate buckskins that were pushed into his gleaming jockey-type boots. His snowy white shirt, starched neckcloth and cuffs were of the finest quality and his brown hair gleamed in the morning sunlight that flooded the room. Her mouth went dry and she had to bite her lips together to prevent herself from sighing.

Oh, why did he have to be so very handsome?

'You are determined to accompany me?' she asked him. 'I am perfectly capable—'

He raised his hand to stop her. 'You are indeed, ma'am, but I insist. We are agreed I might be able to help. My curricle is ready, if you will give me but a few minutes to break my fast I shall take you to Cheapside.'

Beth went off to collect her bonnet and cloak. She was relieved that she would not be venturing forth alone that morning, but all too aware that the more time she spent with the earl, the more pain she would feel at the inevitable parting.

An hour later they arrived at the offices of Spalding, Spalding and Grooch and were shown into a dark, panelled room that smelled of must and old papers. An elderly man in a full-bottom wig stood behind the desk and greeted Beth with a fatherly smile. He cast an enquiring glance at the earl; once Beth had performed the introduction the lawyer invited them to sit down.

'Your note yesterday said you were waiting for news,' said Beth without preamble. 'Are the de Beaunes still in England?'

'I believe so, although my initial information was incorrect. It is only a Madame de Beaune who arrived in London.' He coughed delicately. 'With the current unrest in France it is not inconceivable that her husband has been…detained.'

'She might even be a widow,' mused Beth. 'I believe he was considerably older than his wife.'

'And where is the lady now?' asked the earl.

Mr Spalding looked a little uncomfortable. 'As soon as you wrote to me to say you were coming to London I contacted Madame de Beaune, intimating that I had a client who wished to see her. I had no reply, so yesterday, when I received your note, I sent my clerk with another message. He returned with the information that the lady was about to leave on the Portsmouth mail.'

'Portsmouth!' cried Beth. 'She is going back to France.'

'Very likely,' said the earl. 'But if we set off immediately we may catch her. She could still be waiting for a passage.'

Beth nodded. She turned back to Mr Spalding. 'Did she leave you a forwarding address?'

'Yes, the White Bear.'

Beth looked at the earl. 'Will you take me, my lord?'

'Of course.'

The lawyer began to sort through the papers on his desk. 'If that is all, then I must ask you to excuse me. I have promised to visit a client in Hertfordshire.' He sighed. 'It is a business that will take me out of Town for several days, I fear, and I am hoping to get away today…'

'Yes, yes, of course, we will delay you no longer.' She rose. 'Thank you, Mr Spalding. I shall set out for Portsmouth with all speed.'

She almost ran out of the door and stood, irresolute, on the flagway. She turned as the earl came up to her. 'How long would the mailcoach take to reach Portsmouth?' she asked anxiously as he handed her into the waiting curricle.

He shrugged. 'The best part of the day.'

'Then there is a possibility she may still be there.' She looked up at him. 'How soon can we get there?' He did not answer immediately and she said impatiently, 'Well, sir?'

'If we go back to Darrington House and order my chariot, we could be in Portsmouth by early this evening.'

'So late?'

'There is another way.'

'Well, sir?'

He turned his head to look at her, a challenge glinting in his hard eyes. 'We could go there now, in my curricle. I believe we could make it in less than five hours.'

Behind her, the groom stifled an exclamation, but Beth ignored it. 'If that is the case, then let us be gone!'

Without a word the earl took the next turning and drove through a series of narrow side streets to reach Blackfriars Bridge.

'Which way do we go, sir?' asked Beth, looking at the Thames, its sparkling waters almost obscured by the number of ships and barges going about their business.

'The road via Battersea and Wandsworth will be quicker than fighting through the traffic north of the river.'

There were fewer fashionable carriages once they had left the city and they wove their way between a succession of covered wagons, brewers' drays and ox carts. At length the road became clearer and the earl allowed his team to set a cracking pace. Beth relaxed a little, watching the changing landscape as they bowled onwards in the autumn sunshine.

'You are very quiet, Mrs Forrester. Are you nervous?' asked the earl presently.

'I am led to believe you are an excellent whip,' she replied coolly. 'I am too concerned with making good time to reproach you for going too fast. If Madame de Beaune returns to France, I do not know what I shall do next.'

She could not prevent the note of anxiety in her voice and the earl took one hand from the reins and laid it over her own, clasped tightly in her lap.

'There is no point in worrying about that until it happens.'

Beth did not reply. Her voice was suspended in shock. His grip on her hands had been brief, but it had been such an intimate gesture, bestowed almost casually, as if they had known each other for many years. She wondered if he even realised he had done it, yet that fleeting touch had conveyed such warmth, such comfort and courage that she felt enormous gratitude towards him. She hugged the feeling to her as they drove on mile after mile, barely checking at the turnpikes and tolls.

'You're pushing 'em hard, sir,' growled Holt. 'You'll need to change horses at Guildford.'

'No, they'll make it to Bramshott,' the earl replied without taking his eyes from the road. 'That will leave us with less than twenty miles to travel with strange cattle.'

There was no question of stopping for refreshments and Beth did not suggest it. When they reached Bramshott she descended briefly while the earl haggled with the landlord for his best team; by the time he handed her back into her seat two more spirited horses had been harnessed to the vehicle.

'Holt!' she cried as the earl took his fresh team on to the road. 'You have left him behind.'

'He is staying with my horses. We shall collect him on the homeward journey. It is just you and me now, Mrs Forrester.'

She ignored his teasing tone. 'If we are alone, then perhaps we could talk about last night.'

'There is nothing to say.'

'But—'

'Pray do not concern yourself about Clarice. She is like a cat and will always land on her feet.'

'But she was your fiancée!'

'And what is that to you?'

His words stung her into silence. What should she say, that she was jealous of every woman he had ever known? That would be the truth, but of course she could not admit it.

'Why, nothing, of course.'

'Then we will not discuss it, if you please. Let us instead consider where we might find Madame de Beaune.'

She swallowed hard, trying to bring her mind back to their last stop. 'I spoke to one of the maids there, sir. She tells me there is an inn called the White Bear at the crossroads, just north of Portsea Island.'

'Then that might be where we shall find Madame de Beaune. Well done, ma'am.'

The sudden praise almost undermined her. She sat bolt upright, her eyes fixed on the road ahead. 'It seemed sensible to make enquiries.' She scolded herself for the quiver in her voice.

'This has been a trying day for you, Mrs Forrester. You must be tired.'

'I am too excited to be tired, my lord. I hope by the end of the day to have the evidence I need of my brother's innocence.'

'You have gone to a great deal of effort for your brother.'

She turned to look at him. 'And would not you do the same, sir? Simon's life is at stake. If it were merely his good name, then perhaps he could quit the world, live retired and ignore his accusers, as you have done—' She broke off, realising what she had said.

'And just what do you mean by that?' he bit out.

Beth squirmed in her seat, wishing herself anywhere but here. 'I—um—I heard that you…that there was…a scandal. That is why you rarely come to London. Why you live mainly on your north-ern estates…'

The horses never checked. Whatever his anger he did not allow it to affect his driving. 'I wondered if you knew about that,' he said at last. 'Since we embarked upon this escapade you have never once asked me anything about myself. I am not a vain man, Mrs Forrester, but I was piqued that you showed so little interest in *me*. Unless, of course, you thought you knew everything about me.'

She answered stiffly, 'What you did in your past is no concern of mine, my lord.'

'Indeed it is not.'

Beth bowed her head, mortified.

'And just what is it you think I am guilty of? Come, madam,' he cajoled her when she waved a dismissive hand. 'You have said too much not to tell me the rest. Perhaps Clarice added some juicy detail last night—'

'No!'

'Very well, out with it. What is it you know?'

'Nothing! I should not have spoken. I beg your pardon.'

With a muttered oath he brought the curricle to a stand. 'But that is not good enough, madam. I want to know just who you think you are travelling with today.'

'Please, my lord, I spoke out of turn. Can you not forget it?' She turned away, only to find herself being gripped by the shoulders and forced to face him.

'No, I can not,' he ground out. His eyes, hard as flint, cut into her. 'What have you been told about me? Am I a monster? A mur-derer? Mayhap a libertine who preys upon vulnerable women.' His hand came up to cup her face. 'But you already know that,' he purred. 'Are you afraid now that I might take advantage of you?'

'No, you would not do so.'

He laughed harshly. 'Look around you.' He waved hand. 'We are alone, miles from anywhere. Why should I not take what I want from you?'

Anger blazed in his face, but Beth saw something else there too: pain. She had hit a nerve and wounded him, deeply. His anger was not wholly directed at her and that gave her the courage to meet his look.

'Of course I do not believe that of you,' she said quietly. 'I would not have come so far with you if I had believed you would hurt me.'

His grip on her arm tightened. She bit her lip to prevent herself from crying out.

'So what do you believe of me?'

'I heard…' She looked away and whispered the word, 'Treason.'

He released her and she rubbed her arms.

'You know the worst of me, then.'

'I know no details,' she muttered. 'It cannot be so very bad, since you are a free man—'

'Mayhap you should have asked me about it.'

'You have not encouraged me to think you would confide in me,' she retorted, showing spirit. 'You brushed aside my questions at the soirée and refused to explain to me about your fiancée. What would you have told me if I had asked you about…about this?'

'The worst that can be said of me is that I was a damned fool!' he growled, gathering up the reins.

They set off again and Beth thought miserably that the fragile friendship they had been building had been shattered by a careless word.

'I can only judge you on my own experience, my lord,' she said quietly. 'I believe you are a good man.'

'I hope you never have cause to think differently,' he said shortly.

Guy was thankful that driving a fresh team gave him an excuse to keep his attention fixed on the road. He silently berated himself for allowing his anger to surface. He was no longer a callow youth to lose his temper over such a trifle. He had long ago become inured to the slights and innuendo following the scandal that had forced him to withdraw from public life. Apart from his closest friends, he did not care what anyone thought of him, although he was contemptuous of those women who set their cap at him, so anxious for a title and a fortune that they cared little that the name was tainted with scandal.

The truth was that Beth Forrester had undermined his defences. As they travelled together he had begun to believe they were just a man and a woman, enjoying each other's company. But all the time she had thought him a traitor. No wonder she had believed she could buy his silence by offering herself to him! Guy glanced down at the figure sitting upright and silent beside him and his anger melted away. What right had he to criticise her? He had chosen to retire from society rather than work to clear his name; he could hardly blame the woman if she believed ill of him. He said, by way of making amends, 'We should be at the crossroads very soon. Odd that the lady should give that as her forwarding address if she was departing from Portsmouth.'

'I had wondered about that,' she replied thoughtfully. 'Unless her experience of Portsmouth made her loath to put up in the town again.'

'Well, I hope we may soon know the truth.' He raised his whip to point towards a large building in the distance. 'If I am not mistaken, that is the inn ahead of us.'

Five minutes later they clattered into the yard of the White Bear. It was a large old building with galleries on two storeys surrounding the yard and was full of bustling activity when they arrived. The ostlers were huddled in one corner, talking amongst themselves, and did not immediately dash out to take charge of the curricle team. The earl, aware of Beth's fretting impatience, called to them to hurry and once the horses were under control he jumped down and ran around to help Beth to alight.

'Not the most efficient hostelry I have ever visited,' he remarked as he gave her his hand. 'Not even the landlord to welcome us.'

'Perhaps they are very busy today,' she remarked, setting off immediately for the inn door. 'Let us hope the service is better inside.'

He followed her into the inn and past the noisy taproom. As she hesitated outside the coffee room a harassed-looking waiter came out, wiping his hands on his apron. He gave a nod in their direction and asked civilly if he could be of assistance.

'We are looking for a Madame de Beaune,' said Guy. 'We understand she is staying here.'

The waiter froze, his brows coming together. He said slowly, 'Madame de Beaune, you say?'

'Yes.' The man continued to stare at them and Guy added sharply, 'Well, is she here? Out with it, man.'

The waiter swallowed, and looked around, as if seeking assistance.

'Please,' said Beth. 'We have travelled all the way from London, please tell us if she is here.'

'Well…aye, she is, in a manner of speaking.' The waiter was no longer wiping his hands on his apron, he was wringing them. 'She's here, but she…she's dead.'

Chapter Fourteen

Beth swayed at the waiter's announcement and felt the earl's steadying arm slip around her waist to support her. Before she could speak a portly gentleman in a brown frockcoat and grey wig appeared and the waiter turned to him.

'This lady and gentleman have just arrived from London, sir, and were asking after the French lady.' With that the waiter hurried away, grateful to have shuffled off responsibility.

'I am Sir Jeffrey Farnborough, the magistrate,' announced the portly gentleman, coming forwards. 'May I ask what your business is here?'

'Perhaps first we could find the lady a seat?' the earl responded. He was still supporting Beth, holding her close against him, and she dare not free herself, afraid that her legs would not support her.

Sir Jeffrey took one look at her face and nodded. 'Aye, of course. This way.' He led them through a winding passage to a small dining room well away from the entrance. 'Very well,' he said, shutting the door. 'What was your business with Madame de Beaune?'

The earl guided Beth to a chair and hovered over her solicitously. 'Leave this to me,' he murmured quietly before straightening to address the magistrate. 'We met Madame on her previous visit to England in '87,' he said easily. 'She was travelling then with her husband, who had come over on business. We planned to renew the acquaintance. Unfortunately we were delayed getting to town and Madame had already departed, but she left us a note telling us she would be here.'

'And do you have the note with you?'

The earl lifted one eyebrow at the magistrate's question. 'I'm afraid not. It was very brief, I did not think I should need to refer to it again.' He said, anticipating the next question. 'Perhaps I should introduce myself. I am Lord Darrington. And this is Mrs Forrester.'

'Well, I am sorry, my lord, madam, but it seems you have wasted your journey. As the waiter informed you, Madame de Beaune died last night.'

'May I enquire the cause of death?' asked the earl, gently swinging his quizzing glass.

'She was murdered, my lord.'

Beth's eyes widened, but she kept silent.

'Indeed?' Lord Darrington raised the quizzing glass to his eye 'How shocking. Would it be indelicate to enquire how…or why?'

'As to that, sir, we know a thief stole in during the night. Poor woman disturbed him going through her luggage and he stabbed her. The man in the next room heard the rumpus and set up the alarm, but the killer was too quick. He jumped out of the window and was away.'

'How very dreadful,' murmured Beth.

The magistrate shook his head. 'As you say, madam, dreadful. Well, I must get on. If you have just arrived, I suppose there is nothing you can tell me to help me with my case. Do you know her family, for instance?'

'No,' muttered Beth.

'We understand she had only recently arrived from France,' put in the earl.

'Ah, an *émigré*.' Sir Jeffrey gave a loud sigh. 'A sad end, then. So you'll be going back to London now, I suppose.'

'Yes, but not quite yet,' replied the earl. 'After such a shock I think we need a little time to reflect. If you do not object, Sir Jeffrey, I plan to order some refreshment. May I offer you…?'

'Thank 'ee, but no,' said the magistrate, puffing out his cheeks. 'I must get on. There is a deal to do before I am finished here.'

He took his leave; as the door closed behind him, Beth turned her gaze upon the earl.

'Why did you not tell him the truth?'

'That you wanted to question the woman about a previous attack? I thought it might complicate matters.' His eyes searched her face. 'You are still very pale. Sit there while I order refreshments for us.'

'Oh, no, I am not hungry.'

'Nonsense. We have not eaten since early this morning. It will put heart into you.'

He strode out of the room and Beth was left in the silence. She was very shaken by all that she had heard and not a little apprehensive. She told herself that there was nothing to fear with so many people bustling about the inn, but she could not ignore her relief when the earl returned.

'The landlady is even now preparing a meal for us and I have ordered coffee to be fetched immediately,' he announced. 'I will send for wine if you would prefer—'

'No, no, a cup of coffee would be very welcome,' she said.

Even as Beth spoke a young maid appeared with a tray, from which she deposited cups, a jug of milk and a coffee pot on the table in front of her.

'Coffee, my lord?' Beth tried to lift the pot, but her hands were shaking so much that she quickly put it down again.

'Here, let me.'

'I beg your pardon.' She watched him pour the coffee into a cup and hand it to her. 'I despise such weakness.'

'It is the shock of what you have just heard,' he replied.

'I admit I am surprised Sir Jeffrey was so ready to share the details with us.'

'I suspect he is more used to dealing with the occasional theft than a murder. Perhaps he needed to talk about it.'

'Poor woman, such a dreadful thing to happen.' Beth put down her cup. 'I beg your pardon,' she said, her voice breaking. 'It is very selfish of me, but I cannot help thinking that now there is no one to speak for Simon…'

The earl drew closer and handed her his own handkerchief.

Gratefully she wiped her eyes and fought back her tears, determined not to break down in front of the earl.

'If only we had come here yesterday!' she muttered, clasping her hands in her lap, the handkerchief buried between them. 'To be so very near and to fail…'

The earl leaned across and caught her hands in his own. 'You must not give up hope yet, madam. There may be other ways to help your brother. In spite of my seclusion I am not without influence.'

She looked up at him, his image blurred by tears. Her hands twisted beneath his own and she gripped his fingers.

'Would you really help us, sir? After all I have said…'

'Hush.' Freeing one hand, he took up the handkerchief and gently wiped her cheeks. 'I am very tenacious, Mrs Forrester. Once I am determined on a course I see it through.'

He was smiling at her. Beth wondered why she had ever thought his eyes hard, for now they were blue-grey, warm and soft as a dove. But there was nothing soft about her reaction to his smile. It warmed her soul, putting all her fears and worries to flight. He caught her chin between finger and thumb. She did not pull away, but gazed up trustingly, a fluttering excitement growing inside. His thumb stroked her lower lip and she closed her eyes, a sound between a moan and a sigh escaping from her. Her whole body was tingling. The warning bells clamoured in her head: she should pull back from this madness. She made a feeble attempt to free herself from his grasp.

'My lord.' Her protest died before it was uttered and the words escaped as a sigh.

'Guy,' he murmured, so close that his breath kissed her cheek. 'Call me by my name.'

She could not breathe, her body was in thrall to his will. She could not pull away and in a wild moment of elation she realised she did not want to. They were sitting so close she could feel the warmth of his thigh pressing against her own. Guy. She would say his name and he would kiss her, pull her into his arms and she would be lost. The thought of it sent the blood pounding through her veins. Her heart was leaping to her throat, constricting her breath while the aching longing between her thighs was so intense she thought she might faint. Only a thunderbolt could prevent him taking her.

The door crashed open.

'Here we are, m'lord—dinner!'

The waiter's cheerful announcement brought Beth jolting back to the present. She jumped away from the earl, her cheeks burning. Lord Darrington showed no such embarrassment. He shifted in his chair and watched calmly as the servant began to set the table.

'You are lucky to get this,' the waiter informed them. 'Such excitement there's been that the Cook went off in hysterics. It was only the landlady throwing a bucket of water over her that brought her back to anything like her old self.'

'I doubt if it is every day that a murder takes place here,' remarked the earl.

'Never seen anything like it before in my life,' affirmed the waiter. 'I know the old woman was very demanding, and didn't speak a word of English, but she didn't deserve to be stabbed to death now, did she?'

'Old woman?' said Guy. 'How old?'

The servant shrugged. 'Couldn't rightly say, three-score at least, I do reckon. And a poor do for the young mistress travelling with her—widow-woman of the old lady's son, I heard. I don't say I agree with how the French king and his lords was treating the poor people, but I don't hold with running amok and killing folk, neither.'

Beth sat very still. A glance at the earl saw that he, too, was giving the waiter his full attention. He said, 'So who was the younger lady—did you know her name?'

'Aye, my lord, she was Madame de Beaune, too, of course. That upset she was, she left the inn as soon as it was clear the old woman was dead and no one knows where she's gone.'

'Sir Jeffrey said nothing about a younger woman,' put in Beth.

'Probably doesn't know.'

'But he is the magistrate,' protested Beth.

The waiter gave her a pained look. 'Well, if he didn't ask I doubt if anyone told 'im. After all, what good would it do to go fetching the poor young lady back here now? *She* didn't murder her mother-in-law and she was that scared she would be murdered, too, there was no stopping her when she said she was leaving.'

'And just how did she leave?'

Beth marvelled that the earl could speak so calmly when her own excitement was barely contained.

'Hopped on the Southampton stage, she did.' The waiter grinned. 'Paid her shot and disappeared.' Placing the last of the dishes on the table, the waiter nodded to them and went out, whistling.

Beth fixed her eyes on the earl.

'Do you think…?'

He nodded. 'Yes, Mrs Forrester, I do. The Madame de Beaune we seek is still alive. All we have to do is find her.'

Beth furrowed her brow. 'Simon said the de Beaunes had been visiting Madame's sister, who was married to an Englishman and living in a village not far from Portsmouth.' She looked up. 'There cannot be that many gentlemen with French wives.'

'And it is conceivable that Madame was making her way there. We could start by making enquiries along the route taken by the Southampton stage.'

Beth nodded. She picked up her fork.

'Let us get on with our meal, then, and get to it.' She paused. The earl was watching her, a faint smile curving his lips. 'Is something wrong, my lord?'

'You realise we will not be able to get back to London tonight?'

'Of course.' The heat rose to her cheeks. 'Are you thinking of my reputation, sir? We will face that problem later. Now it is much more important that we find Madame de Beaune!'

They did not tarry over their meal and were soon on their way. After he had handed her into the curricle the earl gave Beth a blanket.

'I—er—purchased it from the landlord,' he said. 'We have no idea how long we will be travelling and it may grow chilly later.'

He waved aside her thanks as he ran round to take his seat beside her, setting off from the White Bear at a rattling pace that had Beth clutching at the side of the carriage. When they had travelled a couple of miles Beth voiced a point that had been nagging her.

'Did you notice, sir, that the waiter said the younger Madame de Beaune was worried she might be murdered, too? I wonder…perhaps I am refining too much upon it, but—do you think this assault might be linked to the attack upon the de Beaunes in Portsmouth?'

'It does seem too much of a coincidence that the poor woman should be involved in two such brutal events,' he replied. 'If that is the case, then we need to find the woman and get her to safety.'

Beth squeezed her hands together.

'If there is a connection, then do you think…might it have some bearing on Simon's case, too?'

'It's possible,' agreed the earl. 'But we should not get too far ahead of ourselves. First we have to find the lady. If our theory is correct, she may have alighted anywhere along the stage route between here and Southampton. It will mean slow going, we will need to make enquiries regularly.'

'I know that.' Beth nodded. 'She could well alight at any crossroads and we may miss her altogether.'

'We shall see.'

It was easy enough to follow the route of the stage and whenever they reached an inn the earl stopped and ordered refreshment. His easy manner and generous payments encouraged his hosts to answer his seemingly casual questions about whether anyone had alighted from the stage that morning, or if there was a gentleman living in the vicinity with a French wife.

Beth admired his methods, but she would have liked to take a more active part in their search. She had been her own mistress too long to enjoy sitting quietly and allowing the earl to take command. Indeed, she found Lord Darrington far too masterful. Sitting beside him in the curricle, she was all too aware of him: conscious of his solid, muscular frame when their bodies occasionally collided with the jolting of the carriage, watching his hands as he deftly controlled the reins and remembering how they felt against her body. She dared not allow herself to dwell on that, for it made her go hot and cold; instead of keeping a proper distance, she wanted to shrink closer to the earl, to lean against him and draw comfort from his presence.

That would not do, of course. He would misinterpret her wish for comfort and think she wanted more from him. Which she did not, she told herself firmly, rigidly maintaining a gap between them on the seat. She would have to be extremely careful: she had no maid with her; there was not even a groom to act as chaperon. It had been foolish to set off on this wild chase with only Lord Darrington for company, but she argued with herself that if she had not done so they might have lost their chance to find Madame de Beaune. She squared her shoulders. She was a respectable widow and over the years she had learned how to dampen the ardour of any man who became too familiar. If necessary she would use the same tactics on the earl. The rebellious voice in her head mocked her, reminding her of how little success she had had so far in keeping the man at bay.

That was different, she told herself crossly. *Then I was unprepared. Now I know my weakness I will be able to guard against it.*

'You are very quiet, Mrs Forrester. Are you tired?'

She started. Just the sound of his deep, mellow voice sent her nerves skittering uncontrollably. Beth pulled herself together.

'A little,' she replied, pleased to find her voice was quite calm. 'It seems all I have done since we left the White Bear is to drink cups of ale or sweet wine. I vow I do not think I could take anything else!'

Her companion laughed. 'But it was in a good cause—you saw how readily our questions were answered, even if the answers were in the negative. The town ahead of us should be Wickham—we may have more luck there. We will also order dinner.'

She would not allow herself to enjoy the novelty of having a man look after her every need. Instead, she chose to resent his calm assumption of authority.

'Will we indeed, my lord?' replied Beth sharply. 'I am not at all sure that is what I wish to do!'

'Now is not the time to be missish,' he retorted as they drove into the square and pulled up outside the largest inn. 'I doubt there is another town of any size between here and Southampton and even if you are not hungry, I am.'

Beth opened her mouth to reply and shut it again, realising the truth of his words. Lord Darrington grinned at her and flicked her cheek with a careless finger.

'It galls you that I am right, does it not, Mrs Forrester?' He did not give her time to answer, but jumped out of the curricle, handing the reins to a waiting ostler before coming around to hand her down. 'And now you are angry with me,' he remarked as she preceded him into the inn.

Beth pointedly ignored him. The landlord appeared and with much bowing and smiling he escorted them into a private parlour, where she listened in growing irritation as the earl bespoke rooms and gave orders for dinner to be served as soon as possible. Insufferable man, would it have hurt him to consult her on where they would stop, or the meal they would eat? She jerked apart the strings of her cloak and cast it over a chair, tossing her bonnet after it. She heard the landlord leave and the door close after him. A quick peep showed her that the earl had unbuttoned his greatcoat, but not removed it. He was standing by the door, watching her. She kept her back to him and after a moment she heard him sigh.

'Believe me, I only have your welfare in mind, madam.'

'I have no objection to taking dinner here,' she replied frostily, 'but I *do* object to your deciding what we shall do with no reference to me. *And*,' she continued, her pent-up nerves finding some relief in anger, 'I also object to being called *missish*! You would not treat me thus if I were a man! It is not that I am ungrateful for your services, my lord, but I find you arrogant, overbearing and determined to take charge—'

She broke off as the earl caught her arm and jerked her around to face him. They were standing chest to chest and when Beth looked up she was taken aback by the fire sparking in his eyes.

'I am tired, hungry and in no mood for tantrums,' he ground out.
'Tantrums—!'

'I said I would look after you as I would my own sister,' he carried on relentlessly. 'If she was to treat me to such a tirade, I would put her across my knee and spank her!' His eyes narrowed. 'In your case I am more temped to ravish you to within an inch of your life!'

The deepening glow in his hard eyes robbed her of breath. Nervously she licked her lips.

'Y-you would not dare.'

His face was only inches from her own. He was slowly pulling her closer, his head so near now that when he spoke his ragged breath fanned her cheeks.

'When you do that with your tongue it's not what I would *dare*, madam, it's what I can withstand.'

Her eyes widened, but she could not look away. Their bodies were almost touching and her heart was thumping so hard she thought he must feel it. The images his rough words had conjured sent tremors of excitement running through her, right down to her toes. Her senses were overwhelmed; she felt the heat of his body reaching out to her. It was all she could do not to tremble beneath his unyielding grip. She swallowed, watching his eyes slide to her throat, like a predator deciding where to take the first bite.

'You cannot r-ravish me,' she struggled to keep her voice steady. 'I will not let you.'

He leaned even closer. 'Your permission is not required.'

Beth swallowed. He was in earnest. She closed her eyes. He was going to take her. Here. Now.

And what shocked Beth most was that she wanted him to do it. She summoned up all her remaining will-power and forced herself to look at him.

'That, my lord, would be the actions of a libertine.' Her tone was strong, matter of fact.

'You know my reputation, madam.'

His mouth as he murmured the words was so close that she could feel his breath on her cheek. The temptation to give in was very great. She fought it down.

'Yes, but I know you too well now to believe it.' He raised his head. His grip on her slackened a little. 'You would not force yourself upon me against my will.'

'But would it be against your will?' he countered.

She gave the tiniest shake of her head and slipped out of his grasp. 'No, but it *should* be. It would be very wrong.' Her head went up as she heard the rattle of dishes outside the door. 'If I am not mistaken, here is the waiter with our dinner, my lord.'

She made her way to the table and waited for him to pull out a chair for her. When he did so she sat down, trying to convince herself she was relieved that danger had been averted.

They watched in silence as a waiter and serving maid laid covers on the table and spread out the dishes for their meal. The fading daylight made the room mercifully gloomy and when a boy arrived with a taper the earl twitched it from his hand.

'I will see to the candles.' Guy was amazed at how normal his voice was. 'Leave everything on the table and we will serve ourselves. You need not return until we call you.'

The servants hurried away. Dazed, Guy looked at the taper, trying to think what he should do now. A glance at Beth showed that she was staring straight ahead of her, her breast rising and falling rapidly. She was more shaken by their encounter than she would have him believe. He walked around the room, lighting the candles.

'I should have told him to put dinner back an hour.' Guy tried to keep his tone light. 'What unfortunate timing.'

'No.' Her voice was so low he had to strain his ears to catch her words. 'No, I am glad we were interrupted before we could do anything we might regret.'

He was about to make a playful retort, but a glance at her face showed him that she was distraught. He said gently, 'For my part I would not regret it.'

'Perhaps not, but I am as good as married to another man.' She said sadly, 'I beg your pardon. I fear I have been a widow too long.'

Guy marvelled at her composure. Any other woman would be

railing at him for trying to seduce her, but not Beth Forrester. She knew her own power as a woman.

'You do not deny the attraction between us.'

She reached for a glass of water and he saw that her hand was not quite steady.

'I can not deny it, but that does not mean we must give in to it.'

'Because of Radworth?'

'Yes. I have promised to marry him. Forsaking all others.'

'But you are not yet married.'

'The contracts are signed. We are as good as wed.' She turned to look at him, anticipating his arguments. 'Would you have me cast Miles aside for a momentary passion? Events have thrown us together, my lord. I have accepted your help to save my brother, but once that is done we will go back to our own worlds. It is doubtful we will ever see each other again.'

Her words fell upon Guy like icy water. She was right. The physical attraction was strong, but it would not last. How could he commit himself to a woman whose very existence had been unknown to him a few weeks ago? How could he ask her to give up a good marriage and the chance of lasting happiness for a few nights of lustful pleasure? He nodded.

'You are very wise, Mrs Forrester. And very honourable.'

She shrugged. 'I am merely being practical, my lord. Shall we eat?'

Beth could taste nothing. She was outwardly calm, but her body was aching with desire for the man opposite. She was grateful for his forbearance. He carved delicate slices of ham for her, poured the wine and talked on unexceptional topics that helped her to regain her equilibrium. She might have thought him insensitive, had she not seen the slight tremor in his fingers when their hands met on a dish, heard the occasional hesitation in his voice as he weighed his words to avoid saying anything that might embarrass her.

Slowly the tension eased. She could talk to the earl, even look at him without blushing; when the landlord came in to make sure they had everything they needed, she was in command of herself enough to remember their quest.

'I believe an acquaintance of mine lives in this area. A French lady.' She gave the landlord a rueful smile. 'Unfortunately we lost touch—she married a country gentleman and I am afraid I cannot recall his name...'

'Ah, that could be Mrs Graveney, at Bourne Park.'

'That sounds very like it,' agreed Beth, trying not to sound too eager. 'I would very much like to make her acquaintance again. Is the family in residence at the moment?'

'Oh, aye, they rarely go away, save for the occasional visit to Bath to take the waters, Mr Graveney being prone to a touch of gout, you see.'

'And just how far is it to Bourne Park?' put in the earl.

The landlord scratched his head. 'No more than three miles, sir, just off the Southampton road. Funny how things go,' he remarked as he began to gather up their empty dishes. 'I hired my gig to another lady this morning, who was wishful to go to Bourne Park.'

Beth's eyes flew to the earl, excitement bubbling up within her.

'That could be Mrs Graveney's sister,' she said brightly. 'I know she was planning to visit very soon.'

'Aye, that will be it.' The landlord grinned at them. 'Pity you didn't arrive earlier, I think the poor lady would have been glad of your company—she seemed uncommon nervous to be travelling alone, her being foreign and her English not being that good.'

Beth could hardly contain herself until the man was out of the room again.

'It can only be Madame de Beaune,' she said excitedly, as soon as they were alone. 'There is a moon tonight—if the landlord is right about the distance we could be there in an hour.'

'Are you proposing to call upon a country gentleman at ten o'clock at night?' The earl raised his brows. 'He would not thank you for it.'

She put her hands together, prayer-like, and rested them against her mouth.

'I know it,' she said slowly, 'but what if the attack at the White Bear was intended for the younger Madame, and not for her mother? What if the killer has followed her here? If anything else should happen…'

Beth knew she was pleading, but she was not ashamed of it. After a moment the earl nodded.

'Very well. I will have the horses put to.' He smiled at her. 'Put on your cloak again, Mrs Forrester. We are going to Bourne Park.'

Driving in an open carriage at night was a new experience for Beth. They travelled through a world devoid of colour—everything was shades of grey in the dim light of the new moon. She kept her cloak pulled around her to protect against the chill air. They saw no other traffic and everything was still save for the occasional flight of a night bird, and once an owl swooped past on silent wings. The landlord's directions proved accurate and some forty minutes later they found themselves at the gates of Bourne Lodge. The gates were closed and the drive curved away into a wall of trees so they could not see the house.

The earl handed the reins to Beth and jumped down. Beth watched him walk up to the gates and heard the rattle of a chain.

'Locked.' Even as he spoke there was a commotion in the park. Two snarling, barking shapes appeared out of the darkness and hurled themselves at the gates. The earl stepped away. 'Guard dogs. Someone is protecting themselves.' He glanced back at Beth, who was trying to calm the startled horses. 'Can you handle them?'

'Of course. They are not going to bolt with me.' They had just grown quiet when a coarse shout from the park made the team throw up their heads again, snorting nervously.

'Who goes there?' She could just discern a man's figure approaching the gates, his face a pale blur. As he came nearer the moonlight gleamed on the barrel of his shotgun. 'Who are you?' he demanded. 'What are you doing here?'

'If this is Bourne Park, then we would like to see Mr Graveney,' said the earl, raising his voice to make himself heard above the howling dogs.

'Quiet, Samson, Ajax!' The man cuffed the nearest dog and the noise subsided to a muted growl. 'That's as may be, but the master's retired for the night and given orders that no one's to be admitted.'

'Very wise.' The earl reached into his pocket and drew out a small silver case. There was a flash as he flicked it open. 'Perhaps you would be so good as to give your master this card and tell him I shall call upon him in the morning.'

Beth was relieved to see that he kept his hands well back from the bars and the snapping jaws of the two dogs. Silently the man reached out and took the card.

'Thank you.' The earl tossed him a coin. 'That is for your trouble. And there will be another for you if you are here to open the gates for us tomorrow morning—and those animals are chained up.'

'That's for the master to say,' muttered the man, pocketing the coin and the card.

'Of course.' The earl climbed up beside Beth and took the reins from her. 'But I think he will see us.'

With that he deftly turned the team and they trotted away.

'I do not think we need fear for the lady's safety tonight,' he remarked as they sped back through the darkness.

'I hope you are correct.' She shuddered. 'I would not like to enter the park with such dogs on the prowl.'

'Nor I. But I am very hopeful that we have tracked down the elusive Madame de Beaune. There is nothing more to be done until the morning, so I suggest we go back to the inn for a cup of hot punch before we retire.'

Beth's thoughts had been so taken up with finding Madame de Beaune that it was not until they were sitting by the fire in their private room that she began to feel self-conscious again in the earl's company. They had discussed possible ways in which the murder at the White Bear might be connected with Simon, but nothing seemed to fit.

'Perhaps we must accept that it was an unfortunate coincidence,' remarked the earl as he leaned near the fire, stirring a small kettle of steaming punch.

'I cannot believe it,' replied Beth, frowning. 'That someone should attack young Madame and steal her necklace, then two years later she should return to England and her mother-in-law is brutally murdered. There *must* be a connection.'

'If not, then it is a sad indictment on our country.' The earl paused to taste the punch. 'There is one link we have not considered,' he said, pouring more rum into the pot. Beth waited. 'Miles Radworth.'

'Miles?' She laughed. 'What has he to do with it?'

'He was at the inn with your brother and the de Beaunes. Providential that he should turn up on the quay after the attack.'

'Providential indeed,' retorted Beth, her colour heightened. 'He did his best to help Simon.'

'Did he?'

The earl handed her a small mug of punch and she did not reply immediately. She considered his question while she inhaled the pungent aroma of the hot rum and lemons, thinking back over all Simon had told her.

'Yes, he did,' she said emphatically. 'He told the constables they were making a mistake when they accused Simon and, after, he travelled all the way to Malpass to bring us news of Simon's death.'

'That is a lot of trouble to go to for a chance acquaintance.'

'It speaks of a generosity that I cannot begin to match!' she retorted. 'When I think of how I have betrayed him…'

'You have not betrayed Radworth,' he replied curtly.

'No, but I was sorely tempted.'

'If there was no temptation, there would be little honour in resisting.' He smiled at her over the rim of his cup. Hot, aching desire seared through her and she wondered how long her resistance could last when Guy was so close.

She kept her eyes lowered as she sipped at the hot, sweet liquid.

'It is late and you are tired,' he said, putting down his cup. 'Come, let me escort you to your room.'

She picked up her cloak and accompanied him through the gloomy passages. The candles burning in the wall sconces made their shadows dance beside them like clownish attendants. A helpful bootboy directed them to the second floor.

'It appears we are next door to each other,' murmured Guy, opening her door. She hung back as he walked in before her, returning moments later with a candlestick bearing a small stub of candle, which he proceeded to light from one of the lamps in the passageway. 'Here.' He handed her the candlestick. 'Goodnight, Mrs Forrester.'

Beth retreated into her room, locking the door behind her. She heard the squeak of a hinge and footsteps in the room next to hers. That would be Guy. She leaned against the door, unable to stop herself from smiling. When had she begun to think of him as Guy and not the Earl of Darrington?

It was difficult to remember when he had stopped being an unwelcome guest and become so indispensable to her comfort. Somewhere deep inside a tiny flame of hope flickered. Perhaps, when all this was over, there might be a way...

No! Quickly she thrust the thought aside. She dared not even consider the future until Simon was safe. She moved away from the door to inspect her room by the light of her single candle. Dark panelling stretched from ceiling to floor, unalleviated by any decoration save a small mirror on one wall. A large canopied bed took up most of the floor and a small washstand occupied one corner. She was making her way around the bed towards the window when she saw a line of light at the base of one wall. As she drew closer the candlelight revealed a raised edge to the panelling and she noticed a handle and below it a dull metal lock and key...

She jumped back with a gasp as the panelled door swung open. Guy stood in the aperture, a solid, black figure outlined by the lighted room behind him.

'If you planned this...' she began, her eyes narrowing suspiciously.

'No, no, I assure you, I bespoke separate rooms for us.' There was the hint of laughter in his voice. 'I fear the landlord may have misunderstood me.' He looked around. 'Why have you not lit your candles?'

He took the candlestick from her nerveless fingers.

'I—I was about to do so.' She said nothing more; she was not going to admit she had been standing in the darkness, thinking about him.

He went around the room, touching the flame to every candle.

'There.' He held out the candlestick. 'Now you can see to go to bed.'

She reached out, their fingers touching around the metal holder.

Would he kiss her? He was looking down at her, his eyes dark and unfathomable.

He is waiting, she thought suddenly. *He is waiting for a sign from me.*

She drew herself up to her full height. 'Goodnight, my lord.' She pointed towards the open door.

'Are you sure you want me to go?' His rueful smile was almost her undoing.

'I am sure.' She put her hand on his chest and pushed him gently but inexorably towards the opening.

'Very well, madam.' He stepped back into his own room, saying as she shut the door between them, 'You only have to call if you need me.'

She closed the door and turned the key. It gave a satisfying click.

'What...' Guy's voice came muffled through the panelling '... Do you not trust me?'

Despite her raw emotions a gurgle of laughter escaped her. 'Good fences make good neighbours, my lord!'

She prepared slowly for bed. With no nightclothes she decided she would sleep in her shift, but her gown and petticoats needed to be shaken out and folded carefully over a chair in readiness for the morning. She was still smiling when at last she climbed into the bed, thinking of Guy. Was he asleep in the next room, or was he lying awake, just as she was? She curled on her side, nestling her cheek against her hand. He would not coerce her; she was free to lock the door and keep him at a safe distance and that is what she would do. But as the bed grew warmer and she gave herself up to sleep, Beth found herself wishing that she could spend the night in the earl's arms.

Chapter Fifteen

Sunlight filtered into the bedroom through dusty windows and Beth lay still for a few moments. Excitement stole over her when she remembered that they were to go to Bourne Park that morning. She dressed quickly, humming a little tune as she tidied her hair. It was a long time since she had felt quite so happy. It was because they had found Madame de Beaune, she told herself as she picked up her kerchief and arranged it around her neck. It had nothing to do with the fact that the earl was waiting for her downstairs.

His smile, when she joined him for breakfast, was conspiratorial.

'I trust you slept well, Mrs Forrester?'

'Very well, thank you,' she answered, unable to suppress the twinkle as she responded.

His every look was a caress, heightening her awareness, sending the blood singing through her. She poured his coffee; he carved wafer thin slices of ham and beef and put them on her plate. *We might be a long-married couple.* The thought appeared only to be dismissed. Beth was aware that they were walking on a tightrope of normality. One wrong word, one touch and they would fall headlong into each other's arms. That must not happen, Beth knew there was far too much at stake for her to risk her happiness and that of her family with a passionate affair. So she smiled at the earl, drank in every word, every look and stored them all away. They might be all she would have of him.

* * *

They drove to Bourne Park in a blaze of autumn sunshine. When they arrived they found the gates standing wide and no sign of the night watchman or his hounds. The house was a square gentleman's residence built of brick and Portland stone with a flight of shallow steps rising to a solid door set beneath a pillared portico. Beth was insensibly encouraged by the gleaming paint, shining windows and neat garden which hinted at an orderly and well-regulated household.

As they swept around the gravelled drive the butler appeared at the door and a servant ran out to catch the horses' heads.

'We are expected,' murmured Guy, handing Beth down.

They were shown into an elegant morning room where they were greeted by a ruddy-cheeked gentleman in a brown bagwig who announced himself to be Mr Richard Graveney.

'My man told me you called late last night, my lord,' said Mr Graveney, once the introductions were complete. 'Not the usual time for a courtesy call.'

'These are unusual circumstances,' replied the earl. 'We believe you have a visitor, sir, a Madame de Beaune.'

'Indeed?' Sir Richard's face gave nothing away, but his tone was reserved.

'We have come from the White Bear at Widley,' put in Beth. 'We arrived the morning after—after the dreadful events there.'

'And how do you think I can help you, ma'am?'

'We know that the younger Madame de Beaune fled from the inn yesterday morning. I have been told her sister lives in the area, and is married to an Englishman.' She smiled a little. 'That led us to you, sir.'

'We called late last night because we have reason to believe your sister-in-law may be in danger,' added the earl. 'Our concern was somewhat relieved by our…reception.'

Mr Graveney stared at them in silence for a few moments, then walked over to the window, a crease furrowing his brow. After staring out at the park for a few moments he seemed to come to a decision.

'My wife received a letter from her sister, disclosing that she and her mama-in-law had fled the terrors in France and were seeking refuge. Of course we wrote back, offering them shelter. My sister-in-law arrived yesterday, in a state of great distress. She told us old Madame de Beaune had been murdered and she had fled the scene, fearing for her life. She begged us not to reveal her whereabouts to anyone.' He bent a frowning look upon the earl. 'What is your interest in all this matter, my lord?'

'Possibly none,' replied Guy. 'We wanted to talk to Madame concerning something that occured a couple of years ago—'

Their host waved an impatient hand. 'Out of the question!'

'Please, sir.' Beth pleaded, her voice low and urgent. 'We would not have come if it was not of the utmost importance! My brother's life is at stake.' She had his attention and continued quickly, 'You may know, sir, of the attack on Madame and her husband as they were leaving the country after their visit to you two years ago?'

'Of course, they wrote to tell us of it once they were safely back in France. Dashed thief escaped punishment, too.' He sat down. 'Drowned, I believe.'

'He was no thief and he did not drown,' she replied, struggling to maintain her calm. 'He was my brother, who tried to fight off the attackers and was then wrongly accused.'

Emotion clogged her throat, she could not speak.

'Perhaps you will allow me to explain,' said Guy.

Briefly and succinctly he relayed the events as Simon had told them and when he had finished they waited. Beth's nerves screamed at the ensuing silence until she could bear it no longer.

'We require only a few moments of Madame's time,' she murmured, fixing her eyes upon Mr Graveney's solemn countenance. 'If she would give a sworn deposition of what really happened in Portsmouth, it would prove my brother innocent.'

'And where is your brother now, madam?'

She bit her lip.

'He is a fugitive,' said Guy. 'If he is brought to trial without Madame's testimony, then there will be no chance of justice for him.'

Mr Graveney looked solemn. He drummed his fingers on the arms of the chair. At last he turned his fierce stare upon the earl.

'This is all very well, but am I to believe you?' he barked. 'Am I to trust you? This lady I have never heard of, but you, my lord, your reputation precedes you. I remember there was a particularly unsavoury scandal—'

'That was ten years ago,' said Guy, his voice curt.

'Aye, but it involved government secrets,' replied Mr Graveney.

'None of which were disclosed by me,' retorted the earl. 'I made an error, but it was a youthful indiscretion for which I paid dearly by retiring from government and public life—'

'Indeed?' Mr Graveney tapped the folded newssheet lying on the table beside him. 'You may spend most of your time at Wylderbeck, my lord—and I have no idea what you get up to *there*!—but although your name is mentioned infrequently in the society pages, when it does appear it is always linked with the more…dashing hostesses. Your character, sir, is dubious, to say the least!'

'Please, gentlemen!' Beth jumped to her feet as the atmosphere grew dangerously explosive. She addressed herself to her host. 'Whatever you may have heard of Lord Darrington, sir, all I can say is that in his dealings with me and my brother he has always acted with the utmost integrity. When my lawyer told me that Madame de Beaune was in England I determined to seek her out and was prepared to do so alone, but the earl would not allow that. His assistance in this matter has been…invaluable.'

The angry red mist that had threatened to overwhelm Guy was receding. The look Beth gave him was so full of trust and confidence his heart swelled and he lifted his head proudly.

'I still have many friends in government who would vouch for me, Mr Graveney, and if we had time I would furnish you with as many references as you could wish for. However, every moment we delay the life of Mrs Forrester's brother is at risk, so I would beg you to consider that, sir, and allow us to speak to Madame de Beaune.'

Another long, agonising moment passed before Mr Graveney finally nodded.

'Very well. I will go and talk to my sister-in-law. If she is willing to see you, then I will bring her here. If not, then I must ask you to leave immediately and you may set your attorney to approach us in the proper manner.'

Beth nodded. 'I understand.' She sat down again as he walked out of the room. Guy was watching her, but she would not look at him.

'Beth, what he said—about my past—'

Quickly she put up her hand. 'Not now.' She gave him a fleeting smile but avoided his eyes. His past did not matter. For the present he was helping her to clear Simon's name. And the future—she dare not even think of it yet. Last night's dreams must be put away.

The silence hung heavy between them, but at last they heard steps outside the door and their host returned, accompanied by two ladies. The older of the two in her cambric gown and with a lace cap tied over her grey curls he introduced as his wife, and once curtsies had been exchanged Beth turned her attention to the woman she had been seeking for so long. Madame de Beaune.

Beth judged her to be not much more than twenty, but fear and suffering had aged her, dragging down the corners of her mouth and adding grey shadows around her eyes. The low neckline of her chemise-style gown was decorously filled with a muslin fichu and she wore a black lace cap over her dark unpowdered curls.

'Madame.' Guy stepped forwards and bowed. 'I beg your pardon for disturbing you at such a time.'

She gave a distracted little wave and retreated to sit beside her sister. When she was settled she turned to Beth.

'I received a note from your lawyer, Madame Forrester, saying you wished to see me. And now my brother-in-law says you wish to talk to me about my previous visit, *hein*?'

'Yes, Madame,' said Guy. He glanced at Beth. 'Mrs Forrester's lawyer has been trying to locate you and your husband for some time, but of course with the current unrest in France this has been very difficult. Forgive me—is your husband still there?'

Madame shuddered, hunting for her handkerchief, and Mrs Graveney quickly put an arm around her.

'My brother-in-law is dead, milord,' she said quietly. 'Murdered during the riots in Paris. That is why his mother and Cecile decided to leave France and come to England.' Her voice faltered. 'They thought they would be safe here.'

'They should have been safe,' muttered Mr Graveney, shaking his head. 'We live in such lawless times!'

'I am very sorry for your loss, Madame,' said Guy. 'If there was any way we could postpone this meeting we would, but Mr Graveney may have told you we need to talk to you urgently.'

Madame wiped her eyes. 'Of course. I will do my best, milord.'

'I believe there was a young man at the inn where you dined while you were waiting to board your ship for France, a young man who came to your aid when you were attacked?'

The woman nodded and when she looked up there was a faint smile in her eyes. She suddenly looked less haggard.

'*Mais oui.* Monsieur Wake…Wakeford. You see, I do not forget. He was very brave, for he was alone and there were two men to fight. Fernand, my 'usband, was already on the ground and could not help…'

'Perhaps, Madame, you would tell us what happened?' Beth urged her gently.

She nodded, her fingers nervously twisting the ends of her muslin fichu. 'We were walking to the packet when two men attacked. I screamed, but no one came. They knocked poor Fernand to the floor, then set upon me.' She shuddered and clasped at her sister's hand. 'They tore the necklace from my throat and I fear they would have done more if Monsieur Wakeford had not come up. One man ran away, but the other stayed to fight. Monsieur Wakeford knocked him down—he wounded him, I think, but I cannot be sure, because as soon as I was free I ran to help Fernand.'

'And what happened after that, Madame?'

She shrugged. 'I do not know. Fernand was anxious that we should not miss the sailing. He was very…*dérangé* following the attack and wanted only to go home. He did not notice until after we had sailed that his watch had been stolen. That saddened him more than all the rest.'

'But what happened on the quay?' Beth sat forwards, pressing her hands together. 'Please think, Madame. It is important.'

Madame de Beaune put her fingers against her temples and rubbed them. 'I do not know. Someone else had come, a man who promised to guard the thief while Monsieur Wakeford escorted us to the packet, I remember.'

'But you are quite, quite sure that Monsieur Wakeford was not one of the attackers?'

Another smile transformed her countenance. '*Mais non*, Madame,' she murmured softly. 'He was a…how do you say it? A hero.'

Beth sat back, anxiety sliding away. 'Thank you, Madame.'

'And your attacker,' said Guy. 'The one who ran away. Did you see his face? Could you recognise him?'

'Really, my lord,' protested Mr Gravency. 'How can you ask that, after all this time—?'

Madame raised her hand. 'No, no, Richard, I will answer. It was very dark, milord, and both men had their faces covered, like so.' She lifted the muslin fichu across her face so that only the eyes were showing.

'Can you remember anything about them at all? Anything unusual?'

'No…they wore ragged jackets that stank of fish.' She pursed her mouth in a little moue of distaste. 'One—the man Monsieur Wakeford captured—he was short and he carried a knife, which made it all the more brave of Monsieur to fight with him, I think. The other—' she lifted her shoulders '—he was tall. That is all I remember, except I did knock off his 'at.' She put a hand up to her curls. '*Cheveux en brosse*—his 'air, it was very…small.'

'Short,' Beth suggested. 'Like a brush.'

'*Oui.* I am sorry I cannot 'elp you more.'

'You have been *very* helpful,' Beth assured her. 'And would you be willing to sign a sworn deposition of all you have told us? It is very important, you see, because my brother is accused of the attack.'

'*Mais oui.* I would like to help Monsieur Wakeford.' She looked at her brother-in-law. 'As long as I do not have to leave the house…'

'My attorney lives in the village—no more than ten minutes

away. I will send for him now and we will get this settled all right and tight.'

The earl bowed. 'Thank you.'

'Good.' Mrs Graveney smiled upon them all. 'While we wait for him, we shall have some refreshment.'

She rang the bell and almost immediately the butler brought in a tray with ale for the gentlemen and sweet ratafia for the ladies.

'Thank you again for your assistance, Madame,' said Beth as soon as the servant had departed, 'I know this has been a distressing time for you.'

Madame de Beaune shrugged. 'Per'aps if we had waited to talk to you in London then Belle-Mère would not be dead.'

'If only you had asked me to send a carriage for you!' put in Mr Graveney sadly.

She paused to wipe away a tear. 'Belle-Mère was a very proud woman. She did not want to be a burden to anyone. We fled to England with very little,' she explained. 'We brought with us letters from our bank in Paris and Belle-Mère insisted we should take them to the banks in London, but they all told us the same thing, that they were worthless. We sold a few jewels to pay for our lodging, but Belle-Mère would not allow me to hire a private coach and outriders to bring us here. She said we would attract less attention on the public coach…'

'And why should you want to travel secretly?' asked the earl, frowning. 'Why did you leave London so suddenly?'

'I thought we were being watched. There was a man in the street outside our rooms. I saw him again when we called upon Sir Henry Shott, and also when we went to the bank. Belle-Mère would not believe it, she said it was nerves, but then we left town, and stopped at the inn…'

She broke off, tears suspending her voice and her sister gathered her into her arms.

Mr Graveney looked at them, then turned to the earl, saying solemnly, 'I do not know if there is any truth in all this. I have no idea why anyone should try to harm my sister-in-law, but you see now why I have taken the precaution of setting the dogs loose of a night.' He pursed his lips. 'I would appreciate your discretion in this matter, my lord. My servants are all long-standing members of my household and are sworn to secrecy—we have set it about that we have a Madame Rendoit residing with us. I am even now deciding how best to arrange for the burial of the poor murdered woman. It must be done anonymously, through a third party.'

'I think that is very wise,' agreed the earl. 'Of course we will respect your wishes. However, in the long term—'

'That need not worry you,' broke in his host. 'We are leaving for America shortly. We have had enough of this god-forsaken land. I have no doubt that it will not be long before the discontent in France spreads to these shores—' He broke off, glancing up as a gig trotted past the window. 'Ah, here is our man, now. We shall soon have this matter neatly tied up.'

An hour later Beth and the earl were driving away from Bourne Park, Madame de Beaune's deposition tucked securely into Beth's reticule.

'I cannot believe we have it at last,' she murmured, unable to suppress a smile. 'I cannot wait to get back to Simon to tell him.' She glanced at the earl, saying shyly, 'Are you willing to escort me back to Yorkshire, sir? I would be very grateful…'

'Of course. My travelling chariot is at your disposal.'

'How soon can we be away?' she asked him. 'Could we leave tomorrow morning?'

He looked down at her, his brows raised. 'If we go directly to town now, then that is possible. But you will wish to see Spalding first, and leave Madame's deposition with him…'

'No!' She clutched her reticule to her breast. 'You will recall he told us he was going out of town and I am loath to leave Madame's letter with a clerk, or to wait around for Mr Spalding to return. I will leave a note for him, but I shall take the letter to Simon. We will then go together to our own J.P., Sir John Marton, in Thirsk.'

He shrugged. 'Very well, if that is what you wish.'

'It is, and I wish to get back to Malpass as soon as possible.'

He was silent for a few moments, calculating the journey times.

'It is gone noon now, so we shall not be in town before dark. It will be very tiring. Are you sure you want to do this?'

'I am, sir.'

'Then we need not stop at the White Bear. We will go directly to Bramshott and pick up Holt. Once I have my own team in harness we will be able to make much better time.'

The curricle swept on, mile after mile. The earl had nursed his horses, but even so by the time they reached Bramshott they were heavily lathered with sweat and blowing noisily. They stopped only long enough for the team to be changed before setting off again with Holt in the rumble seat. Beth sat beside Guy, rigidly upright, her eyes fixed on the road. The piece of paper in her reticule seemed to call to her and she clutched her bag tightly in her lap. She was carrying Simon's freedom. The autumn day drew to a close and Beth was thankful for the rug across her knees, which helped to fend off the chill evening air. They travelled mainly in silence; even if she had not been lost in her own thoughts Beth would have been reluctant to distract the earl, whose gaze remained steadily on the road ahead as he guided his team. They dined on the road, a hasty meal that Beth would happily have forgone, but Guy insisted.

'You need to keep up your strength, ma'am, especially if you mean to travel again tomorrow.'

They had finished dining and were facing each other across the small table, the evening sun streaming in through a window and making candles unnecessary. Beth looked closely at him, observing the lines of strain about his eyes.

'I am being very selfish, sir. After all, I need to do nothing but sit beside you—would you like to rest a little longer?'

'No, I am as anxious as you to get back. I am looking forward to sleeping in my own bed.'

Guy was watching her as he spoke, and the look she saw in his eyes combined with his words to conjure an image of them lying naked together, a tangle of pale limbs in the moonlight. Beth sat back, pressing her hands to her hot cheeks.

She said distractedly, 'I have not yet thought how I am going to explain all this to Miles.'

'Ah, yes. Radworth. I had forgotten about him.' Guy poured the remains of the wine into their two glasses.

She wrapped her arms about herself, shivering a little. 'I am still not sure why I could not tell Miles about coming to London.'

'You do not trust him.'

Beth sat forwards and reached for her wine glass, staring into its blood-red depths.

'I thought I did. He has done nothing to make me think ill of him.' She pressed her fist against her heart. 'But there is something in here that urges caution.'

'What a pity it did not urge you to be more cautious when he asked you to marry him. Why did you accept?'

'I think,' she said slowly, 'I think I was lonely. I was a widow, Simon was drowned…Grandmama and Sophie were dependent upon me.' A wry smile tugged at one side of her mouth. 'At six and twenty I thought myself past the age of falling in love. I could see a time when I would be alone.' She looked up and met his eyes. 'A bleak prospect.'

For a long moment they did not speak. She could not read his expression, but was thankful she could detect no pity in his look. That would have been unbearable.

'Bleak indeed,' he murmured, draining his glass. 'Shall we go?'

Chapter Sixteen

The long twilight had set in as they sped on through the towns and villages towards London. Beth watched the world shrink as darkness closed in around them. She moved a little closer to Guy, allowing her head to rest against his conveniently placed shoulder and for the last few miles of the journey she sank into a deep, exhausted slumber.

She woke up only when the curricle drew to a halt outside Darrington House and she heard the earl calling her name. She opened her eyes to find him smiling down at her.

'Oh, dear, I beg your pardon,' she muttered, yawning. 'I meant to keep you company during the drive!'

'It is no matter, we made the journey safely.' He came round to lift her down, his hands lingering on her waist, holding her to him. 'Just in time. It is beginning to rain. Let us go inside.'

Burley was at the door to greet them, declaring that there was a cheerful fire in the morning room.

'Good, we will go in. And bring a bottle of wine, Burley.'

Beth hung back. 'I should like to retire…'

'Not yet.' Guy's grip on her arm tightened. 'I would be grateful for a few more moments of your time, Mrs Forrester.'

Silently she accompanied him to the morning room and sat down by the fire while Burley bustled in with wine and glasses.

Guy stood at the edge of the hearth, staring down into the flames. Even after Burley had gone out he did not speak.

Beth said gently, 'It is very late…'

'I know, but all the way back to town I have been thinking, and I want to tell you—about Clarice and my…crimes.'

Her breath caught in her throat. Did she really want to know everything about this man? He might tell her things about him she did not wish to know, he might tell her he was still in love with Clarice. It would be better to keep her distance.

Too late for that.

'Very well,' she said quietly. 'I will hear you.'

'Thank you.' He sat down opposite, but did not speak immediately. His brow was furrowed—was he trying to think what to say to her, how to vindicate himself? No, she did not believe that. He was steeling himself for an explanation that would cause him pain.

'Guy,' she said softly, 'you need not do this.'

He looked up. 'I must.' He rose and began to pace about the room. 'Ten years ago… No. I have to go back further than that. Twelve years ago, my estimable father died and I became earl. I had just returned from the grand tour, I was five-and-twenty, inexperienced in women and politics, but I was an enthusiastic admirer of Chatham—I, too, believed we could disarm the American colonies with generosity, rather than pursue a course of aggression and taxation that could only lead to war. I was happy to work with Chatham, meeting with Dr Franklin and discussing terms for reconciliation, but the mood of the people was against us. It was at this time that I met Clarice Bellington. She was young and beautiful. I admit I was captivated. I allowed myself to be distracted—after all, it was clear that the Opposition could not win the argument over America and war was inevitable. Clarice's family moved on the edge of government circles and were violently opposed to Chatham's attempts at reconciliation. She told me she did not share her parents' views. As we became better acquainted I found—I *thought*—we had many interests and ideas in common. I thought her then quite…perfect.

'I asked for her hand and was accepted, despite the differing views between our families.' His lip curled. 'What parents would hold out against an earldom and a fortune? We became betrothed, I was fêted by her family and friends—it was a coup for them to bring the Darrington name and fortune into the ranks of those ranged against Chatham. True, I never made any secret of my support for the old lord, but neither did I speak out, nor did I distance myself from those in Clarice's family who openly wanted war with America. Clarice revelled in the role of political hostess— her status as my future wife allowed her to cultivate the society of great men—Sandwich, Gower and the like. She enjoyed the political dinners and I...I indulged her.

'Then private letters began to be quoted in notices and broadsheets. They concerned the transactions between the King and German princes for the hire of mercenaries to fight for us. Oh, it did not put lives at risk, but it embarrassed the government. And it was serious enough to be considered treason.' He paused. 'It was believed that Clarice was involved, but before she could be questioned she left me and fled to France. Only then did I begin to see her association with me in a different light. Through me she could move in higher, more important government circles. And before you have to ask me, yes, we were lovers, but she was sleeping in beds far more important than mine.'

In the heavy silence that followed Beth searched for some words of comfort to offer him. At last she said lamely, 'You were well rid of her, then.'

'Aye.' He sat down opposite her, resting his elbows on his knees as he leaned forwards and stared into the fire. 'But the damage was done. We were betrothed, and of the two I was known to be the more sympathetic to the Americans. It was even suggested that I had encouraged her.' His jaw tightened. 'I was implicated by association and became an embarrassment to those in Opposition. Perhaps I should have stayed, bluffed it out, shown myself a loyal subject. My close friends knew the truth and believed in me, but they had their own careers to consider and dared not defend me too openly. Chatham sent me a note of support. If he had been in town to advise me, perhaps I could have stayed, but he was very ill by that time and confined to his house. So I retired from public life, took my broken heart and disgraced name back to Wylderbeck Hall.'

'But surely the blame should have been laid squarely at Clarice's door?'

He gave her a pitying look. 'The men responsible for losing the letters were hardly likely to admit that they had been duped by a woman. If she had stayed in England, of course it would have been different, but once she disappeared the matter was hushed up. Those guilty of indiscretions kept their good name and their government posts while I, whose only fault was to fall in love with a beautiful woman, was thought at best a fool, at worst a traitor.'

'And you loved her.'

'Yes.'

Beth's heart ached for the young man so pitifully deceived, but a small worm of jealousy still gnawed at her peace.

'And now?' she forced herself to ask. 'Do you still…love her? It would be quite understandable if you were angry with her, after the way she hurt you,' she rushed on, 'but that does not mean you are over her.'

'Oh, I am well and true over Clarice.' He pulled her to her feet.

'But you have never married…'

'Do you blame me for being cautious?' he murmured, drawing her closer. His voice was deep and warm, wrapping about her like a blanket. He put his fingers beneath her chin, forcing her to look up. The fire she saw in his eyes robbed her of speech. His mouth found hers; she gave herself up to the fierce, yearning passion that burned through her body, a passion that blazed all the brighter because she had been fighting it down for so long. Guy had bared his soul to her and she wanted to console him, to cocoon him in love and wash away the last traces of pain inflicted by another woman.

Their embrace was long, hot and passionate. Beth gave him kiss for kiss, tongues tangling in an ancient ritual that drew on Beth's very soul. When at last it ended they were both gasping for breath. Guy kept his hold on her and began nibbling at her ear, the sensation making her swoon with pleasure.

'Tell me to stop now,' he muttered, his lips moving from her ear to her throat, the light butterfly kisses causing even more havoc with her senses. 'Order me to stop and I will ring for Mrs Burley to take you to your room.'

'And if I do not?' The words came out on a sighing breath, all she could manage as he continued to kiss her throat.

Guy raised his head, his eyes glinting down at her. 'If you do not,' he murmured, his voice enveloping her like the softest satin, 'if you do not stop me, then I am going to carry you upstairs to my room and cover every inch of your beautiful body with kisses.'

'Oh.' Beth gave a soft cry. 'Oh, Guy. Yes, *please*.'

She saw the triumph flare in his eyes. He swept her up in his arms and headed for the door.

Beth buried her face in his shoulder. Breathing deeply, she could smell his very male scent beneath the more familiar scent of wool and the soap from his snowy-white linen. She marvelled at how easily he carried her, the morning room door causing him to pause only a moment, then they were crossing the empty hall and up the stairs, their path lit only by the dim glow of candles. She did not raise her head until he negotiated another door. She heard him kick it shut behind them and looked up to see that they were in a large, high-ceilinged chamber dominated by a huge tester bed hung with richly embroidered hangings gleaming blue and gold in the fire-light. There were no candles alight in the room, but they were un-necessary.

Gently he put her on her feet, He was holding her against him, his face so close that she found herself marvelling at the beauty of the long dark lashes that framed his eyes, observing the fine lines around his mobile mouth. Beth's lips parted; the tip of her tongue flickered over them. Immediately the earl swooped on her. He pulled her roughly against him, kissing her ruthlessly. Her head was thrown back against his arm and she gave herself up to him, tangling her tongue with his, driving her fingers through his hair, holding him to her. She made no protest as he tore the kerchief from her neck and began to trail burning kisses over her skin. Her breasts tightened and pushed, aching, against the front of her low-cut jacket. She clung to him as he hustled her against the wall. As he captured her mouth once more his hands were gathering her skirts, lifting them aside until he could caress the bare flesh of her thigh.

She gasped and a laugh trembled through her. He was going to take her here, now, and suddenly she knew she wanted this more than anything in the world. Her body was singing with desire. Impatiently her hands sought the buttons of his breeches and she tried to unfasten them, but she fumbled, distracted by his fingers moving up her thigh. Beth arched her body, muscles straining as she offered herself up to those searching fingers, gasping as his caresses became more intimate, more insistent.

Then there was no fabric between them, his flesh was against her, inside her. She cried out, clinging tightly to him as he thrust ever more urgently. Heady excitement overwhelmed them. Beth was gasping and crying while Guy's rasping breath grew faster, culminating in a shout as his body shuddered and he gripped her fiercely, crushing her against him.

Beth buried her face in his neck, holding on to Guy as she felt the tension drain out of him. A small, silent laugh shook him.

'I had not intended to take you like that.'

Her arms tightened. 'It was wonderful.'

He raised his head. 'Truly?'

Smiling mistily, she cupped his face with her hands and drew him down to her, placing a gentle kiss upon his lips. He responded immediately, deepening the kiss until they were both burning once more with desire. He swept her up and carried her across to the bed, laying her down as carefully as if she had been delicate porcelain. Impatiently Beth reached for him, pulling him down with her, hungry for another kiss. He obliged, measuring his length against hers, ravaging her mouth and face and neck until that was no longer enough and they began to scramble out of their clothes. She did not remember pulling the pins from her hair, but it was loose about her shoulders.

Coat and waistcoat were discarded. Guy turned away to struggle with his boots and breeches. By the time he turned back he found Beth had removed her petticoats and shoes and was sitting on the bed in her corset and chemise, about to unfasten her garters and remove her stockings.

'No.' He caught her hands. 'Let me.'

He pushed her back on the bed and took one stockinged foot in his hand. Slowly he ran the other hand from ankle to knee. she trembled at his touch. He pulled away the ribbon garter and began to roll the stocking down, a little at a time, placing a kiss on each inch of flesh as it was revealed. He finally reached the toes, kissing and caressing them until Beth was writhing and moaning softly, then he turned his attention to the other leg, forcing himself to go slowly, drawing out the anticipated pleasure for himself as well as Beth.

'I told you I would kiss every inch of you,' he muttered, drawing off the silk and discarding it. He knelt on the bed and pressed a kiss on the soft flesh behind her knee.

She shuddered. 'I am on fire for you,' she moaned, arms reaching for him.

He laughed softly. 'Then you must burn a little more, my love.' His hands caressed her thighs, his mouth following the trail of his roving fingers. She threw her arms wide, clutching at the bedcovers as her body moved restlessly, opening for him, offering up her most delicate places for his kiss. She gasped as he continued with his relentless pleasuring. She groaned, biting her lip to prevent herself crying out. It was too much, she could no longer control herself. Her body pulsed and tightened in an ecstasy that she had never known before. She was convulsed in pleasure, again and again and again.

Beth subsided, spent and trembling, and lay quietly, cradled in Guy's arms.

'Oh,' she breathed at last. 'Oh, I never knew it could be like this. But, Guy, you did not share it…'

'Hush.' He kissed her. 'There is time yet for me. After all, we haven't even finished undressing.' He sat up, his hands on her waist. 'Turn over and let me get you out of this damned corset.'

Obediently she turned on to her front, resting her chin on her hands. Guy knelt up and straddled her, his fingers working out the laces of her corset, pulling them free with slow steady strokes.

Occasionally he stopped, leaning forwards to brush aside the hair from her shoulders and drop a kiss on the back of her neck. Beth closed her eyes, her body resting, but not sleeping, for as the corset loosened she felt the excitement building again. At last Guy pulled the stays away. She shifted, ready to turn and remove her chemise, but Guy stopped her. Silently he pushed the chemise up past her waist. She felt the soft linen of his shirt cool against her back. His hands caressed the soft swell of her buttocks, then slid around to her stomach, lifting her on to her knees before him, his fingers driving downwards between her thighs. A white-hot ache curled low in her belly. She could feel the heat of his body, hard and aroused behind her, and she responded again, lifting, opening, pushing herself up and backwards against him. His fingers continued to stroke and caress, even as he entered her. She was dizzy with elation, her spirit soaring, and all the while he was moving with her, in her, against her. His hands slid up beneath the loose chemise to cup her breasts and he kissed her neck as she arched back towards him. There was a cry, but Beth did not know whether it was she or Guy in the final, writhing, frenzy of excitement that overtook them. As the tension eased he was clinging to her, his body warm against her back, then with a sigh he gently pulled her down on to the bed. Beth lay with him curled protectively about her, wrapped in his arms, the soft billowing folds of his shirt keeping the cool night air from their bodies.

Guy held her close, nuzzling her neck, breathing in the sweet perfume of her skin, burying his face in her silky hair. His senses were still bewitched, the blood singing in his veins. He ran his hands over her skin, marvelling at the smooth, rounded contours of her body. The fire had burned low. They should slip between the sheets and keep warm, but she was lying so peacefully in his arms that he was loath to break the spell. He pulled her closer and closed his eyes.

He awoke a short time later to find her turning restlessly in his arms. The fire had died, but the room was washed with a pale moonlight. Desire stirred as she pressed against him.

'I have never known the like,' she murmured. 'I wanted it to go on and on.'

'And it will,' he said softly. 'I have yet to see you naked.'

He eased himself away from her and stripped off his shirt. Following suit, Beth sat up and drew the chemise over her head. Guy caught his breath as she stretched up, arms raised and momentarily tangled in the material. He reached for her, cupping her breasts in his hands and burying his face in their softness. She trembled, leaning into him. Her fingers drove through his hair, insistently pulling him up towards her until she could capture his mouth with her own. He reeled at the passion of her embrace as they fell back on to the covers. She was exploring his body, discovering him, first with her hands and then her lips, kissing every inch of him, gently teasing his senses. When he groaned and arched beneath her touch she gave an exultant laugh. He lay back and closed his eyes.

'It amuses you, does it,' he muttered, 'to have me at your mercy?'

She was kneeling over him, her hair tumbling around her shoulders, tickling his chest as she leaned towards him.

'Of course. It is where you belong, sir.'

The mix of laughter and husky, wanton passion in her voice was incredibly arousing.

'We'll see about that!' He reached up and pulled her, laughing, into his arms.

She responded eagerly to his kiss, pressing warm and pliant against him. With the first, heady urgency of their passion spent they gave themselves up to a slow and sensual pleasuring of each other in the darkness until at last, sated, they fell asleep in each other's arms just as the first streaks of dawn were lightening the sky.

Chapter Seventeen

Beth woke up slowly to the sound of the rain pattering against the window. Her first thought was that she was cocooned in a warm protective coat, her second the knowledge that it was Guy wrapped around her. Memories of the night flooded back and a delicious lightness filled her being, pooling low in her belly and causing her thighs to ache with desire.

She had given herself to Guy and she could not regret it. She loved him. Beth hugged the thought to her. With Guy beside her she could face anything. There were problems, of course—Simon's freedom was not yet secured, but with Madame de Beaune's letter that was only a matter of time. And she would have to tell Miles that she could no longer marry him. That would be painful, but she hoped he would understand.

She rang for Tilly, but when she had finished dressing and there was still no sign of her maid she went in search of her. An enquiry of Mrs Burley informed her that Tilly had not been seen all morning, so Beth made her way up to the servants' quarters, where she found her maid still in her bed and groaning pitifully.

'Ooh, miss, I feel so bad,' she complained. 'Me stomach's that sore and I daren't leave the room lest I disgrace meself.'

Beth took a cloth over to the jug of water on the washstand and damped it.

'Poor Tilly,' she said, putting the damp cloth on her forehead. 'Is it something you have eaten?'

'I don't know, miss, but with you and his lordship away Mrs Burley don't do much cookin' so me and Fitton went out to the pie shop yesterday morning, and I didn't finish all o' mine so I kept it to eat last night. It did taste a bit funny, though.' She turned quickly and retched into the chamber pot.

Beth went downstairs to find the earl dressed and waiting for her in the breakfast room. He held out her chair for her. As she sat down he put his hands on her shoulders and bent to kiss her cheek.

'You left me sleeping. I missed you.'

'I beg your pardon, my lord—'

He sat down beside her. 'So formal? Will you not call me Guy?'

She responded with a shy smile. 'Guy, then. I beg your pardon if I have kept you waiting. My maid is not well. I think she has eaten some bad meat and is now far too ill to be moved today.' She sighed. 'I do not want to delay our journey a moment longer than necessary, so I shall have to leave her enough money to buy her ticket—'

'There will be no need for that,' he interrupted her. 'Fitton will be following with the baggage wagon, and Holt is going to take my curricle on to Wylderbeck. One of them may wait behind for your maid to recover.' A smile glinted in his eyes. 'Which one shall it be?'

Her lips twitched. 'I do believe Tilly is quite partial to Fitton's company, my lord. If you do not object to his delaying his journey, I think that would answer very well.'

'Then it shall be done. Would you like me to ask Mrs Burley to send one of her girls with you, to act as your maid?'

'That will not be necessary. I can manage to dress myself.'

'And I will manage to *undress* you,' he murmured, sending the heat rushing through her veins again. He laughed. 'I beg your pardon! Now, you must eat something before we set off, so what will you have?'

Realising the good sense of the earl's suggestion, Beth set herself to breaking her fast, refusing to join the earl in drinking ale and instead sipping at a glass of water.

'How long will it take us to get to Malpass?' she asked, pushing aside her plate.

'With good weather, and as long as you do not object to travelling in the dark, we could reach the Priory by late tomorrow night.'

She rose and walked to the window. 'Will this incessant rain affect us, sir?'

'I hope not. We shall be keeping to the main road, which is in very good order.' He came up behind her and put his hand on her shoulder. 'It is only a little rain, Beth. It will not stop me getting you safely to Malpass.'

She dropped her head to one side, rubbing her cheek against the back of his hand. 'I am sure, sir, that if anyone can get me there it is you.'

The rain beat down steadily as they clattered out over the cobbles, patterning the carriage windows with rivulets of water and obscuring the view.

'On our way at last,' said Guy, reaching for her hand. 'Happy?'

'I shall be happier when Simon is free. And when I have spoken to Miles.'

'Ah, yes, Radworth. How will you explain to him that you set off for Richmond to buy your wedding clothes, but instead you went to London?'

'Oh, pray do not joke about it,' she begged him. 'I shall, of course, have to lay the whole story before him.'

'Everything?'

She bit her lip. 'I shall tell him I…I can no longer return his affection.'

'And what will he do then, do you think?'

Beth freed her hand from the comfort of his grip and twisted her fingers together. 'I think,' she said slowly, 'that he will insist upon the marriage settlement being honoured. He will take the Priory.' Her voice quivered. 'I very much fear that I will lose Malpass for ever. I had hoped Miles would agree to make the Priory over to Simon, once he knows he is a free man, but now…' She gave a little shrug. 'I suppose it seemed sensible for Papa to sign every-thing over to me, when he thought Simon was drowned.'

'It also meant that the Crown could not take the estate, should Simon be found guilty of murder and or robbery.'

'True, but Papa did not know Simon had been accused. We made sure we kept that from him.'

'But Radworth knew.'

Beth blinked. 'What has that to say to anything?'

'It was entirely in Radworth's interest to make sure the estate came to you.'

'That's nonsense! Miles had never been to Yorkshire before he brought us news of Simon.'

'But perhaps, once he had seen Malpass, he decided to have it, at all costs.'

A heavy silence filled the coach.

'You think he proposed merely to gain the Priory?' she said coldly. 'That is not very complimentary to me, sir.'

'Do you think he loves you?'

She sat up very straight. 'Yes, I do.'

'Then why were you so loath to tell him that Simon was alive?' he said softly. When she did not answer he sat forwards. 'Beth—'

'No!' She flinched away from him and huddled herself in the corner. 'That is a despicable thing to say. I know no ill of Miles Radworth.'

'Praise indeed!'

She glared at him. 'I would stake my life that he knew nothing of the Priory or the family when he came north to tell us about Simon. For nigh on two years he has been on hand to support us, even neglecting his own estates in the south and hiring a house in Fentonby. That is not the action of a bad man.'

'It is certainly the action of a patient one,' returned the earl mildly. 'Tell me, Beth—in all the time of your courtship, has he *never* tried to take you to his bed?'

'He has tried to…to kiss me.'

'A veritable Lothario!'

Her cheeks flamed. 'Not everyone is as…as impetuous as you, my lord!'

'Imp—! Beth, no man who professed to love you could keep his hands off you for so long, believe me!'

'No,' she said, putting her hands over her ears. 'You are trying to tell me that Miles is a fortune hunter and I will not believe it!' She lifted her head, blinking away the tears. 'Is it not enough that I am going to end our betrothal. Must you seek to vilify him, too?'

'I do not seek to do anything,' retorted Guy. 'I want you to be on your guard, Beth.'

'Thank you,' she replied stiffly, 'I am quite capable of making my own mind up about Miles and I am sure there is no harm in him.'

Guy relapsed into silence. He applauded her loyalty, but his instinct was to distrust Miles Radworth. Perhaps Beth was right and he was a good man, perhaps it was jealousy that made him so uneasy, but he doubted it, and if his suspicions were correct, then their arrival back at Malpass could be fraught with danger.

There was little time to dwell on what the future might hold, for the journey north proved to have dangers of its own. They had not been travelling long before the coach slowed and the footman came to the door to inform them that the road was flooded. It proved passable, but the rain continued to cause problems and they made slow progress to Godmanchester, where the floodwaters kept them at the inn for three days.

Beth was anxious to get back to Malpass and show Madame de Beaune's deposition to Simon. She was obliged to curb her impatience, for all the reports coming in spoke of floodwater all around them, carriages swept away and livestock drowned.

'We are best sitting it out,' Guy told her. 'We are safer here than trying to find a way through the floodwaters.'

Beth knew it was true, but the wait fretted her; the only time she forgot her troubles was at night, when Guy would take her in his arms and kiss away her cares. They grew so close, so comfortable together, that she wondered how she had ever lived without him.

* * *

Eventually word came through that the road was passable and they set off early the next morning to join a long procession of carts, wagons and carriages crossing the medieval bridge at Huntingdon. Beth watched horrified as they travelled all day through a landscape mired by the floods. Uprooted trees littered the riverbanks, hedges and roads were filmed with mud and buildings displayed the telltale brown watermarks, sometimes as high as the upstairs windows, and the occupants had carried their furniture and belongings into the sun to dry out.

As they moved farther north they left the floods behind them and gradually Beth's mind turned back to her own problems.

They had spent one more night on the road and after another long and tiring day's travel the earl's carriage drove into Thirsk as the autumn sun was setting.

'Would you like me to hire a gig for you?' asked Guy as they slowed to enter the town. 'You might want to avoid awkward questions and return to the Priory alone.'

'And what would you do?'

'I will put up in Fentonby.'

She reached out her hand to him. 'Thank you, but no. I think it is time I put an end to this pretence. Besides,' she said, smiling, 'I would miss you too much.'

He kissed her fingers. 'I am glad of that. To tell you the truth I do not want to let you out of my sight.'

He leaned out to give instructions to Thomas. Beth clasped her hands together, another few miles and she would be home. She wondered how Sophie had coped without her, looking after Grandmama and Simon. She hoped her brother was getting better. When she had left the fever had abated and he was beginning to look and act more like his old self—his recovery would certainly be helped when he heard her news. She had sent a note by express when they stopped overnight at Retford, telling Sophie to expect her. It was the first correspondence she had dared to write, fearing that any letter might fall into the wrong hands and the truth would be discovered, but now she was aware of a growing excitement.

She clutched her reticule to her. She could not wait to show the letter to Sophie and Simon. Tomorrow they would ask Sir John Marton to call and then… She did not know how the process of law worked, but she was sure that Sir Thomas would agree to Simon remaining at Malpass while his name was cleared. She looked out of the window, her eyes searching the darkness for familiar landmarks. They rattled through Fentonby and she looked out for the elegant town house that Miles had rented. Poor Miles, she was not looking forward to her interview with him, but it must be done, and then she would be free to marry Guy. She swallowed, clamping down the excitement and hope that bubbled within her. She must not anticipate too much yet, there were still hurdles to be crossed and she was foolishly superstitious that if she took her happiness for granted it would all be snatched away from her.

'Here we are.'

Guy's words brought her back to the present. The carriage slowed to turn into the Priory's gateway and a moment later she was fumbling with the carriage door.

'Here, let me.' Guy gently moved her aside to open the door and jump out. She could hardly wait until he had put down the steps before descending.

'Where is everyone? Surely they should have been looking out for us! Perhaps they did not receive my note.'

Picking up her skirts, she ran up the steps. The door opened to her touch and she hurried inside.

'Sophie! Grandmama!' She hurried into the great hall, tossing her cloak, bonnet and reticule on to the settle and not noticing the gloves and riding crop already resting there. 'Oh, there you are! How glad I am to see you both, I—' She stopped. Her grandmother was sitting in her usual armchair, regal as ever, if a little paler, but Sophie was kneeling at her feet, her face buried in the black skirts. She looked up at Beth's words, her face white and her eyes swollen with crying.

'Oh, Beth,' she cried, her voice choking on a sob. 'It's Simon! He has been arrested!'

Chapter Eighteen

'Is that you, Elizabeth?' Lady Arabella peered short-sightedly across the room and held out an imperious hand. 'Where have you been, girl? It is most irregular for you to disappear in that way!'

Beth hurried to her grandmother, leaving Guy to follow.

'She is very shocked,' murmured Sophie. 'I told her you had gone to London, but I do not think she understood me.'

'I am here, Grandmama,' said Beth softly, kneeling beside the old woman and taking her hand. 'I have been away, but I am back now, and I will take care of everything.'

'Where is Simon?' demanded the old lady querulously. 'You told me he was dead. Now Sophie says it is not so. If he is alive, I want to see him.'

'We will bring him back soon, I promise.' Beth looked at her sister. 'I do not understand. Why was there no one at the door? Where is Kepwith?'

'We are all in disarray—the soldiers insisted on searching the whole house. Two of the maids fell into hysterics and one of the footmen objected. He was knocked down and cut open his head. Mrs Robinson is with him even now,' replied Sophie, wiping her eyes. 'Kepwith went off to the kitchens with—'

She broke off. Guy's head snapped up as a soft, familiar voice came from the other side of the room.

'Here we are. I found all the herbs I needed for my special tisane, Lady Arabella. This will settle your nerves.'

Clarice Cordonnier came into the hall, carefully carrying a saucer and cup from which issued a pale column of fragrant steam.

'What the devil are you doing here?'

Guy could not restrain the fierce exclamation. A glance at Beth showed him that she was on her feet, staring at the woman.

Clarice merely opened her eyes wide at him. 'I rode over this afternoon. I hired a horse in Fentonby.'

'Mrs Cordonnier was here when Simon was taken,' explained Sophie, wiping her eyes.

'I have been comforting the family.' Clarice put the cup and saucer into Lady Arabella's outstretched hands. 'There you are, my lady. Sip it slowly and you will soon feel better.'

'And just how did you get here from London?' demanded Beth.

'I caught the night mail and then hired a carriage to Fentonby. I have to say, I did not expect you to be quite so far behind me.'

Her mocking glance made Guy clench his jaw in anger.

'I'll wager you are up to no good!'

She gave a soft laugh. 'How suspicious you are, Darrington. After Mrs Forrester's kindness to me in London I wanted to be of use to her. From our conversation I thought the family might be in some trouble, so I came north to see if I could help.' Her smile widened. 'After all, ma'am, you advised me to use Darrington's money wisely.'

'But how did you find the Priory?' asked Beth.

'You said your family lived close to Fentonby, and by good fortune Miss Sophie was in the town on the very day I arrived!'

She bent her honeyed smile towards Sophie and Guy wanted to place himself between Clarice and the other women, as if by doing so he could protect them.

'Then thank you for your help, but we will not take up more of your time,' said Beth. 'Kepwith will see you out.'

There was an uneasy silence.

'I invited Mrs Cordonnier to stay,' muttered Sophie. She flinched as Guy smothered an oath and gazed anxiously at her sister. 'She s-said she had met you in London, that she was a close friend of Lord D-Darrington…'

'Perhaps I stretched the truth a little,' murmured Clarice, still smiling. 'But with the family in such disarray I thought I might be able to help...'

Beth drew herself up. 'Thank you, but I think you should leave us now, madam.' Her tone was quiet but firm. She nodded towards the butler, who had come silently into the room. 'Kepwith, you will send a note to the stables, if you please. Mrs Cordonnier's horse is to be brought to the door *immediately*.'

'I quite understand that you will want to be alone with your family,' purred Clarice. 'But surely you would not send me off so late at night...'

Her wide-eyed, helpless look had no effect on Guy, who said merely, 'There is a good moon, you will not lose your way.'

In no way discomposed, Clarice merely gave a soft laugh.

'I did not think there would be any harm,' said Sophie, turning a beseeching look upon her sister. 'She seemed to know so much about you and Lord Darrington and she was so easy to talk to.' She paused, then said miserably, 'I was very lonely here, you see, so much anxiety...'

Lady Arabella looked up from sipping her tisane. 'It was very wrong of you to leave Sophie here alone, Elizabeth,' she said severely. 'The poor child has not been herself.'

Beth patted her shoulder. 'I shall not go away again, Grandmama, I promise.'

'And why is Darrington with you? I thought you had gone to stay with Maria Crowther in Ripon.'

'Hush, Grandmama,' murmured Sophie. 'I told you there was a change of plans and Beth went to London instead.'

'I am quite *désolée* to be leaving you, Miss Sophie, but I can see that you have no need of me, now you have your sister and Lord Darrington to support you.' Clarice moved across to the settle to pick up her gloves and riding crop. 'Pray send me word to let me know what happens about your poor brother. Goodbye, Lady Arabella.'

Sophie's murmured reply was incoherent. Lady Arabella looked up, the tea cup rattling in its saucer. Beth moved swiftly to take it from her as the old lady became agitated.

'Where is she going? It is very late to be travelling.' The faded eyes fixed themselves upon Guy. 'Darrington—is that you? You should escort the lady, my lord.'

'She will do very well without my company, ma'am.'

'It appears I will have to do so, at all events,' remarked Clarice. 'No, no, Miss Sophie, pray do not apologise. I am not at all offended, I assure you. Your butler is here to tell me my horse is waiting. Pray, do not trouble yourselves to see me out.' With that she treated them all to another dazzling smile and sailed out of the house.

'She comes to Malpass and within days Simon is arrested.' Guy frowned. 'I'll wager there is a connection.'

'If only we had been here sooner,' muttered Beth. 'Sophie, how is it you are on such friendly terms with Mrs Cordonnier after such a short time?'

It was Guy who responded, giving a bitter laugh.

'Do not blame your sister too much, ma'am, the woman is adept at worming her way into people's affections!'

'She was so very kind,' agreed Sophie, 'and Miles did not think there would be any harm in it—'

'*Miles* knows her?' exclaimed Beth.

'I introduced them,' Sophie admitted. 'Miles rode over to the Priory when Clar—Mrs Cordonnier was taking tea with me. He escorted her back to Fentonby.' She sighed. 'I was relieved to see him go. You know how he hovers around here. I was always worried he would discover Simon.'

'Well, certainly someone did!' retorted Guy.

'I do not think it can have been Miles,' Sophie replied. 'He has not been here since that day and he sent me word yesterday morning that he was off on one of his buying trips, this time to Scotland, and will not be back until the end of the week.'

Guy frowned at Sophie. 'Are you quite sure you did not say anything to Mrs Cordonnier about Simon?'

'Not directly.' She looked nervous. 'We talked of so many

things… We got on so well, you see…of course I *mentioned* Simon, but I never told her he was alive, or anything about his being a fugitive! But she did find me coming out of the cellars, once. I told her I had been looking for an old travelling trunk and I think she believed me.'

Beth put up her hand. 'Never mind that now, tell me about Simon. When was he taken?'

'The soldiers came late this afternoon. They had orders to search the house—they said they had information that Simon might be here.'

'It is plain that someone has laid information against your brother,' Guy stated. 'If it wasn't Radworth, then my money is on Clarice Cordonnier.'

'No, no!' cried Sophie, distressed. 'She was as shocked as we were when the soldiers came hammering on the door. She was the one who insisted upon seeing their authority, and she looked after Grandmama while I tried to stop them—'

'They did not hurt you?' cried Beth, alarmed.

Sophie shook her head. 'Not at all, but they insisted upon searching every room, even the wine cellar. They found the door through to the undercroft, but Simon heard them. He is so much better now that he had taken to dressing himself and walking around the undercroft to exercise himself. He…he tried to escape through the door on to the drive.' She began to cry again. 'There were more soldiers waiting there for him.'

'Where did they take him?' asked Guy.

'To the lock-up in Thirsk.'

'Then he will be under Sir John Marton's jurisdiction,' said Beth, brightening. 'If only we had known, we could have called in there on our way home!' She hugged her sister. 'Dry your eyes, Sophie, we will have Simon back with us before morning.'

'But…but how? Why?' A sudden look of hope filled Sophie's face. 'You found the de Beaunes?'

'Yes! We have a deposition from Madame de Beaune, confirming Simon is innocent.' Beth scrambled to her feet. 'We will take it to Sir John tonight. I cannot bear the thought of poor Simon being locked up for any longer than necessary…'

Her words trailed away. She was hunting in her reticule, her search becoming increasingly more frantic. A cold hand clutched at Guy's heart when she turned to look at him, her face deathly pale.

'I…I don't understand. It's gone.'

'Clarice!'

Guy dashed across the room, almost colliding with Kepwith, who was coming back into the great hall. Guy pushed past him and wrenched open the front door. He flew down the steps and stopped, staring at the now empty drive. He did not turn when he heard hasty footsteps approaching, nor when Beth's hand clutched at his arm.

'She has stolen the letter?'

'I fear so.'

'But…why? She cannot know what was in it.'

His hand came up to cover her fingers. 'She saw an opportunity to make mischief.'

'Can we go after her?' Beth said urgently. 'Can we catch her?'

'With a couple of fast horses, perhaps…'

'Then let us try!' She pulled away from him and he followed her back into the house, listening as she gave her orders. When she turned back to him there was a fiery glow in her eyes. 'Give me a moment to change into my riding habit while the horses are saddled.'

'Beth, are you sure you want to do this? We have been travelling for days.'

Her head went up at that. 'Simon is my brother. Who else should do it?'

'Let me go alone—'

'No. We do this together, Guy.'

Fifteen minutes later they were galloping away from the Priory. A blustery wind had blown up and clouds scudded across the sky, occasionally covering the moon and plunging the road into darkness, but neither Beth nor Guy curbed their headlong flight. Beth's nerves were taut as a wire, knowing that every moment was precious. It was doubtful that Clarice would ride back to Fentonby at quite such breakneck speed, for she was on a hired horse and an unfamiliar road. Beth had the advantage of knowing every curve and dip of the highway. If they could only catch Clarice before she had time to hide the deposition.

When the road disappeared into a small wood Beth slowed the pace.

'It would not be sensible to gallop through total darkness,' she told Guy as he drew rein beside her. 'Also, my horse is blown—this will give her a chance to recover.' She paused. 'Clarice might think this a way to be revenged upon you. Would she…will she destroy the deposition, do you think?'

'I doubt it.'

'But that would be the most terrible vengeance I could conceive, to take away Simon's chance of freedom.'

'But Clarice is nothing like you, my dear. I have no doubt her revenge will follow a more…mercenary line.'

'You think she will sell the deposition back to me?'

'At an extortionate price, yes. It would go against the grain to pay.'

'But what choice do we have?' Beth sighed. 'Madame de Beaune was going off to America with her brother—it could take months to find her again!'

'Beth—'

'No, my mind is made up. I must retrieve the letter—I cannot bear to think of Simon being locked up for even a day!'

They were emerging from the wood and the path shone before them like a silver ribbon in the moonlight.

'Very well, then.' Guy's horse leapt ahead. 'Let us be on our way!'

Fentonby was silent, the houses in darkness as they rode into the high street. They made for the Swan, where Sophie had told them Clarice had taken rooms. It was very late and there was no one to be seen through the taproom window, but the door stood open and lamps still flared outside the inn. A sleepy ostler ran forwards to take their horses and Guy ushered Beth inside, where they found a waiter clearing the tables. He shook his head when Guy enquired after Mrs Cordonnier.

'Went out earlier today, she did, and ain't come back yet.'

'Did she speak of having friends in the area?' asked Guy. He slipped a coin into the man's hand. 'Has she had any visitors while she has been staying here?'

The man looked at the coin winking in his hand, then slowly shook his head.

'No, sir. Kept very much to 'erself, she did.'

'Could we have missed her?' Beth looked up anxiously at Guy as the servant turned away and continued collecting up the dishes. 'There is only the one road from the Priory. We were travelling fast, perhaps she took a fall…'

'Unlikely,' said Guy slowly. 'She was always an excellent horse-woman. I think it more likely that she is in hiding. She would know that I would come after her.'

'Then what should we do now?'

'There is nothing we can do but go home and wait.'

'We could call upon Sir John and explain—'

'Without proof he will not be in a position to release your brother. And before you say we should attempt it, unless the man is a saint he will not take kindly to being woken up at this time of night.'

Beth opened her mouth to argue, but one look at Guy's face told her it would be useless. She sighed, suddenly exhausted. Without another word she allowed Guy to escort her back to the horses and soon they were riding back to Malpass.

They accomplished the return journey at a much slower pace and Beth rode silently beside the earl, doing her best to hide her frustration, but after a while Guy said quietly, 'My dear, I am so sorry you had to meet that woman.'

'It is not your fault, Guy.'

'I should never have allowed her into the house!'

'I believed it was your Christian duty to do so.'

'Duty be damned—'

She shook her head, smiling a little at his vehemence. 'It is as much my fault as yours. I thought you were too harsh.'

'Your own goodness makes it difficult for you to see the evil in others.'

'My goodness!' Beth gave a long sigh. 'I sometimes think I brought this on myself, that I am being punished for breaking my betrothal vows…'

'That is nonsense and you know it!'

'I know I am being foolish, but I cannot help wondering—' She broke off, giving her head a little shake. 'I beg your pardon. I think I must be tired.'

'It has been a trying day.' Guy reached across for her hand. 'Come, Beth, do not look so downhearted. We will go back to the Priory and wait to hear from Clarice. All is not yet lost.'

Sophie was waiting up for them when they returned to Malpass. She was disappointed that they had not recovered Madame de Beaune's deposition, but was content to accept the argument that Clarice would want to sell it back to them. What was harder for her to accept was Beth's garbled explanation of why she was travelling with the earl.

'Mrs Cordonnier told me she had seen you together in London,' said Sophie, leading them into the small parlour. 'It made it very difficult when Miles turned up here, I can tell you! I was obliged to tell her that you were on secret business and to ask her not to mention anything about it to Miles.'

'You may be sure that will have aroused Clarice's interest,' muttered Guy, frowning.

'If I had known she was such a wicked woman, I would not have invited her to the house!' retorted Sophie, colours flying in her cheeks.

'Of course you were not to know,' said Beth quickly. She glanced at Guy. 'She has taken us all in at some time. But it is very late and we will need our wits about us tomorrow.'

'Of course,' said Sophie. 'The red room was prepared for Mrs

Cordonnier, so you may use that, my lord. I told the servants to go on to bed—do you want me to show you the way?'

'I will do that,' said Beth quickly. She kissed her sister's cheek. 'Goodnight, my dear.'

She watched her sister close the door behind her, then turned to look at the earl. He was watching her, a faint smile glinting in his eyes.

'Well, madam, will you share my bed tonight?'

'Will you be angry if I said no? Now we are back at Malpass I feel the weight of my betrothal very strongly.'

'I thought as much.'

He held out his arms to her and she walked into them, drawing comfort and strength from him as he held her close.

'Forgive me,' she said, her words muffled against his chest. 'Once I have seen Miles…'

'You do not need to explain it to me,' he murmured, kissing her hair. 'Come—walk me to my room and I will content myself with a chaste goodnight kiss!'

Chapter Nineteen

Beth spent a miserable night, her mind racing between anxiety for Simon, apprehension at seeing Miles again and bitter regret that she had ever let Madame de Beaune's deposition out of her hands. She was relieved when at last the chill autumn day dawned and she could dress herself and go downstairs. An hour spent with her housekeeper discussing menus and household matters did much to calm her mind, but it was the sight of Guy at the breakfast table that gave her the most comfort. He rose as she entered the room and smiled at her, looking so devastatingly handsome and strong that it was easy to believe everything would be well, if he was there to help her.

'Good morning, my lord.' She tried for a cheerful note. 'You are looking very smart, despite the absence of your valet.'

He grinned.

'You know I can manage very well without Fitton, as you can do without your maid.' He held her chair for her. 'However, I hope they will be here by the end of the day. They should not have been so far behind us.'

'Were they, too, held up by the floods at Huntingdon?' asked Sophie, coming into the room at that moment. Her brow darkened. 'I wish that woman had been caught in the flood—I wish she had drowned!'

Beth sighed. 'It is galling that she should have such an advantage over us. If only we had got here sooner!'

Sophie was inclined to be practical. 'Let us not worry about that now,' she said. 'Can we go to Thirsk today, to see Simon?'

'I would like to see him,' admitted Beth. 'I want to assure myself that he is well.'

Sophie's face crumpled. 'He was getting so much better, Beth— the fever had gone and he was beginning to eat well—' She broke off and buried her face in her hands. Beth immediately left her seat and went to put her arms around her sister.

'Sophie, do not distress yourself, this is only a set-back. As soon as—' She broke off as the sound of voices filtered through the door. Someone was approaching. She looked at Guy. 'Mrs Cordonnier?'

He put down his napkin. 'I don't think so.'

He rose as the door opened and a cheerful voice said, 'Don't bother to announce me, I can find my way.'

'Edwin!'

Sophie's cry of delight took Beth by surprise and she stared as her sister raced across the room and threw herself at Mr Davies. He was leaning heavily on his stick, but quickly put his free arm about her.

'There, there, my love, don't cry all over me. When you didn't visit me as promised yesterday I thought I should come and find out what was amiss.' He looked over her dark honey-coloured curls, his laughing eyes resting on Guy.

'So you are here, Darrington! Julia was as mad as fire with you— not for abandoning her at Thirsk, but for not telling her what the devil you were about! And Mrs Forrester, returned from Ripon at last.'

'Good morning, Davey.'

Beth could only admire Guy's cool tone as he greeted his friend. She was still too shocked at the sight of her sister with her arms wrapped around the young man.

'Beth never went to R-Ripon,' said Sophie, wiping her eyes. 'Come and sit down, Edwin, and we will explain everything.'

'Sophie!' Beth shot her sister a warning look. 'I do not think—'

'It is all right, my dear.' Guy interrupted her. 'I would trust Davey with my life. And judging by his reception, I think he has plans to become a member of your family before too long.'

'Well, yes, as a matter of fact,' murmured Mr Davies, reddening. 'We were waiting for you to return, ma'am.'

'You see, I did not even confide in Edwin,' cried Sophie, guiding Davey to the table and sitting down beside him. 'I have been most discreet, so how that woman knew about Simon…'

'She has a nose for scandal,' said Guy bitterly. 'But I can see that Davey is looking confused. Beth, my love, perhaps you would send for more coffee, then I think we should take him into our confidence.'

'So Clarice is back in England!' Edwin Davies shook his head, his boyish countenance very grim. It had taken some time to explain everything and Davey's habitual laughter had long since died away. 'I always knew she would be trouble for you, Guy.'

'Not so much for me,' returned Guy, glancing across the table at Beth. 'If I had disowned the woman when she first stole those letters—if I had told the truth—'

'You were not to know.' Beth tried to smile bravely.

'Oh, yes, he was,' Davey ground out. 'He's too damn—dashed loyal! He could have spoken out ten years ago, instead of giving up a brilliant career, and all for such a worthless woman.'

'Let us not dwell on the past,' said Beth quickly, sensing Guy's own hurt and regret. 'Instead let us decide what is to be done now.'

Before anyone could speak there was a scratching on the door and Kepwith appeared.

'Mrs Cordonnier to see you, ma'am.'

'Oho,' murmured Guy, his eyes bright. 'So we move on!'

Davey stood up. 'Let me at her, I'll give her a piece of my mind—'

'No, it is best that she sees only Beth and myself,' replied Guy. 'You stay here and look after Sophie.' He could not have said anything more likely to make Davey resume his seat. He turned to Beth. 'Well, madam, shall we see what she has to say?'

She led the way to the great hall, resisting the temptation to reach out and grasp Guy's hand. They found Clarice waiting for them, dressed as before in her riding habit, but this time she had not discarded her gloves and was gently tapping her riding crop against her skirts.

'I heard that you came looking for me last night.' Her smile challenged them. 'You did not think I would be so foolish as to let you find me before I had put that letter in a safe place?'

'Was it you who informed upon my brother?' Beth demanded coldly.

'I sent word to the authorities that a desperate fugitive was hidden here, yes. Your demeanour in London led me to believe you had… secrets, Mrs Forrester, so I came north. It was an easy matter then to befriend your sister and to see beyond her pathetic attempts at concealment.'

'I do not believe Sophie gave so much away.'

She shrugged. 'Believe what you will, it is not important. Your brother will be taken back to Portsmouth to stand trial. Without the deposition I do not see much hope for him.'

'What have you done with it?' Beth demanded, but Clarice merely smiled at her.

'You need the letter, do you not, to secure your brother's release? Let me assure you that it is safe, although I shall not tell you where it is.'

'We will make you tell us,' declared Beth. 'We will take you now to Thirsk, to the magistrate—'

'And I shall deny everything. I shall say you have abducted me. An act of jealousy, perhaps, because I was once Darrington's fiancée.'

Guy said coldly, 'How much?'

Clarice narrowed her eyes, as if considering the question. 'Ten thousand pounds.'

Beth stared, dismay chilling her bones.

'I will see you in hell first.'

Clarice merely smiled even more at Guy's bitter retort. 'Will you? Then how will you save Wakeford now Madame de Beaune is gone?'

Beth's head went up. 'How do you know that?'

'I have my sources.' She added sharply, 'And it is no good frowning so blackly, Darrington. I know you would like to murder me, but I have made provision for my safety. If I do not return to my friends by noon, they have instructions to burn your precious letter.'

'No!' Beth looked at Guy. He was still frowning, his eyes hard as granite. She turned back to Clarice. 'I do not have ten thousand pounds.'

'No,' came the soft reply. 'But Darrington does. He would not even feel its loss.'

'And I will not advance you one penny.'

'What, not even for your lover's sake?' retorted Clarice. 'Her brother will hang without that letter.'

'I assure you he will not.'

'He cheated the hangman two years ago. There will be no mob to save him this time. He will be taken south and tried. You may be able to argue that the murder was only manslaughter, but there's the necklace.' Her eyes narrowed. 'Life is considered cheap by the English courts, Darrington, but robbery—they take that very seriously. He will surely hang for it.'

Guy shook his head. 'And I repeat, Wakeford will not hang.'

Beth fought to keep her face impassive. The thought of Simon locked in a prison cell was torture enough—the thought of a trial and its outcome was unbearable.

'It seems we have reached an impasse,' said Clarice, shrugging. 'I will leave you to discuss it. I advise you to act soon. Once Wakeford is taken south for trial, my price will go up. There is no need to call your butler to show me out, I know my way. Do not attempt to follow me,' she warned, walking to the door. 'I do not intend that you should know where I am.'

'But if we should wish to contact you—' said Beth.

'I will not negotiate with you, Mrs Forrester. I want ten thousand pounds to part with that letter, nothing less. If you want to pay me, you may send a message to the Swan. I shall look out for it.'

'You will be disappointed,' Guy ground out, his eyes cold and hard. 'I have no intention of giving in to you.'

'No?' Her contemptuous glance rested on Beth. 'Perhaps you are not quite so enamoured of your hero now, Mrs Forrester.'

With that Clarice turned and swept out of the house.

A heavy silence fell over the hall.

'How did she know that Madame was going to America?' Beth asked at last.

'I am not sure that is what she meant, but it is clear she knows more about this than she could have gleaned from you and your sister.'

'Ten thousand pounds.' Beth shook her head. 'We would have to sell everything to raise such a sum and that will take time.'

'You must not even think of paying the woman.' He reached out and took her hands. 'Beth, I must ask you to trust me.'

'But Simon—'

'He is safe for the moment.'

She pulled away from him. 'But he is in *gaol*! You must see that I will do everything in my power to save him.'

'But that should not include paying Clarice her blood-money.'

'I think your hatred of the woman blinds you to what needs to be done,' said Beth bitterly.

'Not at all. Believe me, Beth, I do not intend to let any harm come to your brother.'

Beth closed her eyes. It was difficult to think clearly. 'What do you plan to do?'

He shook his head at her. 'I must keep my own counsel for now. Your brother will be safe in custody. I will go to Thirsk today to see the magistrate. He shall have whatever funds are required for his comfort.'

'No.' Beth tore herself out of his grasp and turned away. 'You do not need to trouble yourself. *I* will go to Thirsk.'

'The devil you will!'

She put up her hands. It was as if she was in some nightmare and could not think properly. All she knew was that somehow she had expected Guy to help and he had failed her. Her head, her very being, was swamped with an irrational disappointment. She said furiously, 'Simon is my brother, I will decide the best way to help him! I do not need your help with this.' She drew herself up. 'I do not need your help with *anything*!'

She glared at him, challenging him to disagree. Instead he gave a stiff little bow.

'Very well, madam. If that is your final word, then perhaps I should leave.'

'Yes, go!' she flashed back. 'I can manage very well without you!'

Beth was obliged to take a turn about the garden before she could join the others. Her argument with Guy had overset her quite as much as Clarice's demands. She half hoped he would follow her, for as her anger receded she realised she was being unfair and would have welcomed the chance to apologise. However, he was nowhere in sight when she made her way back into the house, where she found Sophie and Davey, still sitting at the breakfast table.

'Well?'

She looked at Sophie's eager face and had to fight back her tears. 'She w-wants ten thousand pounds to return the letter.'

'Ten—' Sophie's hands flew to her cheeks. 'Heavens, we do not have such a sum.'

Davey looked at her. 'Darrington?'

Beth shook her head. 'He…he is adamant we should not pay.'

'And he has the right of it,' agreed Davey. 'You have no way of knowing if she will give you the letter.'

'I would give ten times that much to save Simon!' cried Sophie, an angry flush on her cheeks.

'And so would I, my love,' said Davey soothingly, 'if we could be sure it would save him. I have no doubt Darrington has a plan. Where is he?'

Beth shrugged and said, trying to sound indifferent, 'I am sure I don't know.'

'Well, we need to know what he intends to do,' declared Davey. 'Ring the bell, Sophie, we'll have him fetched here now.'

But when Kepwith came in a few minutes later it was with the news that Lord Darrington had left Malpass.

'The devil he has!' exclaimed Davey. 'Where has he gone, did he say?'

'He left word that he would be staying in Fentonby,' replied Kepwith, his countenance wooden.

'Fentonby!' Davey ran a hand through his fair hair. 'What in heaven's name is he playing at now?'

Beth did not answer. She could not speak at all, but remained rooted to the spot, staring at her butler.

He is gone.

The words rang in her head. She thought back over their last moments together. Surely he knew better than to believe what she said when she was in a temper? Unless he was looking for an excuse to leave: perhaps he no longer wanted her. Beth did not hide from the fact—she had read enough of Dangerous Lord Darrington's exploits to know it would not be the first time he had loved and left a woman. She thought bitterly that he was living up to his reputation.

'What do we do now?' asked Sophie, her lip trembling.

Beth squared her shoulders. 'We go to Thirsk, to see Sir John Marton.'

'I shall come with you,' declared Davey.

Beth was about to refuse his escort, but then she saw the look that passed between Davey and her sister. A pain as sharp as a knife twisted in her heart; she had thought Guy loved her that much, but now she found it difficult to believe.

'Very well,' she said. 'But first, Sophie, we should go and see Grandmama. We will not tell her about the missing letter, only that we are going to visit Simon.'

As the Wakeford travelling carriage lumbered towards Thirsk, Beth could not help comparing it with the earl's swift, elegant chariot, in which she had travelled so many miles with him. The comparison only reinforced the difference in their stations. A tiny, insidious voice whispered that Guy could have loaned her the ten thousand pounds to pay Clarice, if he had wished to do so. Instead he had left her. She blinked rapidly, keeping her eyes fixed upon the passing landscape.

'I do not understand why Lord Darrington should want to move into Fentonby,' observed Sophie as they rattled over the uneven ground. 'Did he not say anything to you, Beth?'

She swallowed hard and replied with creditable calm. 'No. But this matter is really none of his concern.'

'None of his—!' Davey shook his head. 'Of course it concerns him, especially if Clarice Cordonnier is involved.' He reached out to touch Beth's arm. 'Pray do not lose faith in Darrington, Mrs Forrester. If he refused to pay Clarice, you may be sure there is a good reason.'

'Yes,' said Beth bitterly. 'Because he will not be beaten by her a second time.'

Davey began to protest, but Beth silenced him.

'I know you are very loyal to your friend, Mr Davies, but your assurances sound hollow. If he truly wants to help us, he should tell me.' She thought back to the days she had spent in the earl's company, and the long, passionate nights. Surely that had meant something to him. She said, the words quiet and despairing, 'Can he not trust me?'

Davey looked uncomfortable. 'He must think it safer not to trust anyone.'

Beth found this response very unsatisfactory. She lapsed into silence, convinced in her own heart that she had read too much into those few brief days she had spent with Guy: it was quite clear to her now that he did not love her.

Their visit to the magistrate gave Beth little comfort. He heard her story, shook his head over the explanation of the stolen deposition, but finally declared that he was powerless to help.

'I am very sorry, Mrs Forrester, but you cannot tell me where I can find this, this Mrs Cordonnier and a deposition, written by a Frenchwoman who is no longer in the country—it all sounds very implausible. Your brother must answer the charges against him.' Seeing her stricken look, he softened a little, adding gently, 'The most I can do is to keep Wakeford here in Thirsk until he is called to trial. That way at least you will be able to visit him regularly.'

Sir John escorted them personally to the gaol, where they found Simon in good spirits, although looking pale and shaken after his ordeal.

'They are treating me very well,' he told them. 'Sophie managed to pass me a purse before they carried me away, so I have been able to pay for a separate room and decent food. And to be truthful, Beth, I am pleased to be out of that dashed undercroft. At least I have a window now.'

Beth managed a smile as he pointed to the barred opening high up in the wall. The sounds from the street filtered in, taunting them. Resolutely she refused to think of it.

'You do indeed look better than when I last saw you,' she admitted.

'And what news of the de Beaunes?'

His eager question was met with an uneasy moment of silence before Beth told him what had happened, ending with Clarice's visit to the Priory.

'I had hoped Darrington might offer to loan me the money to buy back the letter,' she ended.

Simon merely shrugged. 'You cannot expect him to lay out such a sum for a stranger.'

'You may be sure Darrington has good reason for refusing,' put in Davey.

'Would *you* refuse me such a sum?' Sophie challenged him.

'No, of course not,' he replied swiftly. 'If I had it, which I don't...'

Beth put up her hand. 'Please, do not make yourself uneasy, Mr Davies, I do not doubt *your* friendship.'

'And I would not have you doubt Darrington's.'

She gave a sad little smile. 'No, of course not. I think perhaps I expected a little too much of him.'

It was very late by the time they returned to Malpass and Beth acquiesced to Sophie's entreaty that Davey should be allowed to stay. She gave instructions for a room to be prepared, then went off to see her grandmother. Lady Arabella had retired, but she was not asleep and Beth endured a long and painful interview. She demanded to know why Beth had not told her of Simon's presence in the undercroft and was convinced that if she had been informed, the soldiers would not have been able to arrest him.

By the time she had settled her grandmother, Beth was exhausted, too tired even to pay much heed to Tilly's description of the trials she had endured whilst travelling to Malpass in the earl's baggage coach. She merely told her maid how pleased she was to have her home again and tumbled into bed, falling asleep the instant her head touched the pillow.

The following morning brought another trial for Beth in the form of a visit from Miles Radworth. She had just finished breakfast when he was announced. She made her way to the great hall and as she descended the stairs he came forwards, his hands held out to her.

'My dear, such dreadful news about your brother!'

'You know of it, then?'

He took her hands, lifting first one, then the other, to his lips.

'It is was all over Fentonby when I arrived home last night. There was no avoiding it. My dear, you must tell me everything.'

She looked up at him and read the concern in his face. 'Yes,' she said slowly, 'I think I must. Come along into the library, Miles, and I will explain.'

'…so there you have it,' she finished, spreading her hands. 'I did not go to Ripon, as everyone thought, I went to London, thinking I might be able to help Simon.'

'I wish you had told me, Elizabeth.'

'I wish I had, now.' She sighed. 'Perhaps I should not be in this predicament if I had trusted you.'

'And Darrington insisted upon accompanying you?'

'Yes.' She glanced down at her hands, clasped lightly in her lap. 'I cannot deny that he was very helpful.'

'Because he is in love with you, perhaps?'

Beth kept her eyes lowered. 'No,' she said quietly. 'I do not think he loves me.'

She heard Miles's chair scrape back as he rose and took a turn about the room.

'But you travelled with him back to Malpass—alone?'

'Yes.'

'I see.'

I doubt it, she thought miserably. She prayed he would not ask her any more questions; she did not want to explain just how intimate she had been with Lord Darrington.

'You realise if—when—word of your exploits gets out, your reputation will be ruined?'

Beth closed her eyes. He would cry off, and who could blame him? Besides, she could not be sorry for it, now she knew her own heart.

'Yes. I—'

'In the circumstances I think it best we bring the marriage forwards.' He continued as if she had not spoken. 'So far our betrothal has been a private affair, but now it should be made public. The banns will be called and we shall be married within the month.'

Beth stared at him. 'You still wish to marry me?'

'Of course.' His thin lips curved into a smile. 'An announcement will put paid to any rumours that may arise from your recent—ah—adventures. We will invite everyone to celebrate with us at the Fentonby Assembly next week. My hired house in Fentonby is too small for such a celebration, and the Priory is not suitable for such a gathering, especially in the present circumstances.'

'But, Miles, how can I think of celebrations with Simon in prison—'

'Hush, my dear. You must see that once you are my wife I shall be much better placed to help you. From all you have told me, I think the Cordonnier woman is using you to get at Darrington. She thought you could persuade him to pay her off.'

'She did.'

'Our betrothal will show her she has mistaken the matter and with Darrington out of the way she may well reduce her demands.'

She looked up at him, saying hopefully, 'Do you really think so?'

'I am nearly sure of it.' He walked over to her and held out his hands, saying, 'Well, my dear—what do you say?'

Beth allowed him to pull her to her feet. She had planned to tell Miles she could not marry him, but all that had changed now. She felt battered by the events of the past few days, especially Guy's refusal to help her. The turmoil within resolved itself into a blazing fury. She would show the precious earl how little he mattered to her—she did not need him any more. Resolutely she lifted her head.

'I say yes, Miles.'

She did not move as he lowered his head and pressed his mouth over hers. She waited for his kiss to ignite the flame of desire that had leapt to life so readily whenever Guy had taken her in his arms. Desperately she forced herself to respond, but inside she felt nothing.

Chapter Twenty

Miles did not remain at Malpass for long. Lady Arabella had not yet left her apartment and he declined Beth's suggestion that he should accompany her to Thirsk, saying he had engagements in Fentonby that would not wait. Beth was therefore left to break the news of her forthcoming marriage to her family. She went first to her grandmother's room, where she found Lady Arabella taking breakfast, her maid informing Beth that her mistress had not slept well. When Beth gently explained to her that she and Miles had at last set a date for their wedding, the old lady merely looked blank.

'Are you not going to wish me well, Grandmama?' murmured Beth, kneeling at the side of her chair.

'Nothing will be well until Simon is home again,' stated the old lady.

'No.' Beth blinked back the hot tears that were never far away. 'No, you are right, Grandmama.'

Sophie's response was a great deal more vociferous. Beth had waited until they were on their way to Thirsk to tell her. Mr Davies was with them, but she had accepted that he and Sophie were inseparable.

'You are joking me!' cried Sophie, when Beth broke the news.

'Does Darrington know of this?' demanded Davey.

'I am *not* funning,' retorted Beth, two angry spots of colour burning her cheeks. 'And it is no business of Lord Darrington's what I do!'

'Oh, Beth, what are you about?' Sophie caught her arm and gave it a little shake. 'When you came back the other night, and said that you had been in Darrington's company for the past week—'

'That is neither here nor there,' she flashed. 'If Miles does not object to that, then it is of no consequence.'

She glared at her companions and they sat back, silenced. It could not be forgotten, but it was certainly pushed to the back of Beth's mind when they reached the gaol to learn Simon had been moved to another cell.

'A bigger apartment and clean bedding,' joked Simon, when they were shown in. 'The view is not so fair—this one overlooks the courtyard, whereas my previous room had a view of the sky. Oh, and I have a new gaoler.' He pointed to the burly individual standing guard at the door. 'Logan is perfectly civil, but insists on keeping me within sight night and day.'

'How perfectly horrid.' Sophie shuddered. 'At least you are no longer shackled.'

'No, and the food has improved, too.' He grinned. 'All in all it is not so bad and a lot better than the undercroft at Malpass.'

'I hope we shall have you free soon,' muttered Beth.

'Oh.' Simon looked up. 'Is there news?'

'I am afraid not, but Miles has vowed to help us.'

'Is Radworth still here, then?'

'Oh, yes.' Sophie nodded. 'And at last they have set a date. Miles and Beth are to be married at the end of the month!'

'Really?' Simon beamed. 'Let us hope I shall be free to give you away.'

His brave attempt at humour overset Beth and she collapsed against him, sobbing.

'There, there, sis, no need for this.' He patted her shoulder awkwardly. 'It won't help, you know, and I hate to see you cry.'

She pulled out her handkerchief and began to wipe her eyes, huskily begging pardon for such a display of weakness, but the tears continued to flow for some moments and she did not know whether she was crying more for Simon or herself.

They arrived back at Malpass in good time for dinner; as they entered the great hall, Kepwith held out a silver tray.

'Lord Darrington called while you were out, ma'am. He left this note for you.'

The silence in the great hall was thick with apprehension. Beth knew that Sophie and Davey were watching her carefully. She raised her brows.

'Indeed?' She picked up the letter and broke open the seal. She was concentrating so much on keeping her hands from shaking that she barely understood the message. One thing was quite clear from his first sentence: he would not be lending her the money to pay off Clarice. That was the only thing she wanted to know—his warnings to her to be on her guard she dismissed. Clenching her jaw tightly to prevent any show of emotion, she tore the letter in two and threw it on to the fire.

'There is nothing in it that need concern us.' She dusted her fingers. 'Shall we join Grandmama for dinner?'

Beth found little time for reflection during the next few days as she busied herself with preparations for her forthcoming nuptials. She had sent an express to Mr Spalding in London, asking him to resume his search for Madame de Beaune, and received a note by return informing her that he believed the lady had left the country with her sister and brother-in-law. Certainly Bourne Park was no longer occupied.

This missive was quickly followed by a letter from Mrs Cordonnier, couched in the friendliest terms, but leaving Beth in no doubt that unless she found the money soon, the deposition would be destroyed. When she told Miles he begged her not to worry.

'I will reply,' he said, taking the note from her. 'I shall advise her of our betrothal and that she can expect to receive nothing until after we are married.'

'But Simon could be taken back to London at any time.'

'We will deal with all these matters as they arise,' he said mildly. 'Trust me, Elizabeth.'

With that she had to be content, but anxiety nagged at her as she went downstairs to dinner. She had invited Miles to join the family and when Beth reached the drawing room she found him making polite conversation with Mr Davies and Sophie, while Lady Arabella looked on in disapproving silence. Taking in the scene in one swift glance, Beth was obliged to put her worries to one side and take on the role of perfect hostess. It was clear her grandmother did not approve of her intention to marry Miles, but if he could win Simon's freedom it would go a long way towards helping Lady Arabella to accept him.

It was growing dark as Guy trotted up to the Priory. He thought back to the very first time he had called here, with Davey stretched out on a farm gate. The black outline of the building had towered over them, dark and menacing. Heaven and earth, if he had known the cost of getting involved with Beth Forrester he would have chosen to carry Davey all the way to Highridge rather than come within a mile of Malpass!

'Don't be a damned fool, you know that isn't so,' he muttered angrily to himself as he dismounted and looped the reins over a post near the steps. Visions rose up before him. Beth directing the servants to carry Davey inside, Beth with a lamp in her hand, her eyes large and nervous as a deer when he met her in the corridor in the middle of the night. Beth with her glorious hair over her shoulders, lying naked in the moonlight....

Savagely he dragged his thoughts back to the present as he ran up the steps. Kepwith opened the door, but barred his way.

'I beg your pardon, my lord,' he hesitated, and looked a little embarrassed. 'My mistress has ordered that you should not be allowed into the house.'

'The devil she has! Then tell *your mistress* that I wish to see her out here!'

The door was closed again as the butler went off to deliver his message. Guy looked at his watch. The family dined early, so they should have finished by now. Would she come? As the minutes dragged by, he began to doubt it.

At last the door opened and he looked up quickly, only to have his hopes dashed when he saw who was standing there.

'Davey! Will she not see me?'

'No, she will not.' Davey stepped outside and pulled the door almost closed behind him. 'Radworth is here, but I doubt if she would have admitted you, even had he not been.' He tucked his hand in Guy's arm. 'Let us walk away from here, where we will not be overheard.'

They descended to the drive and walked away from the house, Guy slowing his stride to match Davey's limping step.

'Did she receive my letter?' he asked bluntly.

'Aye, but she burned it.' Davey shook his head. 'She thinks you have deserted her.'

'Because I refused to hand over the money to that bloodsucking woman? I asked her to trust me and the next I hear is that she and Radworth are to be married in three weeks!'

'She is very angry with you, my friend.'

'I thought she knew me better than that!' He gazed up at the darkening sky, his breath escaping in a hiss. 'Davey, when Clarice came here demanding money she had a surprising amount of information, more than she could have gleaned from Madame de Beaune's letter—and before you fire up at me, I do not think that she learned any of it from Sophie!'

'And do you know now who is her accomplice?'

'No, but I have my suspicions. I fear this matter is not purely about the money. Forgive me,' he said quickly, when Davey opened his mouth to speak, 'I have a plan, but it depends upon total secrecy and I will not divulge it to anyone, even you. But believe me when I say I am relieved that you are staying at the Priory.' He stopped. 'I have not asked you about your leg, my friend.'

Davey shrugged. 'It is healing slowly. As you see, I can manage well enough with a stick now.'

'But perhaps that is far enough for today.' Guy turned and they began to walk back towards his horse. 'I am going away for a couple of days. Watch over Beth for me while I am gone, Davey.'

'Where are you going?'

Guy shook his head.

'It is better that no one knows. But I intend to return in time for the Fentonby Assembly.' They had reached his horse and Guy turned and gripped Davey's hand. 'I will be back as soon as I can.'

'Do you have a message for Mrs Forrester?' asked Davey as Guy scrambled up into the saddle.

'Would she receive it?' Even in the deepening gloom he read the answer in Davey's face and said bitterly, 'No, of course she will not, but I shall leave one anyway. Tell her—if you can make her listen—tell her to keep faith with me a little longer.'

Beth looked at the shining gown spread out on the bed. The kingfisher-blue silk gleamed in the candlelight. It was her newest gown, the only one she had bought since her father's death that did not signal mourning.

Less than ever did she want to wear bright colours, but she had promised Miles she would dress appropriately for the Fentonby Assembly and the formal celebration of their betrothal. Miles had told her that, once they were married, he would be able to help Simon. He did not say how, but she clung to that hope. Only the day before he had dissuaded her from making Clarice an offer for the deposition.

They had been on their way back from Thirsk after visiting Simon, and Beth had been desperately trying to think of ways to raise the money.

'Sophie and I could sell our jewels, then there are the Malpass diamonds and the silver from the house—'

'My dear.' Miles raised his hand, saying gently, 'You forget. The contents of the Priory are not yours to sell now.'

She shook her head, saying impatiently, 'Oh, I know I have signed the contracts in readiness for our marriage, Miles, but surely, to save Simon—'

'My dear, saving your brother is uppermost in my thoughts. We shall attend the Fentonby Assembly tomorrow night, I shall be at your side and this Mrs Cordonnier will realise she has me to deal with.'

Dear Miles. Beth could not think that Clarice would be at all impressed, unless Miles was willing to pay her the money she wanted. However, there had been no further demands so she could only hope that Miles was right. She put on the kingfisher-blue gown and allowed Tilly to put up her hair with a single, glistening ringlet hanging over her bare shoulder. All the local families would be at Thirsk tonight, ready with insincere condolences over the fate of her brother and equally false congratulations for her forthcoming wedding. She disliked being the object of so much gossip, but it could not be avoided and Miles insisted this show of solidarity would be beneficial to Simon. Beth could only be thankful that Sophie was going to be there to support her.

She picked up her wrap and made her way to the great hall.

'Grandmama!' Her surprised exclamation echoed to the rafters, but did not discompose Lady Arabella.

'I have decided I shall come with you,' the old lady announced, rising from her chair beside the fire. 'We will show them that the Wakefords have nothing to be ashamed of.'

'No indeed, ma'am.'

'Does Grandmama not look well?' demanded Sophie.

Beth gazed with affection at her grandmother, admiring the severe black gown, high to the neck with white lace ruffles at the sleeves and worn with a black silk apron. She had a black-lace cap over her white hair and was wearing diamonds, a family heirloom consisting of an aigrette that was pinned into the lace cap, dainty ear-drops, a diamond collar and a wide bracelet clasped over the top of one of Lady Arabella's black gloves. The pieces had been passed down through the years; although Sophie might consider the enamelled gold setting adorned with diamonds and sapphires to be out of date and too conspicuous to be worn with the fashionable light muslins, there was no denying that they looked magnificent against Lady Arabella's black silk.

'She looks exceedingly well! But are you sure you want to come with us, Grandmama? It is some time since you ventured out...'

'Then it is high time I did,' retorted Lady Arabella. 'Besides, this might be the last time I shall wear the Malpass diamonds. I have no doubt Miles Radworth will claim them for his own as soon as you are wed. No need to look so shocked,' she added, smiling grimly at Beth's startled face. 'I am well aware that he has tied up the settlements to his advantage.'

'Grandmama, the arrangements are perfectly usual for a marriage contract,' said Beth gently.

'Hmmph!'

Sophie reached out to touch the old lady's arm. 'Do you not *like* Miles, Grandmama?'

'As a matter of fact I do not,' came the blunt reply. 'What's that line from Shakespeare that always comes to mind when I see him? "He has a lean and hungry look." Ah, Mr Davies, there you are. Well, now we are all ready, shall we go?'

The George was Fentonby's largest coaching inn and the Assembly Rooms had been added some thirty years ago. They were generally proclaimed to rival anything in York or Bath. Beth had rarely visited them, despite the fact that Lady Arabella had been one of the chief subscribers when they were built. Many of the great families had moved away from the area and those that were left preferred the more genteel society of Thirsk, so the rooms had been left to the enjoyment of the wealthy tradesmen and farmers. However, news had spread through the town that Mrs Forrester would be attending to celebrate her betrothal and it was with a sinking heart that Beth observed the number of carriages drawn up at the entrance as they turned into the High Street.

'The world and his wife are here!'

'We expected that,' said Sophie. 'Mrs Robinson told me the news of your betrothal was all over the town.'

'It is going to be a sad crush,' stated Lady Arabella, 'I suppose we must resign ourselves to it.' She leaned forwards, peering through the glass. 'Is that Sir John Marton and his wife? And I see

Lord Embleton's carriage. Well, at least there will be some of our acquaintances there.'

The carriage pulled up at the entrance to the Assembly Rooms and the ladies waited while Mr Davies alighted and turned back to hand them out. Since he still needed the support of his walking sick, Davey gave his free arm to Lady Arabella, leaving Beth and Sophie to follow behind. As Beth had suspected, the rooms were very crowded and their progress into the ballroom was slow. Lady Arabella's appearance caused even more delay, since so many people wanted to talk to her. Beth was pleased by their attentions to her grandmother, not least because it meant that she could slip into the room in Lady Arabella's shadow. The press of people and confusion immediately inside the door gave Beth the opportunity to study the assembled company. She spotted Miles on the far side of the room, but made no attempt to attract his attention, for her eyes were drawn to the tall figure of Lord Darrington, who had just come out of the card room. His plain dark coat was no different from many of the younger gentlemen present, but his upright stance and athletic figure commanded attention. His brown hair gleamed in the candlelight and she watched him surveying the crowd, idly swinging his quizzing glass between his long fingers. Davey had told her the earl intended to be present and she had resolved not to pay him the least heed, but she could not tear her eyes from him. At that moment he turned his head, as if aware of her eyes upon him. Quickly she looked away.

'Mrs Forrester, are you ill?' Davey's voice was full of concern.

'It is nothing, sir, really.' But she realised with dismay that he had followed her glance.

'Ah, I see. Madam—'

'Please,' she said quietly, 'do not try to defend the earl! I will not listen to you.'

'I cannot defend him,' he replied. 'I have no more idea than you what he is about, but I would beg you, ma'am, to believe he is not your enemy. Have faith in him.'

'Impossible,' she said bitterly.

Sophie came up to them. 'Let us find seats,' she suggested brightly. 'Grandmama will want a chair, as will you, Edwin. Your leg is not yet healed enough for dancing.'

'True, and very annoying...' he grinned at her '...because I would have liked to stand up with you.'

They went off and Beth was left alone. She was aware of a moment of loneliness. Nonsense, of course, because she was well acquainted with most of those present and once Miles realised she had arrived he would keep her at his side for the rest of the night. She moved around the room, greeting one acquaintance, then another, her skin prickling because she knew the earl was watching her from the side of the room. It seemed that every time she raised her head he was at the edge of her vision. If he drew closer, she moved in the opposite direction. She saw him talking to Sir John Marton and judged it safe to return to her grandmother, but her progress was delayed as her acquaintance came up, eager to offer their congratulations, so that by the time she drew nearer to Lady Arabella Guy was there, laughing at something Davey was saying. Determined not to allow him to spoil her evening, she slipped away again. At every opportunity she smiled more widely and laughed more loudly, to show that she really did not care that he was present.

Miles came up. She schooled her features into a smile.

'You are looking very grand,' she greeted him, her eyes taking in his elegant powdered wig and dove-grey velvet coat. 'I vow you look fine enough for a royal drawing room!'

'But this is a very special occasion.' He lifted his watch and glanced at it before bowing over her fingers. 'I have been looking for you, my dear, but it was the worth the wait. You look...magnificent.' She felt the blood rising to her cheeks under his warm gaze and wished she had covered the low neckline of her gown with a muslin *buffon*. She gave an uncertain laugh and pulled her fingers free.

'Thank you. I was about to take a message to Grandmama. If you will excuse me...'

'I will, reluctantly. But I shall expect you to dance with me later.'

'Of course.' She kept her smile while he kissed her fingers, then moved off in the direction of the benches where Lady Arabella was sitting with Sophie and Mr Davies. She had not gone far when she found herself facing a solid wall of black cloth that was the Earl of Darrington.

Chapter Twenty-One

A fleeting glance at Guy's face showed her that he was looking very grim, the lines of strain accentuated around his eyes and
mouth. She went to move past him, but his hand shot out and caught
her arm. In the press of people no one noticed he was detaining her.

'Why would you not see me? Davey says you did not even read
my letter.'

'I want nothing more to do with you.'

'Nothing! After we travelled nearly the length of England together?'

'I was grateful for your help, I told you as much,' she replied,
desperately trying to remain calm. 'But you declined to help me
any further. Our acquaintance is ended.'

'The devil it is!'

His grip tightened and, with a growl, he pulled her towards a
small alcove at the side of the room. A waiter with a tray of wine-
glasses stood between the decorated pillars that flanked the entrance, but a sharp word from the earl sent him scurrying away.
There were no candles near the alcove and the shadows engulfed
them, robbing everything of colour.

'How dare you drag me here! You have nothing to say to me,
my lord.'

Guy spun her round to face him. He said roughly, 'Just because
I would not pay Clarice Cordonnier her blood money you think I
have abandoned you.'

'What else is there to think?'

He was standing between her and the ballroom, blocking her escape. He said quietly, 'Beth, believe me, I had my reasons for refusing to pay Clarice. Have you so little faith in me?'

'Methinks I had too much faith in you!' she flung at him. 'Oh, I was a *fool* to allow myself to be beguiled by you. If you trusted me, you would have explained your reasons.'

'I might throw the same accusation at you, madam,' he ground out. 'Without giving me a chance to explain myself, you set a date to marry Radworth. I thought you were going to cry off.'

She turned to him, her lip curling. 'And why should I do that, my lord?'

'Because you are going to marry me!'

'When you leave my brother to rot in gaol? I think not.'

His head went up as if she had struck him. 'Do I mean so little to you?'

'Yes!' she flashed. 'I wish I had never met you! I w-wish you would take yourself off now and leave us in peace!'

'And what about your brother?'

'I do not need you—in fact, *I will not allow* you to help me!'

She glared up at him, her breast heaving. Even in the darkness she saw the spark of anger in his eyes. He stepped closer, towering over her, tall, dark and full of menace.

'By heaven, I shall work for your brother's release, madam, with or without your permission!'

'And I say you shall not. Miles will help me to save Simon.'

'Will he, though?'

'What do you mean by that?'

'Do you think Radworth will help anyone who might challenge your claim to Malpass?'

'I—I don't understand you.'

He said slowly, 'I believe your brother is safer in Thirsk gaol. I fear he might meet with some…accident if he were free.'

Fear trickled down her spine. 'You do not think that…that M-Miles—' She shook her head. 'No. No, I will not believe this, this *slander* against Miles. Not without proof.'

'I have none, yet.'

'And you will find none,' she retorted furiously. 'I believe you are jealous, my lord.'

'Yes, I am, since he seems to have your unwavering devotion.'

She put up her head. 'And why should he not? He has given me no cause to doubt him!'

'But has he done anything to deserve it?'

'Of course! And no doubt he would have done more, if I had gone to London with him instead of you!'

There was a pause, no greater than a heartbeat, then he said softly, 'And would you have preferred his caresses to mine?'

The air around them, already heavy with anger, suddenly became charged with danger. She tried and failed to prevent herself from being flooded by memories of the passionate nights they had spent together. They were as one; even now her body responded to his dark presence, she had to force herself not to move closer, to merge into his shadow. The deep resonance of his voice wrapped around her like velvet. Every sense, every nerve screamed at her to give in, to throw herself into his arms.

'Beth—'

Tell him, the voices in her head cried urgently. *Tell him you cannot live without him.*

'Guy, I—'

'So here you are, my dear.'

The mood was broken. Light flared as Miles walked in carrying a candelabra, which he placed on a *torchère* at the back of the alcove.

'You have a propensity for being alone with Lord Darrington, my dear. That will have to stop when we are married, you know.'

Beth clasped her hands—she knew now what she must do. 'Miles, I cannot marry you.'

His eyes moved to Guy, then back to her face. 'But I am afraid you must, my dear.'

'There is no must about it, Radworth,' Guy said coldly.

Miles gave a thin smile. 'Is that so?'

'It is, Miles.' Beth nodded. 'I am very sorry, but I…I was mistaken. I cannot marry you.'

He shrugged. 'Very well.' Beth had been holding her breath and now she let it go, relieved that Miles was being so reasonable. His next words sent her thoughts careering back into turmoil. 'Then I will have you and your family out of Malpass by the end of the month.'

She stared at him. 'You cannot do that.'

'Oh, but I can.' His silky voice sent a shiver down her back. 'The marriage settlements are all signed. You will remember the clause that if the marriage does not go ahead, the Priory and all its contents come to me. You cannot fight that, my dear. It is the law.'

Guy put a steadying arm about her. 'Perhaps the law will take a different view when they learn the truth about you, Radworth,' he said. 'How you were prepared to sacrifice Simon Wakeford to get the Priory.'

Beth's world had been righting itself, but now it began to tilt again. 'I don't understand,' she said, looking at both men.

'Radworth came to Malpass determined to have it,' said Guy. 'He persuaded your father to leave everything to you, did he not?'

'Pure fairy tale, Darrington,' scoffed Miles. 'It is true I let slip to old Wakeford that his son was drowned, but it was his idea to change his will.'

'An idea put into his head by you.' Guy glanced at Beth. 'I believe your instinct not to tell him that Simon was alive was very wise, my dear. He is using you.'

'I cannot believe he would do that,' said Beth slowly. 'To come all this way, and to remain in Fentonby for so long.'

'You are right, my dear,' Miles agreed. 'The earl is air-dreaming. You know I am no fortune hunter. What would I want with the Priory when I have my own property in Somerset?'

Guy shrugged. 'You are a collector, Radworth. You love antiquities and the Priory is full of them. Priceless, you called them. I believe Simon Wakeford described his home to you that night you dined together in Portsmouth and from that moment you coveted the house and its contents. Then when Wakeford was accused of murder you saw your chance.'

Miles spread his hands. 'So that is the worst you know of me—that I covet the house and its contents.'

'Not only that. I think you persuaded Clarice Cordonnier to inform the authorities that Simon was hiding at the Priory.'

'No, he would not do that!' Beth's exclamation brought Miles's cold glance flickering over her.

'As you say, my dear. I have only met the woman once or twice.'

'Enough to discuss with her Madame de Beaune's deposition.'

There was a sudden stillness in the alcove. Beyond the pillars the dancing was continuing, but the music and laughter of the ballroom was a world away from the tension and menace that cloaked them.

'Clarice was too well informed,' Guy continued. 'She knew of things not mentioned in that paper. The necklace, for example, and the fact that Madame de Beaune was dead.'

'She told you that, did she?' Miles shrugged. 'She found the letter purely by chance, you know. The actions of an inquisitive mind. It wasn't until she brought it back to me that I realised its significance. She was very ready to try to obtain money for it, but rest assured, my dear, I never intended that you should buy it back. However, if she could get a few thousand from Darrington, then I had no objection to that. But I made the mistake of discussing the matter with her. That was foolish of me.'

'But how did you come by the information about Madame de Beaune?' Beth demanded.

'Because, my dear, I had people watching the ports, in case the French couple returned to England.'

'But you knew I was already doing that,' said Beth.

'I think Radworth's reasons for finding the de Beaunes were quite different to yours,' murmured Guy. 'Am I right, sir?'

'I certainly did not want them to testify in Wakeford's defence.'

'So you ordered Madame de Beaune to be murdered.'

Beth gasped. Miles merely shrugged.

'Believe that if you like. You will never prove it.' His lip curled. 'I did not know then that Beth had gone chasing off to London with you and that you had met with Madame.'

'But I do not understand—why are you so eager that my brother should not be free?'

'Because he might lay claim to his inheritance.'

'And you were willing to commit murder.'

'I will never admit to that.'

Beth looked at Guy. 'We must tell Sir John, immediately.'

'What will you tell him?' demanded Miles with a sneer. 'I will deny everything. And remember I am well respected in this area. I have been a model tenant since I arrived in Fentonby and have gone out of my way to make myself agreeable. You are Wakeford's sister, so of course you will tell any lies to get him released. And as for having Darrington as your witness, hah! A disgraced peer from a dubious family—his father was a wild-living man who ran through a fortune before he was thirty. The Darrington name was never very honoured, but then your friend here made an unfortunate alliance that cost him dear.' His lip curled. 'It seems he has a foolish propensity for succumbing to a pretty face.'

Guy lunged at Miles, but Beth threw herself in the way.

'No!' she cried. 'Remember where we are! Do not add to the scandal!'

Miles was backed against the wall, breathing heavily. He pushed himself upright and straightened his coat.

'You do right to tell him, my dear. Now I urge you to think twice before you cry off. You will lose everything.'

'When the world learns of your perfidy—'

'*My* perfidy!' Miles laughed. 'You have been careering around the country with Darrington—even staying in his house! What of your reputation, madam? Everyone will think I am a saint indeed not to cast you off! Besides,' he added softly, 'there is the deposition.'

Beth stiffened. 'What about it?'

His hateful smile appeared. 'I have it. If you can persuade your brother not to challenge my claim to the Priory, then I will make you a present of it on our wedding day.'

Beth put her hands to her mouth. Guy put his hand on her shoulder.

'You will not marry him, Beth,' he said grimly. 'Whatever else may happen, you will not marry that villain.'

'I will do anything to save Simon,' she whispered.

'Beth, listen to me—' Guy broke off when there was a loud 'ahem!' and he looked around to find a footman hovering in the entrance.

'Yes, what is it?' barked Guy.

The servant approached and murmured into his ear. Guy turned back to her.

'I must go—someone is waiting for me.'

'But—'

'I have no time to explain now.' He gripped her hand. 'But I *will* explain, you have my word. Trust me, Beth.' He was gone. Out of the alcove and swallowed up by the crowd.

'How very convenient,' murmured Miles.

She put up her chin. 'He said he will be back.'

'Are you sure of that?' He moved closer. 'Come, Elizabeth, let us continue with our betrothal celebrations.'

She turned away, but he leaned over and continued to murmur his insidious words into her ear.

'Marry me and you will have everything. Your family can continue to live at Malpass, Simon will be freed.'

She shrugged him off. 'Never! How can you expect me to marry you now?'

'As you wish,' he murmured. 'Pity, because you are quite beautiful and I would enjoy having you as my bride. But there it is—if you wish to cry off, then your brother will hang for his…crimes, and as the sister of a murderer, are you sure Darrington will want to marry you? He has been trying to re-establish his position, you know. There are calls for him to return to the Cabinet. He won't be able to do that if he is involved in another scandalous liaison.'

He stepped up and held out his arm. 'Come, madam. Be sensible. Do what is right for your family.'

Beth hesitated. A sudden break in the crowd gave her a clear view across the room to where Lady Arabella was sitting, the Malpass diamonds glittering in the candlelight. She must buy time. Time to consider. Time for Guy to come back to her. Slowly she raised her hand and laid her fingers on his arm.

'For tonight we will continue,' she said coldly. 'I cannot think properly.'

He put his hand over hers. 'Very well, my dear. Look, there is a new set forming. Let us join the dancers.'

She allowed him to lead her out and into that same crowd, more dazed than ever.

As they took their places in the set he leaned closer. 'Did I tell you how ravishing you look tonight, my dear?'

She averted her head. 'Please, Miles, people are staring at us.'

'Let them,' he said, carrying her hand to his lips. 'We will soon be husband and wife, will we not? They should not be surprised if we act like lovers.'

Lovers. Beth could barely suppress a shudder at the word. The music began and she went mechanically through the steps, her smile fixed, but all the time she was trying to order her thoughts. Panic was beginning to fill her: she would have to break the engagement. But how? When? It was impossible to say anything tonight, in so public a place. When Miles led her off the floor and they began a tour of the room, gathering congratulations as they went, she felt she was being swept inexorably along in the wrong direction.

Suddenly her wandering gaze alighted upon a group of gentlemen gathered about a voluptuous lady in gold satin, ostrich plumes nodding from her blonde head. She stopped.

'Ah.' Miles followed her gaze. 'Mrs Cordonnier. Shall we speak to her?'

'I would rather die first!'

He laughed softly. 'Very well, we will turn away.'

'I could tell Sir John—'

'And what would be the point of that, when I have told you

that I have the paper now?' His hand tightened. 'Smile, Elizabeth. Remember this is a happy day.'

Reluctantly Beth curbed her impatience and allowed Miles to take her down to supper. She was tired and dispirited. She longed to go home, away from the whispers and curious glances, but Miles was determined to show her off. Her grandmother was also content to stay; when Beth suggested to Davey that he might wish to retire he quickly denied it, saying how much he was enjoying the company. Since he had spent the best part of the evening with Sophie beside him Beth could well believe it. She looked around her, trying to conceal her desperation. Where was Guy?

Miles claimed her hand for the last of the country dances, but as soon as the music ended she begged to be taken back to her grandmother.

'Forgive me, Miles, but these past few days have been very anxious for me.'

Miles patted her hand. 'I understand, my dear. Perhaps it is time I moved into the Priory. I could be of more help to you—and there will be much to do. I will need to draw up an inventory.'

Beth threw up her head, an angry retort springing to her lips, but at that moment their attention was claimed by a flurry of activity at the entrance.

'Good Gad,' said Miles, 'who can be arriving at this time of night?'

Beth's fatigue vanished as she looked towards the door. Guy had returned and on his arm, looking about her nervously, was Madame de Beaune. So *this* was why he had asked her to trust him. They did not need the deposition if they had the lady herself to give evidence!

'What does Darrington think he is about?' muttered Miles, beside her. 'To bring a guest in now, when all the dancing is ended.'

He did not recognise her, thought Beth. But why should he? When he had seen her she had been a pretty French bride, powdered and bewigged. Now she was merely a sober young widow in an unremarkable gown and with her own hair curled neatly around her head.

Beth hid her smile and gave his arm a little tug. 'Come along, then. I will present you!'

Sir John Marton and Mr Davies were talking with Guy and the lady as they approached and Beth slowed her step, reluctant to interrupt, but almost immediately Sir John spotted her and broke off, beckoning her to come forwards.

'Well, well, Mrs Forrester, this is a turn up and no mistake!' cried the magistrate, beaming at her. 'It would appear Lord Darrington arranged for this lady to come here and speak in your brother's defence.'

'And I am delighted to see her,' replied Beth. 'Madame de Beaune, you must allow me to tell you how grateful I am that you have come here. Allow me to present Mr Miles Radworth to you, Madame. You may recall he was with Simon on that fateful night.'

Miles had dropped behind but now he stepped up and made a flourishing bow. Madame de Beaune curtsied.

'Of course I remember you, *monsieur*. You were travelling with poor Monsieur Wakeford.'

'He will not be "poor Monsieur Wakeford" for much longer,' declared Sir John. 'My lord, bring this lady to me in the morning and I will take her statement, If all you have told me this evening is true, then Wakeford will be a free man by noon.'

From the corner of her eye Beth noticed Clarice slipping out of the room. She wanted to call Guy's attention to the fact, but only for a moment. Clarice Cordonnier was no longer important.

She said with a smile, 'That is excellent news! I must tell Grandmama and Sophie!'

'Of course,' said Miles, stepping back for her to pass him. 'But if you will excuse me, I think I should be going. It is getting late.' He began to move towards the door.

'Just a moment!' Guy stepped forwards. 'What has happened to your watch, Radworth?'

'My… I didn't bring it tonight.'

'That's odd, I am sure I saw you looking at it earlier,' remarked Davey.

Guy reached out and hooked his finger around the chain at

Miles's waist. The watch slid out from beneath the flowered waist-coat. Guy held it out, allowing the distinctive face to catch the light.

Madame de Beaune gave an anguished cry. 'My husband's watch!'

'Is it, now?' Guy turned it over and read out the letters engraved on the back. 'F. D. B. Hardly your initials, Radworth.'

'It belonged to my husband, Fernand,' stated Madame de Beaune clearly. 'It is a Breguet. One of the best watchmakers in the world.' Her face paled as she stared in horror at Miles.

'It was you,' she whispered. '*You* attacked us!'

Even as she was speaking Miles pulled the timepiece from Guy's hands and made a bolt for the door, pushing Beth out of his way so that she cannoned into Guy, preventing his pursuit. There were screams and confusion, but just when Beth thought Miles could escape, Davey thrust out his cane to catch Miles's legs and he crashed to the floor. Sir John immediately ran forwards and stood over him, fists curled menacingly.

'I think,' he said sternly, 'we should finish this discussion some-where more private.'

Chapter Twenty-Two

They gathered in a small room on the next floor. Guy took up a position by the door. Having got this far, he would make sure Radworth did not escape now. His glance shifted to Beth, who gave him a faint smile. She was looking a little tired, but still beautiful, her silk gown glinting in the soft light, the blue-green colour accentuating her flame-red hair. She was sitting beside Madame de Beaune, who was staring at the watch as if to assure herself it was really there in her hands.

'Now,' barked Sir John, 'perhaps, Radworth, you will explain yourself. What is this about?'

'A misunderstanding, nothing more. It can all be explained.'

'I think not.' Guy's voice cut across the room. 'Before you try to worm your way out of this, let me tell you that the man you paid to follow Madame de Beaune and murder her has been caught and has already confessed everything.' He glanced across at Beth, adding for her benefit, 'I set two plans in motion before we left London. One was to send word to Bourne Park and persuade Madame to place herself under my protection. The other was to ask Sir Henry Shott to find Radworth's hired killer. He soon discovered the culprit, a man from Radworth's estate in Somerset.'

'That greed should have caused all this!' She shuddered.

Miles was standing by the fire, looking down pensively into the flames. 'It was not greed, it was love,' he said calmly. 'Love, lust, desire—call it what you will. Darrington said I am a collector, but he is wrong. I am a connoisseur. Imagine my delight when I found myself travelling back from France with a young man who was only too keen to describe to me his home, an ancient Priory, full of antiquities. Then in Portsmouth we dined with the de Beaunes. The old man was not excessively rich, but he had two treasures, his young bride and the Breguet. As soon as I saw the watch I knew I must have it.'

'So you attacked them—a woman and an old man.' Guy's lip curled in disdain.

Radworth shrugged. 'Getting the watch off the old man was not difficult, but then Wakeford came along. Chivalrous young fool decided to play the hero. I snatched the woman's necklace and ran off, but I decided to go back, for I had thought of a way I could have all the treasures that had been described to me that night. Once I had removed the old surtout and cap and replaced my wig and tricorn, no one would recognise me.'

'What about your wounded accomplice?' asked Guy.

'The fool thought I had devised some plan for his escape. Once I had persuaded Wakeford to see Madame and her husband to the packet, it was an easy matter to add another stab wound. He was dead by the time the constable arrived.'

'You murdered him.' Beth gasped. 'And placed the blame for the theft upon Simon.'

Miles gave a thin smile. 'The necklace was a mere gewgaw, so it was no hardship to slip it into your brother's portmanteau. You have no notion how difficult it was to persuade the constables to check the bag, but at last they did so, and when Wakeford returned he was marched off to gaol.'

'And you were happy for my brother to be falsely accused.'

He looked across at Beth and smiled. 'I thought it a rather neat ending. I had the Breguet, Wakeford would take the blame, then I would marry his sister and have his inheritance, too.'

'We thought you so kind.' She shook her head. 'I have never known anyone so, so *evil*.'

'But that is not the end, is it?' said Guy slowly. 'You had to make sure Simon would not be acquitted.'

'No.' Beth shook her head. 'How could he do that?'

'Buying strong ale to stir up the mob, then laying on an unseaworthy ship to carry away the freed prisoners. Was that it, Radworth?'

'Precisely. How astute of you, Darrington.' Miles smiled to himself, like a man reminiscing on some past glories. 'It was only a matter of waiting until the news came in that she had gone down with all hands. Then, of course, I came to Malpass, to offer my condolences.'

'And your wicked scheme almost worked.' Beth's lip curled.

'Yes. If only the fools I paid to kill Madame de Beaune had not failed me!'

'They did not fail you,' put in Guy. 'But they killed the wrong Madame de Beaune. That is what made me suspect that you were involved, when Clarice hinted that Madame was dead. I knew that was not true, because she was by then living under my protection.'

'I was very 'appy to stay,' put in Madame, smiling slightly. 'I remember Monsieur Wakeford with great affection.'

'As I am sure he remembers you, ma'am,' Beth replied warmly. 'I know he will be delighted to renew his acquaintance with you.'

'I went to fetch Madame earlier this week and installed her in a house nearby.' Guy spoke directly to Beth. 'We arranged that she would come to the Assembly. I wanted her to confront Radworth, but I received word tonight that Madame was too afraid to travel here without me. That is why I had to leave you. I dare not tell you, I could not risk Radworth becoming suspicious—'

Her smile lit up the room for him. 'It did not matter. I knew you would come back to me.'

Sir John jumped up. 'Well, if that is all for tonight I think we should be going,' he said. 'My lord, I would be pleased if you would give me your company to put Mr Radworth into the lock-up for the night and in the morning I will take him to Thirsk and he will be able to exchange places with young Wakeford. I do not think we need to keep your brother locked up any longer, Mrs Forrester.'

'Perhaps not quite an exchange,' said Guy. 'I greased several palms to find a safe, comfortable cell for Simon and employed a guard for him, too.'

'Do you mean Logan?' said Beth quickly. 'You put him in the gaol to protect Simon?'

'Yes. I was afraid Radworth might try to get to him.'

'As a matter of fact I did,' said Miles. 'You have just explained why my bribes failed.'

'I c-cannot believe what you are saying!' exclaimed Beth. 'You paid court to me and all the time you were—you were—'

'But Wakeford is an irrelevance, my love.'

Beth turned away, distressed. In two strides Guy was beside her. He put his arms around her and held her until the shivering subsided.

'I am well. Please, Guy, you do not need to worry about me.'

She spoke bravely but he was not convinced, and turned to his friend.

'Davey, I would be glad if you could see the ladies home while I accompany Sir John—'

'Madame de Beaune is welcome to stay at the Priory,' said Beth. She added shyly, 'And you, too, Guy. Please come back when you have finished here.'

His heart soared at her words. He kissed her hands. 'Gladly,' he muttered. 'I will be back as soon as I can.'

She gazed up at him, a smile trembling on her lips. 'I shall wait up for you.'

After all the bustle and excitement of the evening, it was a relief to climb into Lady Arabella's large travelling carriage. Its roomy interior comfortably accommodated them all, with Beth explaining to Sophie and her grandmother that Madame de Beaune was to be their guest for a few days.

'You are very welcome,' declared Lady Arabella graciously. 'I do not think I know you.'

'No, Grandmama,' said Beth patiently. 'You will remember I told you that Madame met Simon at Portsmouth. She is come now to testify to his innocence.'

As the carriage trundled its way home Beth and Davey explained everything that had happened.

'From our seats on the far side of the room we had no notion of what all the commotion was about,' said Sophie.

'They say Mr Radworth has been arrested,' stated Lady Arabella.

'Yes Grandmama. It was he who attacked poor Madame de Beaune and put the blame for it all upon Simon.'

The old lady snorted contemptuously. 'Hmmmph! I never liked the man, always thought he had a lack of breeding.' She put her hand up to her neck. 'And I did not like the way he stared at my diamonds. As if he could not wait to possess them.'

'There is no possibility of his possessing anything of ours now,' replied Beth. 'I shall instruct our lawyer in the morning—a contract based upon such villainy and deceit cannot stand.'

'I do not think there will be any difficulty there, ma'am,' affirmed Davey.

'And when will my grandson be home?'

'Very soon, I hope, Grandmama.' Beth clasped her hands. 'I hope by tomorrow evening we shall all be together again.'

The tranquillity of the old Priory welcomed them and Beth immediately went in search of her housekeeper.

'We will need a room made up immediately for Madame de Beaune,' she informed her. 'Lord Darrington will be returning, too, before the morning, Mrs Robinson, but you had best make up one of the other guest rooms for him.' She added, unable to prevent herself from smiling, 'I believe Mr Simon will need his own room tomorrow.'

'Oh dear, oh lord, ma'am, that is good news,' cried the housekeeper, wiping her eyes with the corner of her apron. 'I will not tell you how hard I have prayed for this moment! I was that shocked when the soldiers came and took him away, and Kepwith told me he had been living in the undercroft all this time—! But is he really free, ma'am? Will he have to go to court? What—?'

Laughing, Beth raised her hands to stem the flood of questions.

'I am afraid I do not have all the answers just yet, Mrs Robinson, but I shall know more once the earl returns. Prepare the rooms, if you please, and I will explain everything to you tomorrow.'

In a very short time everyone was settled and Beth sank down on a chair in the great hall, pleased for a little solitude to think over the events of the evening. She asked Kepwith to build up the fire, then sent him off to bed, saying that she would wait up for the earl.

The old house settled around her like a well-worn cloak. She looked up to the ceiling, the soaring rafters disappearing into the gloom. The firelight glinted on the swords and trophies that covered the walls. A feeling of peace stole over her. She leaned back in her chair, gazing at the fire while the steady tick of the clock soothed her into a doze.

Beth had no idea how long she slept, but she woke abruptly as the great oak door burst open and hasty footsteps rang out on the stone flags.

'Simon!' Beth flew out of her chair.

'I knew you would not want to wait until tomorrow,' said Guy, standing behind them and grinning broadly. 'So I persuaded Sir John to let me fetch him home.'

Beth emerged from her brother's bear-like hug and threw herself into Guy's arms.

'So *that* is why you have been so long. You have been to Thirsk and back! Thank you! And thank goodness I ordered Mrs Robinson to prepare rooms for you both before she went to bed!' She disengaged herself from Guy's embrace. 'Simon, come and sit down by the fire. Are you hungry? Thirsty? Shall I ring for Kepwith—?'

'No, no, I want nothing, sis, thank you, save to sleep in my own bed.'

'Your room is ready. Shall I come with you—?'

'No! I have had my fill of being accompanied everywhere! Besides, I am sure I can remember my way.' He planted a kiss on her cheek, bade them goodnight and strode off across the hall, whistling.

Beth watched him disappear up the stairs. 'Despite his incarceration he is so much better than when I last saw him.' She turned back to Guy. 'How can I ever thank you for bringing him home to me?'

'I will show you.' He pulled her into his arms and kissed her, sending all coherent thought flying from her head. When at last he broke away she leaned against him, sighing.

'I have missed you so much. I am sorry I ever doubted you.'

'No, I should have been more open with you.' His words were murmured into her hair.

'We were foolish not to trust one another.' She turned her face up to him for another lingering kiss. 'We must make sure we share everything in future. Let us start with you telling me what happened after we had left the Assembly Rooms. Is Miles safely locked up now?'

'Yes, my love. He will not trouble us again.'

'And what of Mrs Cordonnier?' asked Beth. 'In all the confusion she escaped without notice.' She sighed. 'I know it is very uncharitable of me, but I would have liked to see her punished for her part in all this.'

'She will be,' Guy told her. 'Clarice was waiting at the door when we went out to Sir John's carriage and she launched herself at Radworth, declaring he had promised her two thousand guineas to destroy Madame's letter.'

'But I do not understand. Miles and Mrs Cordonnier—they were working together?'

'Not really. Clarice met Radworth when she visited your sister at Malpass and immediately recognised him for the villain he is. Unfortunately she did not realise that she was just another pawn in his game.'

'So what will happen to her?'

'She was so incensed at Radworth that she admitted everything to Sir John, how she stole the letter from you and tried to obtain money for its return. Sir John bundled her into the coach and took her to the lock-up, too.' He grinned. 'It was quite an—ah—acrimonious journey.'

Beth frowned. 'But tonight Miles said *he* had the letter. He said he would give it to me...he lied about that, too?'

'Yes, my love. He was just trying to make sure you married him. The letter was destroyed days ago. Clarice never had any intention of returning it to you. But she still hoped to persuade *me* to part with ten thousand pounds.'

'And I was so cross that you would not help! Can you ever forgive me?'

'If I had shared with you all my suspicions, you might have understood why I would not pay.' His arms tightened around her. 'We can do better than this, Beth. Shall we start again, my love—my one and only love?'

'Yes, please. Let us put all this behind us. Oh, I do love you, Guy Wylder.'

She saw the look of triumph burning in his eyes and it fanned her ever-present desire for him into a blaze. She tilted up her face, inviting his kiss. He swooped down on her, taking her mouth, demanding a response. Beth's lips parted, she returned his kiss, leaning her body into him, giving herself up to the pleasure of his touch. It liquefied her insides while excitement grew and pooled low in her body. She remained pressed against him, her head thrown back as he raised his head.

'Tell me now if you want me to go, or it will be too late.'

His voice was ragged and husky with passion. Her response was to reach up and drag his head down so she could kiss him again. Her heart was already beating wildly, but when she heard the low growl in his throat it leapt alarmingly, leaving her giddy with desire. In a single movement Guy swept her off her feet, cradling her against him as he carried her across the hall and up the stairs. She clasped her hands around his neck and buried her face against his cravat. He smelled of sandalwood and spices and an indefinable scent that she had learned to associate with him. She tingled with the anticipation of what was to come, her body aching, preparing itself for the feast of sensations he would rouse in her.

When she looked up again they were in her bedchamber. He set her on her feet, kissing her while his fingers swiftly unhooked her bodice. Beth knew no hesitation, no coy shyness. She set about undressing her partner with equal fervour. The fire Tilly had thoughtfully built up had warmed the room and now its rosy glow was all that they needed to light their way to bed. Their naked limbs were pale against the blackness of the hangings as they fell together on to the covers, memories of their earlier union making their kisses eager. Passion surged between them, but they held back, savouring the delicious moments as they explored each other's bodies, kissing, teasing, caressing, tasting, until their senses were so heightened that the merest touch provoked a soft moan of ecstasy.

Beth had never known such intense pleasure. She lay back against the covers, her arms stretched out, fingers clutching at the silk as Guy took her to new heights, working her body with his hands, his mouth, his tongue, until she thought she would die from the pleasure of it. She reached out for him as his hand caressed her breast, the thumb circling one hard, erect nub while his mouth and tongue teased even more intimate areas.

Excitement grew inside her, a wild exhilaration, spreading, increasing until it was such an unbearable pleasure that she was writhing beneath him, trying to pull away from the exquisite torment, but he held her firm. She was a prisoner of her own pleasure. She cried out, begging him to stop, to go on. Momentarily the pleasure ceased as he moved over her, measuring the length of his body against hers. He entered her, matching his rhythm to hers, carrying her inexorably onwards. She was open, receptive. Her legs wrapped themselves around his waist as their bodies moved together. She dug her fingers into his shoulders, feeling the hard muscle beneath the skin, sensing her power over him as they moved ever faster. It was a tense, rigid, dizzying culmination. Guy gasped, his hands holding her in a blood-stopping grip as he pushed into her and tensed, his head thrown back. She half expected to hear a triumphant howl as she clung to him, her own body racked and exhausted by the physical and emotional effort of loving.

His breathing softened. Guy supported himself on his arms above her, looking down. She could not see his face, but she could feel the love and gentleness emanating from him. He lowered his head, searching for her lips. She lifted her face to receive his kiss, light as a feather. Silently, they slipped between the sheets. Beth shivered slightly as the cotton struck cold on her bare skin, then Guy gathered her in his arms, warmed her with his own body and she fell asleep.

It was a beautiful autumn morning. A light frost coated the grass and the rising sun was a gilded orb against the pinky-blue of the clear sky. Beth stood amongst the ruins of the old church. She avoided the chill shadows, enjoying the warmth of the rising sun on her face. A faint mist hung over the river while on the other side of the wilderness it hovered between the trees, dimming the glow of their crisp golden leaves. She picked her way between the tumbled stones, moving away from the standing walls until she could see across the gardens to the Priory, its old stone turned to mellow gold in the morning sun.

Something, not exactly a sound, more a feeling, made her look round. Guy was approaching. He was wearing his greatcoat over his shirt and breeches, but it was unbuttoned and billowed about him. He stopped.

'Do I intrude?'

'You were sleeping. I did not want to disturb you.'

'Thus when I did wake, you were gone.' The smile in his eyes reassured her.

'How did you find me?'

'There were footsteps in the frost. When I realised they were heading through the cloisters I guessed where you were going.' She saw the uncertainty behind his eyes. 'Is anything wrong?'

'No-o.' She wrapped her arms around herself. 'I was thinking. About the future.'

'Well. Radworth booked the church for three weeks' time, I suggest we use it. There is still time to read the banns. Would you object to that?'

She blushed. 'No. I would like that. Very much.'

His relief was palpable and that pleased her.

'I will have to go to Wylderbeck before then. I would like to take you with me. I want to show you my home.'

'Yes, of course.'

She turned and walked back into the main body of the abbey. The air was very still and the sun had crept high enough to shine over the remains of the walls, bathing the area in warmth and light. It came to her that, centuries past, couples would have stood in this very spot, making their marriage vows.

She heard Guy's step behind her and said softly, 'Where will we live, when we are married?'

'I hope you will like Wylderbeck enough to consider it our principal home.'

'I am sure I shall, if you are there with me.'

'I may have to spend more time in London. I have heard that Pitt would welcome my presence. With the current unrest in France I would like to think I might be of use to the government.'

She turned to him. 'Then of course you must go. And I will come with you, if I may.'

'I would not have it otherwise.' He was standing very close. 'You are shivering,' he said. 'You should be wearing more than a spencer over your gown.' He opened his arms. 'Come here, let me warm you.'

It was only a step to reach him. She slid her arms around him, under his coat, feeling the warmth of his body through the thin shirt. Guy pulled his greatcoat around them both.

'What is wrong, my love?'

'I was thinking about the family: Sophie, Grandmama, Simon.'

He rested his cheek lightly on the top of her head. 'If Davey has his way I think Sophie will not be long in following you down the aisle and Lady Arabella will naturally continue to live here.'

'She would want that, I think. If you do not object.'

'Perhaps you should discuss it with your brother.' She raised her head, brows raised in enquiry.

'You had mentioned you would like to make Malpass over to Simon.' Amusement deepened in his eyes as he noted her surprise.

He said, 'It is his birthright. If you wish to return it to him, I have no objection.'

'But…then I should come to you with nothing. Well, almost nothing—my widow's jointure…'

The glint of amusement in his eyes was replaced by a warmer glow. It sent a shiver running through her that had nothing to do with the morning chill and his words, softly spoken, told her everything she needed to know.

'I have everything I need right here. Now and for ever.'

* * * * *

Mills & Boon® Historical

December 2011

THE DISAPPEARING DUCHESS
Anne Herries

New bride to the Duke of Avonlea, shy Lucinda felt her harrowing past was finally over—until word from her enemy forces her to flee. Lucinda leaves in order to save her husband Justin from scandal… But will he give her up so easily?

IMPROPER MISS DARLING
Gail Whitiker

When Alexander Stewart protests his brother's engagement to her younger sister, Emma Darling is furious at his effrontery—but her attraction to him is worse still! For if their siblings' match is unsuitable, a relationship between them is unthinkable…

BEAUTY AND THE SCARRED HERO
Emily May

Major Nicholas Reynolds returned from Waterloo a hero, but his battle-scarred face exiles him from high society. Lady Isabella Knox is intrigued by the man…but can she let herself lose her heart to the most notorious gentleman of the *ton*?

BUTTERFLY SWORDS
Jeannie Lin

During China's infamous Tang Dynasty, betrayed Princess Ai Li flees before her wedding. With only her delicate butterfly swords for a defence, she enlists the protection of Ryam, a blue-eyed warrior who finds it hard to resist her…

Mills & Boon® Hard Back
Historical

*Another exciting novel available
this month:*

THE LADY CONFESSES
Carole Mortimer

A scandalous secret!

Having run away from home to avoid an unwanted betrothal,
Lady Elizabeth Copeland must keep her disguise as an elderly
lady's companion at all times. Even when she's called upon to
nurse the lady's nephew—who rather infuriatingly happens to
be the most incredible-looking man she's ever seen…

Elizabeth yearns to break out of Betsy's drab dresses to reveal
that she's of the same blue blood as the rakish Nathaniel.
But she must not! Unless Nathaniel gets under her guard
and elicits a confession…

The Copeland Sisters
Flouting convention, flirting with danger…